Sarah Tierney is a graduate of the MA in Novel Writing at the University of Manchester, and her short story, 'Five Miles Out', was made into a short film by Andrew Haigh. Sarah has worked as a journalist, editor and copywriter. She lives in Derbyshire with her husband and daughter.

Making Space

Sarah Tierney

SANDSTONEPRESS
HIGHLAND | SCOTLAND

First published in Great Britain by
Sandstone Press Ltd
Dochcarty Road
Dingwall
Ross-shire
IV15 9UG
Scotland

www.sandstonepress.com

The publisher acknowledges subsidy from
Creative Scotland towards publication of this volume.

ISBN: 978-1-910985-44-1
ISBNe: 978-1-910985-45-8

Cover design by Rose Cooper, Valencia, Spain
Typeset by Iolaire Typesetting, Newtonmore
Printed and bound by CPI Group (UK) Ltd, Croydon CR0 4YY

For Al and Marianne

1

It was one of those job interviews that began with someone telling me there weren't any jobs on offer. It reminded me of my love life. Sex I'd thought would lead to dating but turned out to be a one-night stand. A first kiss that was also the last. So why did you get me here? I wanted to ask. Instead I said, 'Oh, okay,' and sat down, as that seemed to be what was expected.

The interviewer was a girl called Natalie, about my age, late twenties, and dressed all in black apart from a strawberry red neck tie that matched her bobbed, dip-dyed hair. She pulled a file from her desk drawer and took out my CV and a form titled 'Interview Candidates'.

'What I can do is put you on the list of people we call when we get particularly busy. How does that sound?' she said.

'It sounds good.'

'Right then. I just need to go through this form.' I watched her write my name at the top, her biro running out before she got through the Mc of Miriam McGregor.

She picked another pen out of her desk tidy. It was a different colour but she used it anyway.

Putting aside the wasted bus fare, I was relieved there weren't any jobs here. The company was called City Business Services. It was housed in a grimy, white office block in an industrial park in Ardwick, just about walkable from the city centre, though you wouldn't want to risk it at night. The shrill ring of telephones interrupted the terse silence of the staff. There was a trio of middle-aged ladies sitting at right angles to each other, a skinny young man wearing headphones in the corner, and a teenage girl with an elaborate updo who'd been the only one to smile when I'd walked in.

City Business Services looked after the financial, IT and administrative affairs of small businesses that couldn't afford to have their own office team backing them up. I'd heard about them through my sister's husband, an ecological consultant who'd used them to produce his website. I sent in a CV that emphasised my admin experience rather than my MA in Television Production, and was invited in for 'a chat' by Natalie who was now quizzing me about my typing speed and experience of Microsoft Office.

She didn't seem that interested in my answers. I felt like she was just ticking boxes, and when I glanced at the form, I saw she actually was. She worked her way down a list of admin skills of which I had a full score. There was a space at the end headed 'Notes on the Candidate'. She hadn't filled it in yet.

Natalie put down the pen and tucked a curtain of hair behind her ear. She seemed out of place in this office, partly because she was talking, quite loudly really, while everyone else was silent. My CV sat on the desk between us.

'So you say you did an MA in Television Production?' she asked.

'Yes, at Stockport.'

'How was that?'

'Good. I really enjoyed it.' I wanted to add something to show it had been more than just a pleasant use of a year, something that made it look like the building blocks of a promising career in television, but there was nothing more I could say.

'So did you decide a job in TV wasn't for you...?' Natalie was studying me with interest now. I shifted slightly in my chair, aware of the other staff listening in. Did she want me to admit to media career failure? Surely the fact I was here was evidence enough.

Natalie lowered her voice. 'I'm actually planning to do a TV Production MA myself. I'm trying to decide between Stockport and Salford.'

So this was why she'd invited me in for the chat. A bit of research before she made a decision. I said, 'I applied for both but Salford said no.'

Natalie nodded, as if I'd confirmed something for her. 'I've heard that Salford is more respected by the industry. I don't want to spend all that time and money then end up back here.' Her voice had crept up but she lowered it again. 'In two years' time, I want to be working on either *Coronation Street*, *Hollyoaks* or *Emmerdale*. That's my mid-term career goal.'

I tried to sound enthusiastic. 'You should go for it.

Apply for both and see what happens.'

'I've already been accepted on both. I just need to decide which one to choose.'

'That's great.'

'Yeah, it is.' Natalie studied the employment section of my CV then pushed it slightly towards me. 'I actually think Salford is looking the most likely.' She smiled and stood up. 'Anyway, thanks for coming in to see us.'

When Natalie telephoned again about six months later, offering a week's work in the office, I couldn't remember what City Business Services was. Such a non-descript name. The type you'd give as a front for a criminal operation, so bland it would hopefully go unnoticed.

'You've not had any luck with a TV job then?' she asked.

Oh, her. I had a flash of the grubby office, her Ribena-tinged hair. 'Nothing definite.' Nothing at all.

'I start part-time at Salford next month. So can you come in tomorrow? You'll be manning the phones and filing.'

The next morning, Natalie introduced me to the rest of the office: a Sheila, a Deborah, a Bernie, and the teenager was Megan. She either forgot or ignored the headphones boy in the corner. Maybe he was a temp, too? She said the owner of the company was a lady called Teresa who only came in once or twice a month. Then we both sat at Natalie's desk while she went through the phone system.

The screensaver on her ancient computer was an inspirational quote. *Be brave. Fear is the only thing*

4

you should be afraid of, slowly shifting colours as it bounced between the sides of the monitor. Natalie was wearing biker boots and a slinky navy blue dress with a peacock feather necklace. I supposed it was quite brave, especially if she'd walked here through the no man's land on the edge of the city centre like I had.

I tuned back into what she was saying. This job was more complicated than your normal receptionist role because the office took calls for lots of different businesses, all directed into one incoming line. The phone system which identified the number dialled was broken, so they had no way of knowing which company the person was calling for. And you weren't allowed to ask because, as Natalie explained, the aim was to deceive the caller into believing the business they were contacting was an established, successful operation with its own receptionist and office staff, rather than a one-man-band who picked up messages by email.

She said, 'So just say something unspecific when you answer. Like "Good morning, how can I help?" or "Hello, good morning" or "Hello, who's calling please?" Unspecific but businesslike. Without giving them a business name.'

The phone rang and Natalie demonstrated. 'Hello, good morning,' she said, her voice rising brightly at the end. 'Neil isn't here right now. Who's calling please?' She scribbled a name on a pad. 'And what is it regarding?' More scribbling. 'I'll pass that on for you. Bye.' She clicked the phone down.

'Try to get as much info as possible,' she instructed. 'Then put it into an email and send it straightaway.'

5

I nodded. Didn't anyone think it strange that the person they were calling for was never there? The phone rang again.

'You have a go,' Natalie said.

I paused then picked up the phone. 'Hello, good morning?' It sounded like I wasn't sure what time of day it was.

'Hi. Is this City Business Services?'

'Er…maybe.' I thought we were supposed to be undercover. A phone-answering phrase came to me. 'One moment please.'

I pressed the hold button. 'He wants to know if this is City Business Services.'

'Say yes and find out what he wants.'

Obviously. 'Hi, yes, this is City Business Services.'

'Are you sure?' The caller sounded half-confused, half-amused.

'Yes.' I wasn't going to explain. 'How can I help?'

'I'm looking for someone to organise some papers for me.' A man. An accent. I couldn't say where from.

'What kind of papers?'

He hesitated. 'All kinds, I suppose.'

I resisted the urge to thrust the phone over to Natalie and say you deal with this. 'So, do you need help with some filing?'

'Yes, filing. Is that what you do?'

'Erm, I think so.'

Natalie raised her heavy eyebrows into her heavy fringe. I had the feeling I'd strayed from the script.

The man said, 'Perhaps someone could come to my house to have a look?'

'Well, okay.' I doubted anyone would. I used my favourite line: 'Can I take your name and number and someone will call you back.'

'Yes, it is Erik Zeleny.' He spelled it out and gave his mobile number. I wrote them on a Post-it note and put the phone down.

Natalie looked at me expectantly.

'A man who wants someone to sort out some paperwork at his house,' I said.

'At his house?'

I nodded. I felt like his unsuitability was somehow my fault. 'I said someone would call him back.'

'I'll talk to him later. He'll lose interest when I give him our rates.' She stuck the Post-it on the corner of her computer screen. *Erik Zeleny is the only thing you should be afraid of*, it read, until the peppy quote bounced away across the screen.

I did feel a little bit nervous. I don't like answering phones and I don't like working in new places. Temping was a bad career choice. Not that I considered it a career. Or a choice. I spent the morning filing invoices and taking phone messages. Most of the enquiries were straightforward. There were just two I couldn't nail down to a particular business. I showed them to Natalie who treated them as a kind of 'Guess Who?' parlour game. Could it be Helen from Physio Fitness? Or Helen from Swift Personal Finances? It was a man calling to change an appointment time on Thursday evening. I imagined him getting mortgage advice when he'd been expecting a sports massage.

In the afternoon, Natalie asked me to sort through

a stack of HR paperwork – P60s, copies of wage slips, holiday request forms – in a walk-in cupboard at the back of the office. That was when I saw the file labelled 'Job Applications'. I checked no one was coming, then flicked through to M.

Miriam McGregor. Natalie's blue ink replaced by black halfway through my name. The neat line of ticks in the section called 'Skills'. Then 'Notes on the Candidate'. *Miriam seems a nice girl with a solid range of office skills,* she'd written. *Dormouse manner, capable rather than bright, possibly depressed.*

I felt my face burning up. Dormouse? Possibly depressed? What was this, my medical notes? And 'capable rather than bright'. How would she know? She'd only spoken to me for five minutes, and most of that time she'd been talking about herself.

I looked for somewhere to sit down. There wasn't anywhere. No, I hadn't looked depressed. I distinctly remembered smiling and being upbeat in that interview.

I stared again at the form. I felt like leaving. Tearing the form in two and calmly placing it on Natalie's desk, then walking out without saying a word. Or just walking out. Yes, that was what I'd do.

Natalie poked her head around the cupboard door. 'Cup of tea?'

I turned the form towards me so its contents couldn't be seen. 'No thanks.' It was four-thirty and I finished at five. I'd drink my own tea at home thank you rather than that cheap Costcutter brand they had here.

'I spoke to Erik Zeleny earlier,' she said. 'I'm going round first thing Monday to see what this paperwork is. I've given him the daily rates and he still wants to go ahead.'

I nodded. Did I look unhappy and unintelligent? I tried to put my features into an expression of interest and enthusiasm. Natalie gave me a funny look.

She said, 'I was thinking this could be a good project for you to handle. It sounds like he wants someone to tidy up some books and magazines. Maybe set up a library system for him.'

'Sounds good.'

'It might mean we can keep you on for longer than a week as well.'

'Great.'

'In fact, it would be useful if you could come to his house on Monday.'

'Great.'

'I'll give you the address before you leave. Are you sure you don't want a brew?'

'Oh, um. Okay. Milk no sugar. Thanks.'

Natalie went back into the office. I slipped the form back into the file.

2

When I got home that evening my flatmate, Jessica, was making something complicated in the kitchen with Gareth, her new boyfriend, my ex-boyfriend. He gave me a tooth-whitened smile when I came in, and I could tell he was thinking, I've slept with both these girls, even though it was only once with me and I could barely remember it because I was drunk.

I suppose 'ex-boyfriend' is an exaggeration. We'd been out a few times, that's all. He was a dentist. I went off him when he said he didn't believe in the existence of chronic pain. It seemed reckless to me, and somehow arrogant. Jessica could have him. Though it would have been better if she hadn't. When she'd said a few months back that she was thinking of meeting him for a drink and did I mind, I'd said it was fine. She didn't ask again and now he was in the hallway some mornings when I came out of the shower, or now, hovering by the sink when I wanted to get a glass of water.

'Shall I shout you when we're done?' Jessica asked,

spatula in hand. She took the glass out of my hand, filled it, gave it back to me.

I went into my room and changed out of my work clothes and into my jeans. We lived just off Upper Chorlton Road in Whalley Range in a Victorian house that had been converted into flats. When we'd signed up for it four years ago, Jessica and I drew lots for the bedrooms and I missed out on the big one with a balcony. Mine was a boxroom with a bed that was somewhere in between a single and a double which meant my sheets were always wrinkled and loose. The room was at the back of the flat, directly off the kitchen-living room, looking out onto a patchy lawn and a mass of brambles that crept further across the grass every summer. At the end of the garden was a silver-green eucalyptus tree that had grown higher and wider than the surrounding houses. The leaves stayed on all year, hissing and shimmering in the breeze, the whole canopy swaying and bowing in storms. I watched it lying in bed as I woke up each morning.

The view of the tree was the room's one redeeming feature. It was cramped and noisy and it didn't give me the sense of retreat I wanted. It was like living in a cupboard off the living room. I would give anything to have my own place. I don't mean buy, just rent. A place where I could close the door on the world and know it would stay out there until I decided to step into it again. Sometimes I locked my bedroom door from the inside. Jessica acted offended by it. I suppose she was right to be.

People didn't usually stay in these flats as long as we

11

had. Some were damp. Others, like ours, had a noise problem from the Social Services accommodation next door. Letters for long-gone residents piled up in the porch. The communal entrance hall steadily filled with left-behind furniture. The building had the neglect that comes from nobody caring because they know their stay is temporary. But the thing that was bothering me now was how settled my room looked. How permanent my life here had become.

When we'd moved in, I'd imagined I would be there for a year or so before something better came along: a new job that would let me afford a nicer flat, a boyfriend who'd want to live with me. At twenty-five, the tiny room didn't bother me. I liked the idea that I wasn't settled, that my living arrangements were unconventional.

I didn't feel like that anymore.

I sat on my bed and tried to ignore next door's TV coming through one wall, Jessica and Gareth's voices coming through the other. My mind kept flitting back to that form. The person it described wasn't me. The person who lived in a room meant for a child and shared a flat with a friend she didn't particularly like wasn't me either. I needed to stop acting like it was. I looked around at my books, my clothes, the IKEA art pictures on the walls. I hated the room and everything in it.

In the kitchen Gareth was stirring something on the hob, one hand on Jessica's waist as she cut up coriander.

'There'll probably be some left over,' she said, with a placating look.

'Thanks.' I edged around them to get the roll of bin bags from underneath the sink.

12

Back in my room, I began putting my belongings in piles: bin, charity, sell, and keep, designating a corner for each one.

First, my wardrobe. Inside were either going-out clothes: above-the-knee skirts, low-cut tops, armless, tight, strappy, sequinned. Designed for bars and being looked at under bad lighting. Or they were dressing-down clothes: four pairs of near-identical jeans from Next, several bulky jumpers, about a million t-shirts with meaningless words on them like 'Camp Kidson 1954' in a faux-faded font. 'Big Sur' in a surfer-style swirl.

There was a time when I wore t-shirts with band names on them and patterned dresses with big boots. At some point, though, this style had become no good. It was too teenage, too studenty so I'd replaced it with the Next jumpers and the boot cut jeans, and these work clothes; silk-lined suits, stiff ironed shirts, plain black trousers, which felt like a costume every time I put them on: Now I'm going to dress like someone with an office job. And thinking about it, so did the other two sections of my wardrobe. Now I'm going to dress like a girl desperate for attention. Now like a girl desperate to be ignored.

I put them all in the corner marked 'charity'. Then I started on my books. I had a lot. They filled two bookcases and were stacked in piles against the wall. Some were from university. TV criticism, film scripts, biographies of directors and actors. Others dated back to my late teens – *Jane Eyre, The Great Gatsby, Lolita, On the Road,* and so on. Over the years, my tastes had

13

become less literary. Many of my more recent purchases featured vampires. My DVDs followed a similar pattern. At uni I'd chosen films by director. Now I preferred to watch HBO box sets. You could wipe out an entire weekend with a twelve–episode series, emerging on Monday morning with no hangover, just a vague sense of dislocation in the world.

I put a few in the corner named 'sell' and the rest in 'charity'. Then I moved the sell ones to charity as well. I didn't want them hanging around for months while I waited for someone to buy them off Amazon.

I worked my way through the whole room like that, sorting through my shoes, my make-up, my knick-knacks. There was a box under my bed full of old letters, birthday cards, and photographs. I pulled it out and took off the lid, then suddenly lost heart. I called my sister Susie then, to ask if she'd give me a lift to a charity shop tomorrow. Most of my belongings were in that corner, and the one labelled 'bin'. Almost all, in fact.

By the time I'd finished, Jessica and Gareth had gone out. It was a Friday night. I ate a bowl of cold curry in the kitchen then got ready for bed.

I didn't have any pyjamas to change into and taking them out of the bin bag felt wrong, like I'd broken a promise. I left them where they were and got under the covers naked. I never did that if I was on my own.

The next morning Susie arrived at just past nine, the only gap she had in her Saturday schedule. She had her phone in one hand, car keys in the other, but still managed to grab my arm when she saw all my stuff packed up in my room. 'I thought you meant just a few bags. Are you finally moving out of this student flat?'

'"Young professionals". Neither of us are students.'

'Sorry. "Young professionals". So, where are you going?'

'Nowhere. I'm having a clear-out.'

'Of everything you own?'

I gave her a bin bag of clothes to take down to her car. Susie was three years older than me but it always felt like more. She had married Tom when she was nineteen. They'd had two children by the time she was twenty-four. She'd never been to uni and done the living with friends thing or the staying in bed till 1 pm on a Tuesday thing. As a result, she looked at my life like it was something quirky and strange and not quite serious. As if it was a fanciful project I was involved in, rather than an actual adult existence.

She once asked me why I hadn't settled down with a decent man, as if decent men came along all the time and offered to set up home with me, and I was just giggling and batting them away. Both my sister and my mum veered between treating me like a child and getting annoyed that I wasn't more grown-up. Today, for example, Susie would happily take over the whole charity shop operation, then later tell me to get my driver's licence so I didn't have to rely on her to help out. It was confusing to be mollycoddled one minute then told to sharpen up the next.

My nephew Alfie was waiting in Susie's Mini outside. He said 'Hi' then went back to pressing buttons on his game console. We loaded the bags around him and filled the boot, then set off through the Saturday morning traffic, passing the Pot of Gold shop with its stacks of washing-up bowls filling with rain, the Booze R Us off-licence selling three bottles of wine for £10. In Chorlton, Susie deftly parallel parked outside Barnardo's.

'Mum, my swimming lesson starts in eighteen minutes,' Alfie said.

'That's loads of time. You've got your trunks on under your jeans, haven't you?'

'Yeah but I still need to get ready.'

'I'll be quick,' I said. I took a box of DVDs and books out of the boot and carried it inside, pushing open the door with my shoulder. A teenage girl with short black hair was standing in my path with her back to me. I said, 'Excuse me,' but she didn't hear. I was getting ready to ask again when a middle-aged man touched her shoulder. 'Chloe,' he said. She looked up and, seeing me, stepped out of the way.

There was nobody at the counter so I left the box on the floor and went to get another load. I did this four or five times, bringing in bulging bin bags, too-full shoeboxes. Susie stayed in the car because you weren't supposed to park there.

By my last trip, my belongings had taken over the bottom half of the shop. Anyone wanting to browse the bric-a-brac on the back wall would have to pick their way through my boxes of Spanish films and Sookie Stackhouse books, between bags spilling out M&S cardigans and machine-wash suit trousers.

I found the public display of my belongings

embarrassing. I looked around for a shop assistant but there didn't seem to be anyone. The man who'd nudged the girl was glancing surreptitiously at my boxes of books like someone waiting to pounce on a table you were about to leave in a busy bar. Have it, I thought, it's yours. He saw my glance and turned back to the bookshelves. Or don't.

Where was the shop assistant? I couldn't just leave it all sitting there. My life in bin bags. It made me feel kind of ill. I started walking, quickly, towards the door. Then someone behind me said, 'Where's all this come from?' and the man said, 'I think from the lady just leaving,' so I stopped and turned around.

They were both looking at me. A redhead with leg warmers over leggings and at least three jumpers. And the man who now had my copy of *Art by Film Directors* in his hands. The teenage girl was the only person not turned my way – she was taking a selfie on her iPhone, a sparkly gold scarf draped around her long white neck.

'Hi,' I said, returning to the counter. I felt like a shoplifter not a charity giver. 'I couldn't see anyone so I thought I'd just leave it here. Sorry.'

The girl smiled. Her name badge said Annie. 'I'd only been gone a minute and when I came back, we'd doubled our stock. Are you moving house?'

'Just having a clear-out.'

'You've done well.'

'I felt like having a fresh start.'

'Oh yeah, I know that feeling. My trick is to rearrange all the furniture in my flat – you feel like you're somewhere new without having the effort of moving.'

I'd planned to do that when I got home but I didn't like to say so. The man picked up another of my books. *100 Films to Watch Before You Die.*

'Are you giving away all of this?' he asked.

Tall with a light tan as if he'd grown up in a hot country and had been out of the sun too long. A blue cashmere jumper I doubt he got in a charity shop.

'Yes.'

'Why?' he asked. 'How?'

'Don't talk her out of it,' Annie said quickly.

How? 'Well, I... It was a spur of the moment thing. I just put it all in bags and boxes.' Was that what he wanted to know? I didn't think so.

'Just like that,' he said.

I shrugged. 'It was easy.' From the way he was looking at me, I was starting to feel like I'd achieved something special.

Susie came in. 'We need to go, Miriam.' She looked at all my stuff covering the floor. 'Are you sure about this? I mean, what are you going to *wear*?'

The three of them were staring at me now.

The teenager, Chloe, came over and pulled my green dress out of a bag. 'This is nice.' She held it up against herself. On me it was thigh-length and try-hard. On her it was below-the-knee and demure.

'Do you want me to buy it for you?' the man asked.

'Will you?' She sounded like she already knew the answer.

'Of course, how much is it?'

Annie considered the dress for a moment. 'Say £3.50?'

I didn't know whether she was asking me or the man.

We both looked expectantly at her. '£3.50 then,' she said. She bagged it up and handed it to Chloe, who took it then gave the man a one-armed hug.

'Thanks, Dad,' she said.

I looked down at my possessions – suddenly they were everything I'd done and seen and been for the last fifteen years. I wanted to take them back; the dress, my books, my favourite films. Then a second later, I felt repulsed by them all again. I hurried out. This wasn't so easy after all.

My room felt strange that night. The shadows were in the wrong places and there were empty spaces where there hadn't been before. The noises from the halfway house next door were clearer, as if my belongings had been acting as a sound barrier. Mario, a long-term resident whose room was through my wall, shouted something that sounded like 'FIRE!', then played a relaxation CD on loud all night. I woke just past four and lay awake listening to whales singing and waves crashing. My thoughts kept returning to everything I'd given away. Things I needed, like shoes and towels. Things I liked, like my full set of *Buffy the Vampire Slayer* DVDs.

But when I woke again, late on Sunday morning, I felt better about the bare bookshelves and sparse wardrobe. If a stranger walked in, they wouldn't be able to work out who lived here. They couldn't pin me down or make comments on my personality and life. They'd look around and draw a blank. And that was how I felt for a moment; like I could be anyone and everything was still to come.

3

When I got dressed on Monday morning I liked the lack of choices in my drawers and wardrobe. I had just three outfits now: jeans and navy blue V-neck jumper; second pair of jeans and grey V-neck jumper; and black skirt with black cardigan, black coat, black ballet shoes. I hadn't realised I'd left myself with so few options but it didn't matter, it was enough. Though when I set off walking through the rain to meet Natalie, I regretted giving away my boots and wished I hadn't left my umbrella on a bus a few days ago. My toes were already wet as I crossed the main road, snarled up with school run cars.

The address Natalie had given me was in Whalley Range but it was nowhere near my flat. I lived on the border with Old Trafford, Erik Zeleny lived east of here, in a neighbourhood I never went to. There was no reason to. No shops or bars, just rumours of muggings and prostitution.

I followed College Road into a quieter, residential area where the traffic drone was replaced by the patter of rain on horse chestnut trees. The drops on my head were fewer but heavier as they fell from the canopy above. There were spent conker shells on the pavement and in the gutter, and the garden hedgerows were full of berries. It was late September and the leaves were starting to turn.

The houses here were set back from the road and had a shabby grandeur to them as if they'd seen better times. This area seemed both rich and poor with no clear boundary between the two. At some point, it must have all been big family homes with well-kept gardens and separate rooms for piano playing and nursery games. Now many were cut up into flats like mine and Jessica's, with columns of doorbells flickering in entranceways and tribes of wheelie bins huddled on the drives.

I passed a derelict mansion with glassless windows and a skeletal roof, then took a slowly curving road towards Sylvan Drive which was parallel with the black railings at the top of Alexandra Park. Number 38 was at the end, in the shade of two huge copper beech trees. I was early so I sheltered beneath them by the front wall. On the stone gate pillars were faint, carved letters spelling out the name of the house but they were so worn away by rain and time, I couldn't work it out. I was trying to trace the vaguest letters with my finger when Natalie pulled up in her black Corsa.

When I'd woken that morning, I'd thought about not turning up. I lay in bed watching the tree swaying, getting upset about her comments on that form. Then I thought about my bank balance and the fact I'd just thrown away most of my clothes, and decided I better get dressed after all.

I forced a smile as she got out of her car.

'Big place,' she said, looking at the house. It was all chimneys and gables and complex networks of ruby-coloured drainpipes. 'He needs to get these trees seen to. They're blocking all his daylight.'

Maybe that was why he hadn't bothered opening any of the curtains. We followed the driveway up to fern-swept steps that led into an archway enclosing the front door. Natalie pushed hard on the doorbell. There was a muffled ringing then silence.

We waited and she rang the doorbell again. Then we heard someone coming around the side of the house, and it was the man from Barnardo's on Saturday. Chloe's dad.

He remembered me, I could tell, but Natalie spoke first, stepping towards him and holding out her hand. 'Mr Zeleny. Hi. I'm Natalie, we spoke on the phone. This is my assistant, Miriam.'

'Hi.' He shook Natalie's hand, looked at me.

'Miriam will be doing the filing for you, if you decide to use our services,' she said.

He was studying me with something like suspicion. I dropped the smile I'd attempted.

'So, shall we have a look?' Natalie said when he didn't respond.

'Actually, I don't think—' He stopped, swallowing his words.

We waited. Natalie said, 'Mr Zeleny?'

He took a deep breath. 'Yes, excuse me. This way, please.'

Natalie raised her eyebrows at me behind his back.

22

We followed him along the driveway which continued down the side of the house, passing an old wooden garage and a car covered in tarpaulin. Behind the house an overgrown lawn stretched back to a red brick wall overshadowed by more beech trees. A bird feeder hung from one. A squirrel clung to it, teeth out.

We went through a back door into a porch where the rain rattled on the roof, then into a big, cluttered kitchen with books and plants and magazines and CDs on the table and work surfaces. As we followed him through, I saw an expensive-looking camera next to an Apple Mac. The screen showed a black and white photograph of a girl in a ball gown on a staircase. He led us down a narrow hallway, narrowed further by paintings and bookcases and hanging coats and scarves, then took us up the stairs to a small room at the back of the house.

By small, I mean full. There wasn't enough space for the three of us to stand on the tiny patch of clear floor-board inside, so I stood in the doorway, trying to get a better look. Magazines were stacked in waist-high piles, leaning against each other, some already toppled over the floor. I saw copies of *Vogue* and *Harper's Bazaar*, *GQ* and *The New Yorker*. There must have been hundreds, perhaps thousands, of them. He didn't say anything, just stood looking at it all, pressing the fingers of his hands together as if channelling all his tension there.

'Right,' said Natalie. 'So what are you thinking?'

'I think…' He seemed lost for a moment. 'I think it needs…'

I get anxious when someone gets stuck like this, as if it's me that's struggling not them.

He gathered himself. 'I think it needs to be tidied and that Miriam will be the right person for the job. I would like her to start as soon as possible. You said the day rate was £160. That is fine with me.'

Natalie turned to me. 'Miriam, er, do you want to ask any questions?'

He had thrown her. I could tell she didn't know what to make of this situation but as long as he was paying, it didn't matter.

There were things I wanted to know, like, what am I supposed to do with all these magazines? And why can't you sort them out yourself? But it seemed unprofessional to ask.

'No,' I said.

'Right then,' she said.

He mumbled, 'Good,' then ushered us out of the room and quickly closed the door. We all traipsed back downstairs into the kitchen.

Natalie looked at the camera and the girl on the Mac. 'Are you a photographer?' she asked.

'Yes.'

'Oh really? What kind of photography do you do?'

'Fashion mainly. Sometimes other products.'

'Really? How creative. Is that why you've got so many magazines?'

'Well, perhaps.' He looked at me. 'So when do you think you can start?'

'Today.' Natalie answered. 'I'll leave Miriam here with you.' To me she said, 'I'll call you tomorrow for an update.'

They stepped towards the door to the porch and I

started to follow then remembered I was staying. My heart was suddenly beating very fast, which was irritating to say the least. It wasn't that bad, was it?

It was. I didn't know him. I didn't feel safe in this big old house. And I wasn't happy about working here with him on my own. I went towards the door, thinking I'd fob them both off with a story about feeling ill. But he was there before I reached it. I came to a dead stop in the middle of the kitchen.

He said, 'Last night, I decided I wasn't going to go through with this.' He was standing in the doorway. There was something apologetic in his tone. 'When the doorbell rang, I was going to tell you I had changed my mind. Then I saw it was you.'

You?

'From the charity shop,' he said.

'I'm not sure about this.'

He paused. 'Neither am I.' He must have realised I was about to leave because he said, 'Why don't you stay for the morning then decide?'

4

I didn't say anything, just took off my wet coat, then, after the decisiveness of this movement, couldn't see anywhere to put it. He took it out of my hands and placed it over a chair seat. He was rubbing the fingers of his right hand together again, like someone rolling tobacco or sprinkling salt.

'Would you like a drink? I am making hot chocolate.'

'No thank you.'

'Are you sure?'

'Oh, okay then.'

He moved around me to get to the cooker, where there was a pan of milk on the stove. He poured in spoonfuls of chocolate powder, letting each one dissolve before adding the next. I stood back against the radiator, a rounded, old-fashioned one with a faint warmth as if it was just coming on or going off. My cardigan sleeves and tights were wet. I should have brought a spare pair. I did a mental stocktake of my sparse drawers. Did I even have any to bring?

I looked around. The kitchen seemed to be where he

worked as well as ate. The table held camera pieces, a bundle of keys, an iPhone, and various USB leads and chargers. The windowsills doubled up as bookshelves. Photography collections, guides to birds and trees, novels, many of them old and worn like something you'd find in a giveaway box in a library. *The Moonlight Rose* by Yosanda Crest. *Last One Standing* by Jack Fenwick. Was this what he read?

Dotted amongst the computer equipment were odds and ends I wanted to pick up and examine. A rough glittering stone containing a curling fossil; a small, intricate sculpture that reminded me of a bird's wing; a little bottle made from wavy, light blue glass. Stuck on the fridge door was a line drawing of a woman's face. The walls around the table displayed exhibition posters from art galleries in London and Prague.

Erik handed me a mug that looked like it had been handmade. I felt the handle give slightly so held it by the rim, the heat burning my fingers. We went back through the hallway where paintings of plants and birds and people jostled for space on the walls, and the telephone sat on top of a pile of junk mail and flyers.

In the room upstairs, I looked for somewhere to put my drink but every surface was covered. The towers of magazines went from wall to wall, with just narrow gaps between them. The only other objects in there were a single bed, covered with its own thin film of magazines, plus a child's desk – one of those with a lid you could lift up. On the desk was a Sylvanian Families House with as many gables and windows as this one, and a collection of the little plastic toys you get in Kinder Surprise. I didn't know whether it was the doll's house or the contrast with my usual surroundings (office, bedroom, bus stops) but this place had a feeling of unreality to me. When I looked out of the window, I couldn't see any other buildings, just the dense canopies of the smooth-trunked beech trees, shading out the garden and making it feel as if we could be anywhere.

A mobile phone rang somewhere downstairs. He ignored it. 'It is my work number. They will leave a message.' He took a breath. 'So, this will be Chloe's room.'

Chloe his daughter who now owned my green dress.

'She wants to live with me,' he said. 'She told me this just last week.'

'Where does she live now?'

'In Sheffield.'

With her mother, I thought. It made sense – the way Erik spoiled her in the shop, the way she took his gifts for granted. He was a divorced father buying affection.

He explained that she'd been offered a place at Manchester University and wanted to live with him rather than go into student housing. 'It is free accommodation, I suppose.'

'It's probably both,' I said without thinking. 'I mean, it's free and she wants to spend time with you as well.'

He looked at me. 'Yes, I think so, too. How old are you?'

'Twenty-nine.'

'You look younger.' He was studying me as if I was someone he was going to photograph. I looked down. Beautiful female faces stared back at me. They were

28

everywhere, in lopsided piles, falling into one another, a dark glinting eye overlapping a precise red mouth. A tanned shoulder nudging a slim thigh.

'Did you take any of these pictures?' I asked.

'Some of them, yes.'

'What do you want me to do with them?'

'I need you to help me organise them so that I can get this room clear for Chloe moving in. Is that something you can do?'

I said I could. He said he would help me. He said we would work on it together, because I wouldn't know which ones were important, and which ones less important. I would have preferred to work on my own. This room would be more stifling than the office, with just two of us here in this cramped space. I would work fast. Maybe we'd be done in a day.

His phone rang again downstairs and he took the mug out of my hand. 'I better get that. Don't move anything yet.'

I looked out of the window at the back garden. A cat was sitting on the garage roof. A squirrel was burying something in the long, wet lawn. I was still considering leaving. I was always considering it, whatever job I was doing. It comes with being a temp. You don't feel tied to anywhere. You're supposed to be there, but you don't belong there, and tomorrow you're supposed to be somewhere else. Most places, I just floated through like a balloon, being batted from one task to the next, then finally being bumped out of the door. I thought of my bed and my warm, heavy duvet. It was only half past nine.

29

When Erik returned he explained that he wanted to organise the magazines into title and date so he would know what he was keeping and what he was discarding. The room was like a badly shuffled deck of cards – some magazines were already grouped together as if there'd been a system once, or he had started this task before. In other places, they were thrown together randomly – *Vogue* next to *Wallpaper* next to *Elle*. They were mostly fashion magazines, heavy, thick and glossy, but also some slimmer publications – *Time* and *The New Yorker* and the boxy bright yellow of *National Geographic*.

I cleared a space at the foot of the bed to sit down, wishing I'd worn jeans rather than my one remaining skirt. We decided I would start at this end of the room, while he tackled the magazines nearest the door. It was such a mess that there was no obvious place to begin. There wasn't even any space to work in. I stacked more magazines onto the bed to make room to organise them, and wondered what Chloe thought about her bedroom being buried like this. She mustn't have stayed over recently unless she had another room somewhere else in the house.

'Is it just you here?' I asked.

'Yes.'

'How long have you lived here?'

'Eighteen years.'

I couldn't tell whether he wanted us to talk or not. I decided to stop speaking, to see what happened. The silence was uncomfortable and I felt my chest tightening up. Then, after a while, it began to feel normal.

Maybe that was what he was doing, making it okay not to speak, because not long after I'd started to relax, he started to talk to me.

'So how long have you worked for City Business Services?'

'I don't really work there. I'm a temp. They offered me a week's work because they were busy.'

He frowned. 'Does that mean they will send someone else next week?'

'Do you think this will take longer than a week?'

He rubbed his hand over his shaved hair. It was black turning grey. His eyes were walnut brown. 'I don't know.'

'Natalie said she'd keep me on to do this job.'

'Good.'

I thought of what he'd said to Natalie earlier about me being 'the right person for the job'. He seemed to have a faith in me I hadn't earned and it made me apprehensive. It was a long time since anyone had had any expectations of me. I felt sure I would let him down.

'Do you like temping?' he asked a few minutes later.

'Not really.' I stopped myself. 'I mean, it's all right.'

He looked across at me. 'You don't like your job. It's okay to say so.'

'This is okay,' I said. 'I like sorting through things.'

'I do too,' he said. 'I like to collect things and sort through them. It is just that I never get time to finish. And now Chloe is coming back. I have to finish.'

'When's she moving in?'

'April.'

'I think we'll be okay,' I said, smiling.

31

'I hope so,' he said seriously, as if April was next week, not six months away.

As the morning went on I got into the rhythm of turning the magazines spineways, finding the date or issue number, slotting them into the right place in their pile. I knew that when I closed my eyes that night, I'd see the *Elle* masthead or hear the promises on the covers in my head. Two weeks to a beach-ready body. This season's hottest handbags. Examining them, I tried to figure out if there was a style or a look I felt a particular pull towards but I couldn't imagine myself in any of the outfits on the models. I was having a 'wardrobe crisis'. Somewhere in here I'd seen a cover offering a quick fix for it.

At lunchtime I took my sandwiches to Alexandra Park. There was an iron gateway opposite the house which opened onto a wide pathway around a lake with an overgrown island at one end. I took a path that led me past a boarded-up pavilion and a glass-strewn tennis court without any nets, then around playing fields circled by poplar trees. After a while I came to a long, straight avenue between two lines of lime trees that ran from one end of the park to the other. I followed it back to the lake near Erik's house and sat on a bench overlooking the stagnant, scummy water. There were ducks and geese and chunks of naan bread floating at the edges.

I ate my lunch slowly, wondering how soon I ought to go back. An hour? Was that too long? I was glad for this break from the polite conversation with Erik, from the small room and its onslaught of words and images. Even his bathroom felt tight and claustrophobic. The bath itself was full of books, like something from an arty interior design shoot. And a stack of magazines meant there was barely space to open and close the door. There must have been another one somewhere with a shower. Probably behind one of those closed doors in the hallway.

A wiry grey dog trotted past with an empty lager can in its mouth. A gaunt man followed with a green army rucksack on his back. I watched them walk around the lake, then got up and reluctantly headed back to the park gates.

Erik was sitting at the kitchen table, tapping away on his Mac.

'How was your lunch?' he asked, as if I'd just eaten in a restaurant rather than on a park bench.

'Okay thanks.'

'Would you like a cup of tea?'

'Yes please.'

We worked steadily all afternoon and by five o'clock the room was a whirlpool of glossy covers, the stacks broken up and scattered by our attempts to order them. I found it hard to leave it like that. If it had been my room, I would have stayed up all night until it started to make some sense. But Erik said I would want to get home, and I didn't like to say otherwise. When I thought about the night ahead I felt my spirits drop. I didn't know why. There was nothing bad coming up, as far as I could tell. It was just more of the same, minus my box sets. I think that's what was bothering me most about my clear-out. I had nothing to escape into when I got home.

Erik gathered together our mugs. Shifted some copies of *National Geographic* so we could get to the door. 'Anything interesting planned for tonight?'

I would be lying on my bed, watching it get dark, trying to ignore the sound of Jessica and Gareth on one side and Mario on the other.

'No.'

He looked like he wished he hadn't asked. Perhaps I should have made something up to make myself sound a bit more chipper. But it was hard to put on an act around him. There was something about him that made me want to tell the truth.

Still, I didn't need to be rude. I said, 'What about you?'

He let the question hang there for a moment. 'No.'

Well, that was that covered. I followed him downstairs. In the kitchen, he took my coat from the chair.

It was then I noticed a pile of my books which had been hidden underneath. He must have bought them from Barnardo's after I'd left. *The Great Gatsby. Wuthering Heights. A Room with a View.*

'You bought my books,' I said.

'You gave them to the charity shop,' he said, as if I didn't know.

I picked up *A Room with a View* and a postcard I'd used as a bookmark fell out. It was from my dad to my grandma when we'd been on a camping holiday in France. I'd taken it from her house when we were clearing it after she'd died.

The date was 17th August 1989 – I know because it was my fifth birthday and I'd read this postcard many times before. He'd written that I'd liked the Pound Puppy they'd bought me.

I looked at Erik. 'It's from my dad. I didn't know it was in there.'

He took it out of my hand and studied it. 'I like it when I find things in books that people have left by accident.' He glanced at me and slipped it back between the pages.

'I didn't mean to leave it,' I said.

He put the book back on the chair.

This was awkward. And weird. I wasn't sure what to do. 'Can I have it back?'

His mouth tensed. 'You gave it to the shop.'

'Not the postcard.'

'You gave it away. It is too late to change your mind.'

For a moment I couldn't think why he was wrong. 'But it doesn't mean anything to you.'

'It does.' He was standing in front of the chair, as if protecting the books from me.

I didn't understand. 'But it's mine.' I felt myself choking up. I had to get out of there. He just looked at me. I grabbed my bag and went towards the back door.

'Will you come back tomorrow?' he said.

I didn't reply. Beech nuts cracked under my feet as I walked down the driveway to the road.

5

I had planned to get the 85 to Chorlton, then the 86 back down to my side of Whalley Range, but when I reached the bus stop I kept walking, passing churches advertising slimming classes, grammar schools boasting of exam success, edging away from kerbside puddles when cars passed. In my head, I was going over what had just happened. Was I right to be upset? He had paid for the book. But he could have given back the postcard when I said I wanted it. It was like he considered it his the moment he saw it. He didn't even think about returning it to me. It was like it was beyond him.

I reached the centre of Chorlton. I didn't feel like going home to the cramped flat yet but most of the shops were already closed. I considered sitting in one of the bars for a while, just until my thoughts settled, then I saw that the lights were on in Barnardo's and people were still milling around inside.

The same pale-faced redhead was behind the counter. She smiled when I walked in, maybe she recognised me, I wasn't sure. I stood between rails of clothes arranged by colour with a disproportionate amount of black and beige. My blue skirt with the long slits up the side was hanging there. And there was one of my hooded tops.

I checked the price tag. £4. Not bad. I touched the sleeve. It was one I wore when I wanted to feel comfy and cushioned from the world. The jumper version of a pair of slippers or winter pyjamas. Should I buy it back? I felt the fiver in my pocket. I edged over to the DVDs and saw half my collection staring back at me.

The shop assistant came over as I was flicking through them. 'You're not having regrets, are you?' She looked genuinely concerned, as if the films had been stolen from me rather than willingly donated.

'No regrets. I'm just seeing if there's anything decent to watch tonight.' The thing I needed most, I decided, was a way to fill the evening.

'We don't usually get good DVDs.' She pushed back an armful of bangles and started flicking through them herself. 'When we do, they go fast. We've sold a few of yours already.'

I looked at my copy of *Diva*. On the back cover was a still from my favourite scene – the moment in the park when the postboy realises his attraction to the opera singer is reciprocated. 'I'm thinking of buying this back,' I said.

She took it out of my hands. 'File under "Obscure French films". Is it any good?'

'It's all right. In an obscure French film kind of way.'

'Maybe I'll borrow it off you if you buy it.'

I couldn't work out if she was making a sales pitch or just being friendly. I looked at the snatches of familiar colours amongst the unwanted clothes and wondered why I'd come in here. 'Maybe it was a mistake to give away so much stuff,' I said.

'Why, what else have you been missing? I bet I can pick out your clothes. What's your name?'

I told her and she introduced herself as Annie and dryly did a little shuffle-toe tap which made me laugh. Then she started searching the shop for 'Miriam-like items'. She pulled out a tiger-patterned minidress with a black lacy trim, raising her eyebrows as she held it against her. Then an oversized, shoulder-padded purple suit jacket, which she said was me all over.

She stood with her hands on her hips, looking around. 'It's actually not that easy spotting your old stuff. What about that leather satchel – was that yours?'

'No. It's nice, though.' I paused. 'I think.'

'Totally it is.' Annie reached up to pull it down from the hook. '£5.50? We're *giving* it away. What else – was there something in particular you wanted back?'

I thought of the postcard with my name on it in my dad's handwriting. It was the surprise of seeing it in Erik's house. His calm possession of something that was mine.

I said, 'It's just that I feel kind of…flimsy. Like there's less of me than there was before.'

'I'm not sure buying your old clothes is going to help with that.'

'What will?'

'Buy some new things. You don't want to go backwards.' She went over to the counter where a grey-haired lady in a puffy anorak was waiting to be served.

I looked at the satchel. Was it my style? I had no idea. I put it back on its hook, and waved goodbye to Annie as I left.

When I got home, I thought about telling Jessica what had happened at Erik's house but in the end I just said I'd had a shit day and she said, 'Tell me about it,' in a way that meant, 'Don't go on about it.'

Jessica worked as an account handler for an ad agency. She described it as 'boring and stressful at the same time' and was looking for something else. We'd met at university and we now agreed that perhaps film studies hadn't been the best choice of subject, career-wise. Jessica was thinking of doing an accountancy course because she was sick of the limited choices and small salaries open to arts graduates. I wanted to retrain, too, but I couldn't think of anything I particularly wanted to do.

Gareth came round while I was making pasta and pesto for dinner. He'd brought wine and two little pots of tiramisu and a DVD of *American Psycho*. Jessica asked if I wanted to watch it with them and I wondered when it had happened that she could invite me into my own living room. I ate my dinner sitting on my bed, checking my emails on my laptop. I'd been half-thinking of going swimming tonight, but I felt empty-tired, as if I was ill or had been crying. I wished our internet signal was fast enough to let me watch programmes online. I read a few news articles then put Erik's name in Google and found he had a website.

On the home page, there were just two links: Commercial and Fine Art, with his email address underneath.

I clicked Fine Art. It loaded a moving slideshow of textured paintings with a depth of colour that seemed to pulse off the screen. They were abstract and I had no idea what they meant but they were arresting, perhaps because they didn't let the eye settle on one shade. One was a deep, complex blue, moving through different tones, darker, then darker still until the colour seemed like a dimension in itself. Another was rich magenta shades that for some reason, made me feel hungry. Another was clear, luminescent yellows. I thought of images of brains that highlight the different parts used to create different emotions. I clicked on the blue painting to enlarge it. There was no title, just a date, about five years ago, and the size, three feet by five feet.

There was a link, Sculpture, on the Fine Art page but when I clicked it there was nothing in it, just a line saying this section will be updated soon. I clicked Commercial. It displayed photographs much like those I'd been looking at all day. Beautiful men and women with expensive clothes and enigmatic expressions. I moved through them quickly. I had never felt the insecurity women are supposed to get from looking at fashion magazines but I could feel something like it starting now.

Through the wall Mario put on one of his favourite football DVDs. Usually I'd have one of my own on to drown it out: *Buffy* or *True Blood* or *Seinfeld*. I'd watched them all so many times I knew what the characters were going to say before they said it. Now I was stuck with the sound of United beating City at Old Trafford. I knew who was playing because I could hear snatches of the commentary, and because Mario sometimes sang United songs at the top of his voice in the early hours of the morning.

A few weeks after we'd moved in here, Mario had been waiting at the bus stop at the same time as me. He was lumpy and unshaven, in a tracksuit and trainers. He looked older than he should and spoke with an openness that belonged to someone much younger. He was 'bi-polo', he said, and he had a kid he wasn't allowed to see. He talked about the mother throwing him out as if it was last week, even though it seemed to have happened many years ago.

A few weeks later, Jessica reported having the same conversation with him when she was waiting outside for a taxi. His child. The mother. The court order. It was the first thing he told her. The first thing he told everyone.

Now whenever I saw him, sitting at the bus stop or standing in his doorway, he called out hello. I don't think he knew I was in the flat directly next to his. I wondered whether he could hear me watching the same dramas unfolding again and again while he watched the same triumphant football match.

6

The street lights were still glowing beneath the thick tree canopies that spread across Erik's road when I arrived the next morning. It was raining, I was soaked again, and I really didn't want to be there. Thinking about my postcard had kept me awake last night. I'd worked myself up into a restlessness that made me sit up in bed, staring at the wall, for about an hour. It was the fact that he had all this power over my life all of a sudden. My finances, my personal belongings, how I spent my day. If I hadn't been completely skint I'd quit and wait for another temp assignment to come through. But I still owed Jessica for the electricity bill, and the rent was due next week. I couldn't afford to walk away.

Erik didn't answer when I rang the doorbell, which annoyed me even more. I peered through the thick green glass for a change of light or a movement that would show he'd heard, then walked to the back of the house, planning to hammer on the porch door. Then, through the kitchen window, over the doubled-up row of books on the sill, I saw him in the hallway. He turned a key in a door to a side room, tested the handle, did the same at the next one. He was oblivious of me watching, and started moving towards the front door. I walked fast back to the steps and up into the gloom of the arched portico so I was waiting there when he opened it. The keys for the rooms he'd just locked were visible against his thigh through his jeans.

In the kitchen my books were still on the table, half-hidden under a grey jumper. He saw me look at them and turned to stir the chocolate heating on the stove. As he poured it into two mugs, he said, 'I thought you wouldn't come back.'

'I wouldn't get paid if I didn't.'

He looked over at me. I was standing against the radiator with my coat on.

'You're angry,' he said.

'I just don't understand why you won't give it back.'

He put the pan down on the stove, turned off the blue gas flame. 'I do not normally have people at my home.'

I didn't know how to reply. It was like the disjointed conversations in one of my French films.

'I'm glad you are here,' he said, looking levelly at me. Then when I didn't respond. 'We should get started.'

Upstairs all the doors were shut apart from Chloe's room. Had he locked them as well? I thought of how he'd taken the book out of my hands as if afraid I might run off with it. I didn't like being under suspicion. I wasn't going to take anything. Except my postcard and that was mine anyway.

I stepped carefully between the magazines to the

space I'd cleared yesterday. He stood near the door and looked around with a tired, submerged expression. Was he going to stay in here all day again? I wanted to be left alone. It wasn't as though he helped much, looking endlessly through the magazines when all he needed was the date or issue number on the cover.

'I'll finish this easily today,' I said. 'You can get on with your other work if you like.'

He straightened his back, focused his eyes rather than letting them drift across the landslide of colours and faces. 'No, I will help. I worked late last night so I don't have a lot to do today. Then tomorrow, I will decide which magazines to keep. It will not take long, I think. And then Chloe can have her room back. She doesn't know I used it for storage. She would not be happy about it.'

I sat down on the floor, not speaking. It would be a long day if I was planning to stay angry with him for seven hours in this small space. I tried to think of something neutral to say. 'So, where does Chloe sleep now when she stays over?'

'She has not slept here for eight years. In fact, she has barely stepped inside the front door in all that time.'

'How come?'

'She says this house has "bad vibes".' He met my eyes for a second then looked away. 'That is why I was unprepared,' he gestured around the room, 'when she said she wanted to move back in. I had no idea she was thinking of it. When we have finished I am going to redecorate this room for her. She will want a wardrobe, I think, and a desk for studying – it could go here, by

44

the window, so she benefits from the natural light. And a rug beside the bed. I have seen one she will like.'

A smile spread into his eyes while he was talking. He doted on Chloe and it made me feel sorry for him. I imagined her playing on it, asking for money for taxis and new laptops, using the house as a crash pad between clubbing and lectures, bringing friends home in the early hours.

'Won't it be a bit strange having her living here after so long?' I asked.

'Maybe, but I'm excited about it. I want to build a closer relationship with her before she grows up.' He paused then added, 'I think it will work out fine. It is a big enough house for two people.'

It was a huge house. It must have been built for a Victorian cotton baron or a factory owner, someone who wanted views of the new park while he shaved in the morning. I wondered how it would feel to have so much space to yourself. To have the quiet and privacy of not just one room but two whole floors.

I began looking for copies of *National Geographic*, picking them out and putting them to one side, ready to be sorted later. Yesterday I had ordered several years of *Vogue, Elle, Time, The New Yorker,* and *Harper's Bazaar*. They went back as far as 2003, with a few that were much older, 1980s, 1990s.

I was a lot faster at sorting than Erik. He got distracted by the photographs on the covers and inside. He'd cut out pictures with a scalpel and say to me, isn't that beautiful, or, look at this colour here, or the light there. I would look, unsure what I was supposed to be admiring. I saw green or blue or yellow, a building, a field, a beach. The pictures didn't affect me in the way they did him. When I tried to explain this, using the words 'aesthetics' and 'sensitive' in a mishmash sentence I was surprised he understood, he said, 'I am an artist as well as a photographer. That is maybe why I notice these things.'

'What kind of art do you do?'

'Sculpture mainly, at the moment.'

I wanted to know more but didn't know what question to ask. And I didn't want to accidentally reveal that I'd seen his website. It was easier when he asked me questions. We talked about where I lived, what I'd studied, how I was still trying to find my way into a career.

He told me that he got his first job as a photographer after he moved to London from Bratislava. He was twenty-two. It was a few years after the Velvet Revolution.

I remembered news footage of mass demonstrations. A sense that something big was happening that I didn't fully understand. I said, 'I can't imagine what that must have been like.'

'The revolution?'

I nodded.

He was turning the pages of a copy of *Time*. Smoothing out each one as he studied the images. 'Perhaps because you've always been free to do whatever you want in this country.'

I didn't feel like I could do whatever I wanted. I didn't have the bus fare. But I didn't want to start comparing hardships with someone who'd lived through Communism.

He said, 'Here, you can say whatever you want. Be whoever you want. In Czechoslovakia, it was not so simple.' He looked up from the magazine. 'The best way I can explain it is, you had an "outside you" that did everything correctly, for the outside world, and you had an "inside you" that you kept hidden, because you didn't know who might be watching.'

My eyes rested on the shape of the key in his pocket. I was thinking about the 'inside' version of him.

He picked up another magazine. 'Chloe finds it hard to understand as well.'

I refocused. 'So who would be watching?'

'The police, or your neighbours could be listening through the wall. Anyone. But I was only twenty when it ended. I didn't have to live like that for decades like my mother and father.'

'Were you expecting it, when everything changed?'

'Not really, because it had been the same for years and years, and then it happened quite quickly. In September, things were normal. By November, the regime was rattled and we didn't know which way it would settle. Then the Communists were out and everything was open to me and my friends. All these possibilities we didn't have before.'

He changed his university course in Bratislava from teaching to art then got an exchange student visa for UCL. It was where he met Chloe's mother. They married and he worked at a photography studio in Soho before getting a job on a now-defunct fashion magazine. He won an award while he was there which gave him enough of a name to be able to set up on his own. He said they moved to Manchester because he had some clients up here, and it was cheaper to live.

He said, 'When we bought this place, Whalley Range was not somewhere you would want to live. It was still like in that Smiths song. And the house was falling to pieces. There were rats, beetles, slugs everywhere. Every morning you would see trails of slime across the floor, even upstairs. And you never knew if you were going to disturb a burglar when you came home. But I have not had a burglary since 2008.'

'What about a slug?'

'I have not had a slug since I got Micka, my cat. I don't think you have met her yet.'

'I saw her in the garden. She ran away when she saw me.'

'She's shy. She gets friendlier when she's more sure of you.' His eyes met mine when he said this and I looked down because I knew he was talking about me.

Dusk had fallen by the time we finished. All the magazines were neatly stacked by name and date in clusters of knee-high towers. I wasn't sure why we'd bothered to organise them so exactly when he was going to throw most of them away but it was done now, and it was satisfying. There was sense to it, a pattern, not the chaos of yesterday. I wanted to stay and just look at them for a while.

'I should have done this a long time ago,' he said. 'I don't know why I didn't.'

'Because you can't pick up a magazine without looking through it for pictures to cut out,' I said. There was a pile of pages he'd carefully sliced free with his scalpel. Advertisements for perfume, jewellery, watches. Photographs of deserts and storm clouds and rivers through forests.

'It is why I needed you here.'

I smiled. 'So, tomorrow, we just need to decide what to keep, and what to throw away, and put the ones for throwing in bin bags. We can fill your recycling bin but we could do with taking them to the tip because there'll be too many. Then I guess that'll be it, unless there's anything else you need me to do.'

He shook his head, swallowed. 'No, nothing.'

Rain drummed onto the windowsill from the over-flowing gutter above. It was time for me to go home, and by bus or by foot, I was going to get soaked. It wouldn't have been a problem in the past but now my wardrobe was so limited, I would need to dry my jeans before tomorrow or I wouldn't have anything to wear.

'Do you have an umbrella I could borrow?' I asked.

'How are you getting home?'

'Walking.'

'Through Whalley Range?'

'Yes.' It would take half the time as going by bus.

'I don't think it is safe for you to walk on your own when it is getting dark. I will come with you.'

'No, it's okay. You don't have to.'

He went off down the landing and I wasn't sure whether I'd discouraged him or not. Surely this rain would put off any potential muggers? A few minutes later, he returned with one of those huge golfing umbrellas. He was wearing a brown leather jacket and he had a rucksack on his shoulder.

The rain fell heavier as we followed the road along the edge of the park. Puddles flooded the pavement and grimy water soaked through my shoes. He held the umbrella over both of us but it wasn't wide enough and I could feel my arm and shoulder getting wet.

'You don't have to walk me all the way home,' I said, after a while.

'I'm going to the swimming baths. It's near where you live.'

Oh. It wasn't for me then, this trudge through a downpour. 'I go swimming at the Aquatics Centre,' I said. 'A man swam beneath me and grabbed my leg in Chorlton Baths.'

'What did you do?'

'I kicked him.'

'Did you report him?'

'No.'

'Why not?'

'I just didn't.'

'So now you won't go there. It is a shame.'

I was glad we didn't go to the same place to swim. It would be embarrassing to bump into him on the poolside or in the water. I imagined him to be a fast lane swimmer, goggles on, sleek, rhythmic front crawl. I did breaststroke. Slow and laboured, only getting the tips of my hair wet.

We were passing the derelict house. I slowed down, and he stopped. We stood at the end of the driveway, looking up at the empty windows and brick-strewn grass. It must have taken years for it to become so dilapidated. The windows breaking first, then roof tiles falling in a winter storm. Graffiti spreading from the outside to the inside, wallpaper peeling, pipes ripped out, the garden growing wild.

'It's like a haunted house,' I said as we started walking again.

Erik said, 'I would take you in there – I know the man who has bought that land – but I think you would be too scared.'

'Damn right.'

He laughed and repeated the phrase to himself, as if trying it out. We crossed Alness Road, which was empty, and Withington Road, which was busy with traffic, and followed it down to College Road. It arched gently towards my side of the neighbourhood, the tarmac cracked and warped by tree roots.

The roads were quiet and we weren't talking. It was just our footsteps on the pavement and the rain pattering onto the umbrella and the warmth of his arm against my shoulder. People hadn't arrived home from work yet and the houses we passed were silent apart from the fast flow of water down drainpipes. Then the line of cars moving along Upper Chorlton Road came into view in the distance and I felt for a moment that I didn't want us to reach it.

I shifted away from him, out of the cover of the umbrella. He looked at me, surprised.

'It's stopped raining,' I said. But it hadn't, not really, and I wasn't sure why I'd moved away so abruptly.

He took the umbrella down uncertainly. 'Yes. Nearly.'

I walked faster then. I wanted to be home. Outside the bars on Upper Chorlton Road smokers huddled under dripping sun parasols and around outdoor heaters. Jessica was sitting in front of Jam Street Café. She waved, looking at Erik. I waved back and kept walking. When our road was opposite, I stopped.

'I live over there.'

'I will see you tomorrow morning?'

'Yes.'

'Bye then.'

'Bye.'

I ran across the road in a gap between cars. Inside, I stood in my bedroom in my wet coat and jeans, unsure what to do next. I went into the kitchen and looked in the fridge and cupboards, then went back into my room and opened my wardrobe door, even though I knew there was nothing hanging inside.

'Who was that you were with?' Jessica asked when I joined her at Jam Street.

'The guy I'm working for. He didn't think it was safe for me to walk home on my own.'

She gave me a sideways look. 'How old is he?'

'I don't know. Forties? Do you want a drink?'

'Got one.'

There was a quiz on in the bar. I opened the door to laughter and cheers. It was a 'name that tune' round and the clip was something I remembered from school discos, some 1990s dance track. I ordered a glass of red

wine and walked out to a blast of Aztec Camera singing
'Somewhere In My Heart'.

Outside, Jessica was making a roll-up. It had stopped
raining completely now and the air was fresh and sharp.
I squeezed onto a patch of dry bench. 'Are you here on
your own?'

'Gareth's on his way. Hey, I went in your room before
to see if you'd got my hair straighteners – where's all
your stuff?'

'I gave it to Barnardo's.'

'Barnardo's? You don't even *like* kids. Why not sell
it on eBay?'

'It's a good cause.'

'You're a good cause. You could have gone on
holiday with that money. When was the last time you
went abroad?'

'When did you?'

She took a sharp, fast drag on her roll-up. 'I'm going
to Spain in January.'

I didn't know that. She was going with Gareth, it
turned out. She hadn't asked me, she said, because she
didn't think I could afford it, and she didn't want to
make me feel bad.

I didn't know why she was explaining. I would hardly
want to go away with the two of them anyway. I felt
like my relationship with Jessica had strayed into some
strange territory of awkwardness and overcompensa-
tion, and I wasn't sure whether she was a good friend
or not. She was the person I spent the most time with,
but was that just because we lived in the same flat?

I could see Gareth crossing the road. An ironed t-shirt

under his suit jacket. Then aftershave that reminded me of sharing his bed. He kissed Jessica on the cheek and sat down. 'How's tricks, Miriam?'

'Good.'

'Miriam's got an older man,' Jessica said.

'Really?' He was so politely interested it was impolite.

'No, not really,' I said.

'And he's tasty,' Jessica continued.

'More so than me?'

I took a long swig of my wine and wished I still smoked. Jessica and Gareth started talking about their trip to Madrid – bars they wanted to go to, what hotel to book. I didn't know how to join in and I thought of the meandering conversations I'd had with Erik that day. I was finishing there tomorrow. Then it would be back to the office in Ardwick. All those women. All those phone calls.

'Mim, we're heading into Chorlton to get some food. Are you staying here?' Jessica was already standing up.

I said I was. I'd only drunk half my wine and I was planning to get another one. I stayed there until about eight o'clock, budging up for smokers, watching passers-by. I could have been waiting for a friend like Jessica was earlier. That's what I'd say, if I saw someone passing that I knew.

7

The sun was shining the next day. We took our hot chocolate into the back garden and sat on the bench against the side of the garage. Erik relaxed his shoulders against the wood and let the warmth hit his face, his eyes closed and his lips slightly parted. 'I haven't quite woken up yet,' he said.

I wondered whether he had worked late again last night so he could help me today. He didn't seem in any rush to get started, though, and it felt strange to me, knowing how much he was paying for my time. I supposed we didn't have as much to do today. We could be finished in a few hours if we focused. But I was in no hurry to get back to the office; sitting here in the sun was fine with me.

I sipped my chocolate and watched his cat stalking through the grass towards a magpie. Erik's iPhone buzzed in his pocket. He dug it out and sighed. 'I have to get this.' He went inside, speaking in another language to whoever was on the other end.

The magpie let the cat get a few feet closer then

unhurriedly flew up to the garage roof. Erik told me yesterday that he'd counted twenty-seven of them sitting up there on Sunday morning, and that he didn't know whether it meant something very good or very bad.

The landline phone started to ring in the hallway. Loud, quivering peals with long gaps between each one. I ignored it at first then reluctantly got up. Erik was still talking on his mobile in the kitchen. He nodded at me, as if to say, answer it.

I picked up the receiver, looking around for a pen and paper amongst the letters and flyers. 'Hello?'

A pause, then, 'Who's this?'

'Do you want to speak to Erik?'

'Yes. Is he there?' A woman with a voice like a dodgem car, fast and abrupt.

'He's on the other phone. Can I take a message?'

'Are you a friend of his?'

'I'm doing some tidying for him in the house.'

'You're a cleaner?' She spoke as if it was her right to know.

I preferred archivist. 'I'm just helping out for a few days.'

'Well, whoever you are, please tell him Caitlin called. I need to talk to him about Chloe.'

'Has he got your number?'

'I should hope so.'

When I told Erik he rubbed the side of his head, as if suddenly tired. 'I will quickly call her then we can get started.'

I waited in the kitchen, wondering whether to go

back into the garden, out of earshot, but his tone was measured and polite so I decided there was no need. It sounded like Caitlin was quizzing him about Chloe's move.

'She will have her old bedroom,' he was saying. 'I am having it redecorated for her.' He was quiet for a while before he said calmly, 'A lot has changed since then.'

When he responded again, he sounded less composed. 'Has Chloe said something? You know this was her idea. I did not talk her into it.' Then, 'She is old enough to make her own decisions.'

Caitlin must have started to speak but he jumped in. 'I know her very well. She is my daughter, after all.' The next time he spoke he sounded defeated. 'Caitlin, I have to go. I am going. Goodbye.' And put the phone down.

I pretended to be examining the photography books on the windowsill. It wasn't very convincing but he didn't seem concerned. He was preoccupied with Caitlin and Chloe and I felt like I was intruding.

'Shall we get to work?' I said.

He kneaded his shoulder blades as if the phone call had caused a physical strain. 'Yes. No. If you like.' He looked at his watch and sighed. 'We have not got very far this morning, have we?'

'We can catch up.'

'Caitlin, she makes me...' He shook his head. 'She is just concerned for Chloe. But it is very frustrating. She is very judgemental.'

I wanted to know what she was judging him about. Had he been unfaithful to her, was that why they divorced? Was he a bad father? No, Chloe wouldn't want to live with him if he was. And I could tell he loved his daughter from the way he was quietly thrilled about her moving in. Did Caitlin resent him having this time with her, even though he had missed so much of her childhood?

'She sounded like a bitch,' I said.

He looked at me in surprise and I wished I hadn't spoken. 'Yes she is,' he said. 'To me, at least.'

And to me. If the phone rang again, I wouldn't answer and hopefully he wouldn't either. I wanted us to get to work, back into the steady rhythm of sorting and organising and our easy conversations.

'Miriam, I'm sorry. I don't think I can do this today. I have a lot to do for a deadline tomorrow, and my head is…' He shrugged. 'I am not in the right mood for it.'

Oh. He wanted me to leave. 'I could work on it without you?'

'No, I need to do it with you. We can pick it up again tomorrow.'

'Okay.' My voice was flat. I tried to cover it. 'I better get a taxi to the office.'

'I have disturbed your day.'

'It doesn't matter. I just prefer working here.'

'They will still want me to pay for your time. Why don't you go and do something else? I will pretend you were here.'

It was bound to cause problems later but I couldn't be bothered to argue. I left quickly before he noticed how abruptly my mood had sunk. I'd expected to spend the day there then walk home with him through the hushed, evening streets. Now the sun was out and the park was busy with joggers and mothers with prams. He was right; he had disturbed my day. But more than that, he'd disturbed something in me, and my thoughts were overlapping and out of place like the magazines in Chloe's room.

Swimming helped when I felt like this. The repetition, the boredom, the slow count up to forty lanes before I could get out and get changed. That afternoon I did laps of the tight rectangle of space set aside for slow swimmers at the Aquatics Centre, looking up at the sky through the high glass roof. At one end of the pool there was a twisting, tubed slide. At the other, a concrete diving tower. I'd never seen either being used, but today, lean, muscled university students were gathering beside the dark blue diving pool. Every other lane, swimming towards the tower rather than the slide, I watched them take their turn.

A Chinese girl wearing a white swimming cap waited to step onto the springboard on the second platform up. At some signal from below she walked calmly to the end, bounced twice, launched herself forward into the air, somersaulted, and sliced through the surface, sleek and smooth.

On the platform below a boy jumped, changed his mind mid-air, ran on the spot, then crashed into the water with a heavy splash. Another stood with his back to the pool, heels over the edge, then launched, and drew his legs to his outstretched arms before he was submerged.

On the third-highest platform were two springboards.

Two boys stepped out and waited, mirroring each other in their broad-shouldered build, blue swimming trunks, and in the tight somersault of their dive.

As I swam my final length, a tall girl in a black swimming costume hesitated on the highest platform, forty feet or so above the pool. She was there for a minute at least, and I wondered whether she was building up courage or planning the shape of her descent in her mind. I was expecting something spectacular; a twist, a somersault, maybe both. But when she finally dived she went straight down, no tricks, just a direct, fast fall.

I couldn't sleep that night. I lay awake and thought about Erik. When my mind fell on him, I mentally flinched. It was like touching something very hot or very cold; I pulled away immediately. But he was still there, no matter how many times I pushed the thoughts away. I could see the thin, deep lines on his hands, the tight skin beneath his eyes, the distance in them vanishing when he looked at me. I felt a nervous disbelief and an embarrassment at the path my mind was taking. I thought of his mouth, just a little bit open, and felt a warm, steady buzz flow through me.

I had never felt like this about someone older before; no crushes on teachers, no film star fantasies. His hair was grey. His clothes were middle-aged. His daughter was closer to my age than he was. I couldn't be thinking of him like this.

But I was, until early in the morning, so that when I woke with my alarm, I felt a weariness with the whole thing and a resentment towards him for taking away my sleep and my flat, numb state of mind. I didn't eat breakfast or drink tea, I didn't even turn on my phone. I just wanted to see him again to see if this was real.

'Miriam.' He said my name slowly, like it was a word that was difficult to pronounce and he was still struggling to figure it out. It was different to how he normally greeted me. I looked down at the doorstep, past him into the porch, back at him. Was I that obvious? Or was he like me, ambushed and made anxious by this sudden, unwanted change in tone?

He said, 'Did the office contact you?'

'No.'

He paused. 'I thought they would.'

I rooted in my bag. 'I haven't checked my phone.' I was still outside. Why weren't we in the kitchen, chatting as the milk warmed?

Erik shifted on the doorstep. 'I emailed them yesterday to say that I didn't need you to help me anymore.'

My phone played its cheerful 'On' tune as the screen lit up.

He said, 'I would have called you myself but I don't have your number.'

'I can give it you now if you want.'

'Well, I guess I won't need it anymore.'

'Oh, well, no.'

Because I was going and we wouldn't see each other again. Because he didn't want to see me again.

I was biting my lip, I stopped, tried to smooth out my face. 'So, am I supposed to be at the office? Not here.'

'I think so, yes.'

I swallowed, tried to think of something to reclaim the situation. 'Did I do something wrong?'

He shook his head. 'No, you were perfect. It is just me. I am not quite ready to start throwing away yet. I, I am just not ready.'

I nodded, I couldn't bring myself to look him in the eyes. He'd stopped speaking. It was my turn to say something or do something. I said, aiming for brightness, 'Okay. Bye then.'

'Bye, Miriam. Thank you for all your help.'

I turned, heard him close the door. At the end of the drive, I crossed the road, stopped, and put my hand on the cold iron of the park railings.

I went back, he saw me through the kitchen window and opened the door again, a neutral smile.

I said, 'I need to get my postcard.'

His smile faded. Now I was a problem.

I said, 'Can I have it? It's important.'

He was set in the doorway, he was going to say no. I felt a panic and anger rising. Then the phone rang in the hallway. He said carefully, 'I will just be a minute.'

He didn't invite me in. I waited on the doorstep for a few moments, then thought fuck it, fuck you, and went inside. I was getting my postcard wherever he'd hidden it. I rooted on the table in the kitchen, on the chairs, on the work surfaces, picking up books, searching beneath magazines, pushing camera leads and batteries around. He was talking to Chloe on the phone, watching me. I heard him say, 'December, that's just, what, two months away.' The postcard wasn't in here. I met his eyes for a second. Had he put it in one of the locked rooms? I went to the first door, expecting it wouldn't open. It did.

I looked inside. My mind reeled. I shut the door again immediately. Turned to him. His face was frozen.

We stared at each other. That wasn't a room I'd just seen. A room had a floor, walls, air, space. That was something solid, impenetrable, and up close to my face. I didn't know what it was.

I could hear Chloe talking on the other end of the line. 'Dad? Are you still there?'

I opened the next door along and found myself up against another wall. There were books and magazines, stacked high and compact, from the floor to the ceiling.

My heart was racing. I shut the door and went into the kitchen, avoiding looking at Erik.

I thought of all the other locked doors. The curtains that were always closed. The chairs that couldn't be sat on, tables that couldn't be eaten at, the bath overflowing with books. Did he have a bed he could sleep in, or did he lie on a layer of magazines, covering himself at night like a tramp under a railway bridge? I looked at the books lining the windowsill and kitchen surfaces. How had I thought this amount of stuff was normal?

Into the phone Erik said, 'No, I mean, of course it's fine. There's lots of room for you.' Then, 'Chloe, I have to go, somebody is at the door, I will call you back.'

He put the phone down. He looked like he was about to speak, then didn't, just shook his head, as if denying what I'd seen.

I said, 'I couldn't find my postcard but, anyway, it doesn't matter. I'm sorry for intruding. I'm going now.'

'Miriam. It's…'

'It's none of my business.'

'Yes, it is. It is.'

'It's not. I'd best just go.'

'I need your help.'

'I don't think I can help with that much stuff.'

He moved towards me. I was stuck to the floor. 'Chloe wants to move in here in December. She doesn't know about this. I don't want her to know.' His eyes were focused on mine. 'Nobody knows what is in my house but you, and I cannot clear it on my own.'

Then he took both my hands in his and they were nothing to do with those blocked doorways and uncrossable rooms. We were looking at each other and I knew I was getting into something. Or I was already in it and it was too late to get out. I had his hands in mine and I couldn't let them go.

8

He dropped my hands and stepped back, creating a space between us where there had been none. He'd only touched me for a few seconds before he'd moved away and I felt the non-touch more. I wanted to move towards him again but I could feel the mood changing fast. He said, 'So now you know. I am a collector. I collect things. I don't throw them away.'

I tried to shift my attention to what was happening now rather than what had happened a few moments ago. A collector? He was a hoarder. 'I thought you were an artist,' I said.

'I collect materials for my art.' He sounded defensive but his expression was guilt.

'You don't need that much stuff for your art.'

'Yes, I do.'

'What do you do? Papier mâché?'

I'd meant it as a joke. I was trying to lighten the atmosphere, stop my voice shaking, but he said, 'Yes. In a way.'

'Oh.'

'I make collages and sculptures from paper.'

I thought of the colour-soaked images I'd seen on his website. They were collages? 'Can I see some?'

He turned away, then seemed to decide something in himself. 'Why not? You have seen everything else.' He took his keys out of his jeans pocket and put them on the kitchen table. 'My studio is upstairs, next to Chloe's room.' He wouldn't let his eyes rest on me. He said, 'I need to clear my head. I will be back in twenty minutes or so.' I had the sense he was trying to stop himself from saying his next words. 'Please don't touch anything.'

'Where are you going?'

'To the park.'

He couldn't show me the paper-flooded rooms himself, out of embarrassment or something stronger; shame. He wanted me to do it on my own.

When he'd gone, I opened the door to the room next to the kitchen. This time, I was more prepared for the fullness. It was dark so I took out my phone and used its glow to illuminate the towers of books and magazines, balanced in piles and stuffed tight into high, free-standing shelves. It's hard to describe how strange it felt, to open a living room door onto this, to step through an entrance into a barricade. I felt affronted by it. It was a stop sign that made me want to retreat but I made myself just stand and look, trying to see if it became more normal with time.

I wanted to see the room as a rational collection of materials for an industrious artist. As the raw ingredients for an ambitious masterpiece. He needed this stuff, he said. And where else would he put it all? I thought of a project I'd done on Peter Blake for GCSE Art when I'd considered The Beatles' Sergeant Pepper's to be the most amazing album cover of all time. Peter Blake was a collector, I remembered. He had a house full of hoarded objects, it probably wasn't so different to this. And didn't Andy Warhol do something similar? I'd also known a girl at uni who knitted hats and scarves; she had filled her room with balls of wool and strips of odd materials, leaving just a small, soft nest to sleep in. Artists were like that. Wool-gatherers. They filled studios, notebooks, hard drives with material. Erik had just chosen to fill his house instead.

I edged out a book from the nearest shelf: *Under the Sea*. A picture book for children from some earlier decade: inside were intricate drawings of bristling starfish and ruby sea anemones, glowing jellyfish and translucent shrimps. I read the spines of the books around it. *Motor Vehicles of the Twentieth Century. Space Exploration. Life on the Farm.* It was a children's section of a public library, circa 1974. The next shelf continued in a similar vein, then there were several stacks of cheap airport fiction like those I'd seen in the kitchen. Romance novels with brave-eyed heroines on the front, chunky horror fiction illustrated by shiny red blood and grasping hands.

Next I looked into the front room. The windows were hidden behind the mass of books and the light was grainy and dim. I reached for a light switch but couldn't find it behind the books piled against the wall. I made out floor space of about half a metre around the door, then the stacks of books began. Some were in shelves, some in boxes, others were piled back against each other, leaning slightly, and towering up to the ceiling. To the left of the doorway, there was a gap between the stacks, not much wider than my shoulders. A pathway leading through them. I turned sideways to edge down it, tensing my body, wary of knocking the books with my shoulders and sending them tumbling down on my head. The path turned a corner defined by a shelf of encyclopaedias and atlases, then, just when the claustrophobia was getting too much, ended in a small clearing with a high-backed armchair by a bay window. Weak daylight fed through a gap in the closed curtains and something glinted on the floor near the chair. A scalpel. Now I noticed slivers of paper at my feet. I picked up the book on the chair. A battered collection of Romantic poetry – Shelley, Keats, Coleridge – with a library catalogue number sellotaped to the spine. The scalpel had been at work inside, slicing through stanzas, turning some pages to nothing more than a mesh of dissected words and shredded sentences. I tried to see what shape he had been cutting out. Something delicate and feathery. A feather, in fact. Lots of feathers. A plywood board leaning against the chair leg was scored with the criss-cross of knife marks.

I put the book down and retreated into the hallway. I wanted to see his studio. I went upstairs, found the right key, and unlocked it, braced for another wall of books but this room wasn't as full as the two downstairs. You could walk inside and look around easily. Thin yellow curtains were closed across the windows but they didn't keep out the light.

Much of the room was taken up with piles of various forms of paper: magazines, brochures, telephone directories, flyers, boxes of postcards and maps, and colourful art paper. Leaning against the wall were several large canvases like those I'd seen on his website. What I'd thought was paint was actually glossy magazine paper, cut into fingerprint-sized pieces and stuck over each other to create a rich bed of colour, its tones always shifting. There was one in blues and greens, like a meadow in a breeze, one in undulating purples and browns like the swaying canopies of the copper beech trees outside. Then one in orange and reds where the paper was cut into the shape of leaves. It was titled A/W 2010 and when I looked closer I saw the paper was cut from images of catwalk models, their suntanned skin becoming the colours of autumn.

But the most striking things in the room weren't these canvases. On the desk by the window was a collection of sculptures of birds: an eerie, dead-eyed seagull; a swift, wings stretched; a blackbird, beak closed. From a distance they looked like taxidermy but up close you saw that the feathers were made of paper. And while a taxidermist tried to imitate life, these seemed to mock that notion. Each bird was misshapen or swollen or broken in some way. Feathers were missing, revealing white bone, or a cavity, or just a gleaming glossy black. Wings were crooked, necks were at a slant. They looked like they would leak were you to nudge them with your toe, or poke them with a stick.

I saw where the poetry feathers had gone: the seagull with a bold stance and a decomposing chest.

The blackbird was made of sheet music. There was a pigeon crafted from phone directories. The swift was made from holiday brochures; I glimpsed sunsets over sea and palm trees in its trailing wings.

What I thought was, this must take him forever. To cut hundreds of intricate feathers for his sculptures, to find the right colours in the right shades for his collages. Then I thought, maybe he's autistic rather than artistic. I imagined him sitting here late at night lost in his task, his thick fingers busy with the scalpel, his eyes calm. But how many years would it take to turn so much paper into birds and trees? As far as I could see, he'd only used a handful of books for each sculpture so why did he have two rooms packed full of them downstairs? The answer wasn't rational, I knew that much. He collected because he had to. It was a compulsion not a choice.

I stepped out and looked at the door to his bedroom. He hadn't said I could look inside but I wanted to know. Dry-cleaned clothes still in their covers were laid over piles of books on the floor. There was a chest of drawers with a thin scattering of magazines. In the far corner, there was a bed. Miraculously, it was clear.

I only stayed in there a few seconds before backing out and carefully shutting the door behind me.

I waited downstairs in the kitchen trying to keep the image of the clean, white duvet cover and the four matching pillows in my head. It was normal. It was sane. He was sane. Hadn't I seen that every time I'd visited? I imagined him leading me upstairs to that one place the paper hadn't reached. At night on the bed you wouldn't be able to see the chaos surrounding us. It would be like before, when everything slipped away, the whole suffocating mess of it, sinking out of sight as he took my hands.

When he returned he said, 'You're still here,' as if I might have taken the chance to leave for good. I'd considered it, but from a distance, as if it was something another version of me could do in another life.

I put the keys back on the table. He looked at them but didn't say anything. He filled two glasses of water and handed one to me. We drank them standing up, leaning against the table and door.

Eventually, he said, 'I need you to show me how you gave away all your belongings and just walked away.'

I didn't want to think about it. The girl who disliked herself so much she had to start again from scratch. 'I just did it.'

He waited.

'I didn't want what they stood for anymore,' I struggled. 'I was just sick of it. I was sick of myself.'

He looked at me and I had no idea what he was thinking. I was saying too much. It irritated me that we were talking about my problems rather than his. 'And this is different. This house. It's not the same thing.'

He said quietly, 'I want to make room for Chloe to live with me. That is the most important thing.'

'When is she moving in?'

'The 8th of December.'

'Why? Uni doesn't start until September.'

'I know. I thought I would have a lot longer than this but she wants to move to Manchester now and get a

71

job until her course starts. She took a year out to earn some money but she's bored of living in Sheffield. Her friends are here already.'

'So we've got about nine weeks.'

'It is impossible to sort through everything in that time.'

I looked up, meeting his eyes. 'The thing is, we don't need to sort through it. We just need to throw it away.'

'That will be difficult.'

'Not for me. I'll do it for you.'

'It is a waste of material. It will take me years to replace it.'

'Then what about Chloe? There's barely space for you to live here. What will she do?'

'I don't know. I don't know.' His fingers were pressed together, turning his fingernails white. 'I don't know the solution.'

'We'll get a skip. Take stuff to charity shops. It won't take us that long if we focus.' I was trying to convince him before I'd even convinced myself.

He said, 'I understand that we have to throw things away. I'm saying that it will be hard.' He turned to the window and took a deep breath as if he couldn't get enough air. Watching him trying to hide his anxiety and failing, I felt sorry for him, which was bad news. When I start feeling sorry for a man, it's a delicate, wanting feeling that doesn't feel like pity at all.

9

Erik was working in London on Friday so I stayed in bed later than usual, trying to catch up on the sleep I'd missed through thinking about him. I listened to Jessica leaving for work, and let myself drift off again, falling deep into a recurring dream I wanted to wake from but couldn't. It always went the same way: I'm trying to call someone on the telephone but every time I dial the number, I press a wrong button and have to start again. And each time I start afresh, the number gets longer and longer, until there's no hope of me getting all the way through it without making a mistake. As I never quite get the number right, I never find out who it is I'm calling. Today it seemed to go on for ages, and when I eventually woke I was tense and frustrated, the dream emotions still there even though the dream was over.

I got up and padded around in my dressing gown, making toast, eating it sitting on the wide sill of the bay window, watching squirrels hopping about on the clumpy grass. I was wondering how Erik would be with me now I knew about the house. We had a secret between us and I liked the feeling of complicity. But the nature of the secret, the strangeness of it, made him seem unknowable and faraway. I thought again of how he'd taken my hands, obliterating this distance. How he'd stepped back a second later.

I thought I was alone in the flat but then I heard someone in Jessica's bedroom, and froze, toast in hand. Gareth came in, in his dentist outfit, an empty mug in his hand.

He looked like he didn't expect to see me either.

'I thought you'd gone to work,' he said.

'I'm not working today.'

'Lucky you.'

He was one of those people who get their sense of self-worth from working fifty hours a week. I didn't answer him, just looked out of the window. Through the corner of my eye I saw him rinse his mug then put it by the sink. Leave, I thought, leave now. He said, 'See you later,' and went.

I remembered waking up in his bed and asking for a drink of water. He didn't move for a moment, then picked up a glass from the floor and filled it from the tap in the bathroom. The glass was scummy, like it hadn't been washed for weeks. 'Is that all right?' he said, showing me that he knew it wasn't. I should have said no. I didn't.

I finished my toast, got dressed, and started to compose an email to Natalie. Yesterday Erik and I had decided I would work directly for him, rather than through CBS, so I needed to tell her I'd found another job and wouldn't be able to work for them anymore. You weren't supposed to do this as a temp – cut out the middleman and work directly for the client – but if Natalie was suspicious, she didn't let on. When she replied, she didn't ask where I was yesterday, she just wanted to know whether my new job was in television. I was tempted to invent a position at some independent TV company but then she would have asked more questions. I typed back, 'I wish. Just working in admin at the university, boring really.'

I didn't like lying but I liked it more than knowing Erik had been paying CBS £160 a day for my work and I was only getting fifty quid of it. He was going to pay me £120 a day. I calculated how much I'd earn in the nine weeks with him and stood at my bedroom window smiling, until a gardener attacking the brambles below with a strimmer thought I was smiling at him and I stepped back inside. I would be able to buy clothes, books, maybe a new box set. I'd heard good things about a zombie drama on Sky. Maybe I could get it cheap on eBay. I went online to have a look, it was there. I read the reviews, they were all very positive, and if I ordered it today, it could be here by Monday. I was about to press buy, but then I suddenly felt tired and I wished I'd not thought of the idea. I switched the computer off.

The thing was, I'd got rid of my belongings for a reason, even if I couldn't say precisely what that reason was. Annie at Barnardo's was right, I didn't want to go backwards, and replacing vampires with zombies was hardly progress.

My wardrobe was a different matter. I was putting a wash on three times a week just so I didn't run out of clean underwear. Jessica had commented on this, and my sister Susie was also concerned. That afternoon, she phoned to say she was stopping by with Mum and when they turned up, they had four big shopping bags of their cast-off clothes with them.

I'd have preferred food like Mum used to bring me when I was at uni. Susie dumped the bags in the middle of the living room and went to look in my bedroom, calling back, 'It's like a cell in here. Are you becoming a nun?'

I ignored her and handed Mum a cup of tea. She said, 'I've brought you a few things that will help until we can hit the sales in December.'

'I'm fine. It's not like I've got nothing to wear.'

She frowned at my bare feet and goose-pimpled arms. My socks and jumper were drying on the radiator. Susie came back from nosing around my bedroom. 'Are you getting into Buddhism again? That time when you gave up meat then realised it meant no alcohol as well and decided not to bother.'

Mum said, 'That was just a phase, Susie. Miriam isn't religious.'

I sat down in the bay window, wondering whether I was needed in this conversation about me or not. Mum started rooting in one of the bags, and brought out a pink and cream striped jumper from BHS. Me and Susie looked at each other and laughed.

'I don't think that's called for.' Mum put it back in the bag. 'Susie said you've given away all your thermals. And what if you get a job interview? You even gave away your interview suit.'

'I've got a new job actually, so I won't be needing an interview suit.'

'Really? Where?' Mum asked.

'I'm working with an artist, helping him organise his, er, art.'

'I thought you were working as a receptionist,' Susie said.

'I was. Then I got offered this.'

'Is he a well-known artist?' Mum asked.

I tucked my feet under my legs. 'I don't think so.'

'Have you got a contract?'

'A verbal contract.'

'Best get it in writing,' Mum said. 'And make sure he's got enough money to pay you.'

'He's paying me £120 a day. So thanks for the hand-me-downs but I won't be needing them. I can go clothes shopping next weekend.'

'Well, we'll leave them with you. Just in case.'

I was fairly certain I wouldn't ever want to wear Mum's chenille tracksuit or Susie's three-quarter-length trousers but I didn't say so. Mum brought a packet of farm shop shortbread out of her bag and I made us all another cup of tea.

When they'd gone I took the hand-me-downs into my room, putting them in the corner that had been 'charity' and now felt more like 'charity case'. Then I had a thought, and looked inside the bag from Mum.

A pair of socks. Thick, fluffy ones, too. I put them on and ate the rest of the biscuits sitting in bed. It was the highlight of my day.

That night I lay awake again, thinking about Erik and that moment in the hallway. I replayed it so he didn't move away, he brought me in closer, and I stood with my head against his chest and neck. It was about two in the morning. Mario next door started shouting, it sounded like 'Fire' again, but nobody else stirred and after a few minutes he was quiet. Jessica and Gareth came home at half-two, keeping their voices low, then laughing, then shushing each other. It took them forever to get into bed.

When I woke, I could hear them in the kitchen. The smell of frying bacon and toast. I could stay in bed until they'd gone out, but how long would that be? I got dressed without dawdling and was out of there myself within half an hour.

I took the bus into town and went to Central Library to see if there were any books that would help me with Erik's house. I searched the online catalogue and found several about compulsive hoarding but they were all marked as 'missing' or 'unreturned'. The hoarders had them and they weren't bringing them back.

I decided I wouldn't use that word in front of Erik. He called himself a 'collector' and I preferred to think of him that way. A hoarder sounded like an intense, eccentric person with bad personal hygiene, and he wasn't like that at all. His bath was unusable but he showered every day at the swimming baths.

And he wasn't intense; his manner was calm with bright, interested eyes. His house was eccentric, yes, but he wasn't. He was perceptive, clever, and rational – apart from in this one, contained area of his life. That was what I found so hard to understand. It was also what made me think it could be cured.

I wanted to talk to someone about it but I couldn't think of anyone who would give me the response I wanted. I needed someone who would be unfazed by the situation. Someone who'd say, oh yeah, I used to know a man like that, he read a book / went to therapy / had an epiphany and now he's fine. But if I told Jessica, she'd be eyes-wide, feasting on the freakiness of it, and comparing it to someone she saw on a TV documentary. Susie would treat it like another Miriam adventure, not taking it seriously enough to offer any useful advice. Mum would say, why are you getting involved in this, and how are the job applications going? The only person I could imagine telling was Annie but I barely knew her. And why I thought she might be helpful, I don't know.

I abandoned the search for useful books and went to the library's DVD section but there was nothing I wanted to watch. I headed over to Fopp to trawl through the bargain films, then looked around the clothes shops in the Arndale hoping to see something to buy when I got paid, but it was the least fruitful window-shopping trip I'd ever been on.

I felt a growing sense of doubt as the day went on. I could enjoy my own company like this for a while, say two or three hours. It didn't matter that I was on my own amongst groups of friends and families shopping together, meeting for drinks, doing Saturday things, not having to think about how they would pass the evening or the next day. But as it got to mid-afternoon, I started to lose my nerve and my sense of okayness. Maybe it was the fading light. I felt the pull of my bed and a few hours spent dozing under my duvet, so I got the bus home and slept. When I woke it was dark but early. Jessica had Gareth over and they'd chosen a film to watch together, their legs stretched out over the sofa, the room cosy and couply until I walked in.

On Sunday I went swimming at the Aquatics Centre then spent some time trying on Susie's and Mum's clothes, seeing if there was anything I could possibly wear next week. If I'd been working in the office in Ardwick, some of Susie's outfits might have been okay but there was nothing I'd want for Erik's house. I tried to recapture some of the lightness I'd felt when I first threw everything away but now I felt weighed down by my lack of choices rather than set free. I put another wash on. Jessica was in the living room, alone for once.

She looked over the sofa back at me. 'Are you okay, Miriam?' she asked.

I was running out of washing powder. I'd have to stop at the shop tomorrow. 'Yes. Why?'

'With dumping all your stuff. And this constant washing. It's a bit OCD.'

I stopped what I was doing to look at her. 'Is it getting on your nerves?'

'It's not that. But the electricity bill is going to be massive.'

I poured the last of the powder into the machine, planning my words. 'That will be because there's three people living here now rather than two.'

She straightened on the sofa. 'He's not here that much.'

'Only every night.'

'What am I supposed to do? We can't officially move in together when we've only been going out two months.'

Was that where it was heading? 'I'm just saying. You have your boyfriend. I have my washing.' I laughed. I hadn't realised how tragic it would sound before it came out of my mouth.

10

On Monday morning, we made a plan. A plan of attack, Erik called it, which I found heartening. It made me think he was prepared for the work ahead. In the kitchen, we moved the books off the chairs and onto the floor and pushed his laptop and magazines down the table, so that there was space to sit and write. He listed the rooms we needed to clear and I wrote them down.

'Downstairs there is the front room, kitchen, hallway and porch. Upstairs...' He stopped, as if he'd lost his train of thought.

I said, 'Chloe's room, the bathroom...'

He took a deep breath and continued. 'Yes, Chloe's room, my studio, the bathroom, and my bedroom but that isn't important. It's what Chloe will see that I am concerned about.'

I added it anyway. 'So that's everything?'

'Yes.'

From the outside, this seemed like a huge house. But once you'd entered, it closed in around you. His collection had made it shrink by filling every corner, then every room. I wondered which space it would seep into next if we didn't start to reverse the process. The kitchen probably. There were books and magazines in here but they didn't dominate the room. It was mainly odds and ends that you might find in anyone's house. Post, a jug of pens, a pot of red geraniums, his passport, his briefcase, his camera, his laptop. It was where he put everything that wasn't made of paper.

I refocused on the plan in front of me. 'We forgot the other downstairs room.'

'Oh, well, that one's full.'

I looked at him. They were all full. 'We still need to include it.' I added it to the list, not glancing up to see his expression. 'So we've got nine weeks. And six rooms, seven including your bedroom, plus the hallway, landing and porch. That's about a week on each one.'

He was pressing together his fingers again, turning the tips white. Perhaps laying out the size of the problem on paper like this wasn't a good idea. But we needed to know how long we had, and how hard we would have to work. I knew that once we stepped into those rooms it would become difficult to think clearly. We'd lose sight of what we were doing amongst all those books and magazines. I wrote dates next to each room, leading up to 8th December, then stuck the plan on the fridge door.

I said, 'So today, let's get Chloe's room finished.'

He rubbed his lips with his knuckles. 'Where will we put everything?'

'In bin bags in the back garden for now.'

'They will get wet.'

'What does it matter? We're throwing them out anyway.'

He said, 'I don't have any bin bags.'

'I'll go now and buy some from the shop.'

'I'll go later, at lunchtime.'

I sighed. He held my gaze. I had no chance of staring him out.

I stood up abruptly. 'Okay, let's get started.' I went into the hallway and up the stairs. He didn't follow but I kept going anyway, opening the door to Chloe's room. I hadn't been in there for nearly a week but Erik clearly had. Many of our neat piles had been dislodged and divided and magazines were spread across the bed again. It didn't look as bad as on that first day, but it wasn't far off.

I picked my way over to the window to let in some air. The ice cream van that toured this neighbourhood at all hours was parked nearby. It played a laconic version of 'Whistle While You Work', slow and halting like a musical jewellery box that's running to a stop.

A few minutes later, Erik came upstairs, looked at me standing amongst the disturbed stacks of *Vogue* and *Elle*.

He handed me two black bin bags. 'I found these,' he said.

'Thanks.' I sat down on the bed, magazines slid against me. I felt lost for a moment. It had been logical and organised in here when I'd left.

Erik said, 'I was sorting through them, trying to decide what to throw away and what to keep. But I got so confused, I realised it was impossible. That was when I called Natalie and told her I didn't need you anymore.'

'That's why you need me. Because you think it's impossible.'

'Yes, I know.' He looked at me sitting on the bed. 'So, what do I need to do?'

The idea was to discard three-quarters of the magazines but Erik kept losing sight of why we needed to throw them away rather than just sort through them. He clung to them. He took them out of my hands and went to put them 'somewhere safe', which usually meant his studio next door. I felt like we weren't clearing the room, just shifting its contents to another part of the house. I pictured us spending years like this, sweeping magazines and books from one room to the next, from floor to floor then back again, the hoard never actually getting any smaller.

It was tiring; the endless, steady persuasion, the dilemma each magazine set off in him. I picked up a stack of *Vogues* and put them in a bin bag, hoping he would just let me get on with it but of course, he stopped me.

'I haven't checked through those yet.'

I held the bag shut. 'There are too many to check.'

He fixed his eyes on my closed hand. 'There are ten, twenty at the most.'

'There's a whole room full.'

We went through a similar discussion about ten times that day, always ending with him taking the magazines off me so he could sort through them and carefully slice out images, before carrying these cuttings, and sometimes the entire issue, into the studio next door.

I needed a sign to hold up every five minutes, saying 'Chloe. 8th December'. He couldn't see the bigger picture. Or he could glimpse it, sometimes, but then it evaded him a moment later, and he was buried again. I couldn't imagine how it felt to be so attached to something that you couldn't just let it go without going through this long, exhausting process first. I wondered whether his wife had left him because of this.

'Have you always been a collector?' I asked. We were eating Vietnamese takeaway in his kitchen. The table and chairs were full again so he was leaning against the fridge, while I leaned against the radiator.

He thought for a moment. 'No. There was not the space before.'

When Chloe and Caitlin lived here. 'What about when you were a child?'

'There was no space there either. We lived in a flat. And what would you collect in Czechoslovakia? There was just one of everything. No variety like there is here.'

'Was that why you started collecting things later, do you think?'

'I have explained this. I collect materials for my art.'

I didn't say anything. It was obvious to me that there was more to it than that. I pictured Communist-era Czechoslovakia as a grey, monotone place with only three patterns of wallpaper in the entire country, and a couple of state-sanctioned books per family. Arriving in London, where there were no empty spaces and everything was coloured in, must have been intoxicating for someone who responded so keenly to visual stimuli. Advertisements on everything from the back of your train seat to your table in a coffee chain. Free magazines thrust in your hands, catalogues saying 'pick me up', a daily supply of flyers and coupons and junk mail pushed through your letter box. Shelves and shelves of cheap books to be bought. I saw this overstimulation as an onslaught but Erik thrived on it. He wanted to take everything home.

'Let me show you this.' He went to the other side of the kitchen and brought back a slim, expensively produced brochure for an exhibition at a gallery in London. He flicked through it until he came to a page with his name on it, and a picture of one of his collages. On the opposite page, there was a description of his art.

I read it silently. *Erik Zeleny subverts and celebrates the culture of consumerism. His is not an attack but an attempt to get to the heart of what is promised and what is delivered – whether that is fulfilment or emptiness, a simulacrum of happiness or happiness itself.* It praised him as a talent to watch and suggested his work was a good investment piece. The date on the cover was from seven years ago.

'I like your collages,' I said. It was true. They did things to my brain chemistry. The scale of them, the way the colours moved, the way you could almost step into them, like they were a shower or a swimming pool.

'Thank you. I have moved on from those now, though. I am working on a collection of sculptures of birds. My work is becoming less abstract. I don't know why.'

I wanted to ask about the birds. What did they mean? Why were they all injured or dying? But it seemed too personal. I couldn't say my questions out loud.

Instead I said, 'It's interesting that you make adverts for your day job and cut them up into little pieces at night.'

He smiled. 'Is it interesting? I'm not sure.'

'Are you trying to change the system from within?'

He laughed, which made me laugh. 'I have lived through one revolution. I do not need another one. No, I was just trying to be honest about what we want and how we don't get it, but not in too direct a way. I think if art is too direct it becomes boring. It's a lecture. It's propaganda. It's not an exploration.'

'So are you anti-consumerist? Even though you protested against Communism?'

'Are you? You're the one who only has three changes of clothes.'

He'd noticed. I said, 'I haven't got around to replacing what I threw away.'

'It isn't a criticism. I like it that you gave away every-thing you own. It is what people dream of doing.'

'It's not a dream you'd want to live out.'

'You seem to be doing okay.'

'I'm not. My feet are always wet because I don't have any winter shoes. I'm cold in bed because I threw away my pyjamas. I've no DVDs to watch. I've got nothing to do in the evenings. My life is empty. It was empty even before I gave everything away.' I stopped. I hadn't realised how much my streamlined existence was getting to me. Erik was looking thoughtfully at me, his shoulders still leaning against the fridge door.

He said, 'It's not empty. You have a job.'

'Here?'

'Yes. And you have a hobby.'

I was puzzled. 'What's that?'

'Swimming.'

'That's not a hobby. It's an exercise chore.'

'You have your friends and family.'

'Hmm.'

He considered me for a moment. 'I think you think your life is empty because you don't have a boyfriend.'

I froze. I didn't know how to respond. Because it was true? Or because he was talking about boyfriends and I wanted him as mine, and maybe he knew it?

'I don't think like that. It's more than that.' I didn't know what I was saying. 'I mean I don't know what I want from life. I don't know what I want to do with it.'

'You're in your twenties. It's normal.'

I noticed he'd shifted the conversation onto me again. I said, 'You were married when you were in your twenties.'

'Yes but it didn't mean everything was solved, that's it, happily ever after.'

'Did you think it did at the time?'

'Maybe I thought like that, I can't remember. It was a long time ago.'

I wanted to know more but he turned away, I knew he was going to, and went to stroke Micka who was watching us from her cushion in the back porch.

The next morning, I made a suggestion I'd been mulling over in the night. 'I think we should fill up your car with magazines and take them to the tip in Stretford.'

Erik looked vacantly at me, as if he'd had trouble sleeping as well. He was slowly stirring a pan of hot chocolate on the stove. 'Stretford.'

'It's not far.'

'I don't think my car works.'

I'd been expecting something like this. 'You're making excuses.'

'We just don't need to do that yet.'

I hadn't slept properly again. I snapped. 'Erik, I know you're paying me but at the moment, you're paying me to do nothing. You need to let me throw something away, otherwise it's pointless me being here. Where are your car keys?'

He'd not seen me lose my temper before but it didn't seem to faze him. 'You want to drive my car?'

'I want to fill it with stuff so you can drive it. To the tip.'

'It's already filled with stuff.' He turned back to the hot chocolate. 'Of course.'

Of course. I went outside. Micka was lying on top of the garage. She lazily stood up and trotted away when she saw me approaching. There were wet fallen leaves on the plastic sheet covering the car. When I untied the bindings and pulled it off, they stayed stuck to the plastic. Now I could see through the windows. Stacks of magazines on the driver's seat and passenger seat. The back seat and footwells were full as well.

Back in the kitchen the hot chocolate smelled sweet

and homely. There were two mugs on the table, steam rising.

'At least it's already loaded up,' I said.

'What's in there?'

'Magazines.'

'Really?' Erik said flatly. 'I mean, which ones?'

'If you can't remember, they can't be that important.'

He seemed to decide something in his head. 'So do you want to go this second or can we drink our chocolate first?'

'We can drink these first,' I conceded. He handed one to me and I said thanks.

'You're welcome.' He looked down at me, calm but considering, as if processing something new in me he hadn't noticed before.

The car battery was dead. We had to get the old man from next door to bring his Volvo onto the driveway so we could connect them with jump leads. I'd seen Frank in his front garden a few times, pottering around with bits of wood and piles of sand, or taking his Labrador for a wheezing, slow stroll to the park.

'Having a clear-out?' he said, looking at the magazines on the back seats.

'Just making a bit of room,' I said.

'You can come and help us next if you like. It's funny how things pile up.'

Erik was attaching the jump leads to the battery. 'My daughter Chloe is moving back in with me.'

'Chloe. She used to bring her dolls round for tea.'

Erik smiled. 'She's eighteen now.'

'Then she won't be interested in us oldies anymore.' Frank leaned over the engine, checking he had got the leads fixed up right.

Erik said, 'She remembers you. She remembers your dog.'

Until now I'd only thought of the bedroom as Chloe's, but it was her house and her neighbourhood. I wondered whether Erik took her to play in the park when she was little, whether they bought ice creams from the van. Did she go to the primary school on College Road, collecting conkers and chestnut leaves as she walked home?

Erik and Frank were sitting in their cars, engines going. Erik beckoned for me to get in and we backed down the driveway, the sat-nav on his phone talking over the U2 CD he'd pushed in. I wondered how long it was since he'd been out in his car. Perhaps he would drive me home now it was working again. Yesterday, he'd walked me back at the end of the day. The sky had been grainy and heavy as if it was going to rain but it was just dusk arriving, taking us by surprise. We'd not talked much. I'd felt drained by the attempts at clearing and the shifting moods between us.

Now he drove us through Chorlton and up Chester Road, doubling back on himself to get to the entrance to the tip. There were signs on either side of the narrow track telling us to drive slowly, to not stop, to only dispose of household rubbish, to be aware of criminal prosecutions for discarding industrial material. We were in a queue of cars. When we reached the forecourt in front of the recycling containers, there was nowhere to park.

Erik's hands were tight on the steering wheel. 'It's too busy,' he said. 'This was a bad time of day to come.'

I looked out of the side window, wishing I hadn't suggested this. A van backed out, leaving a space. Erik didn't move.

'You can park there.' I gestured towards the gap.

'I don't think this is a good idea. There are too many people. Why did I let you talk me into this?'

I tried to keep my voice level. 'Because this is what you hired me for.'

'I know, but it's too busy. Let's come back another day.'

'We can't. We're holding up the queue.'

He glanced in the rear-view mirror. Three cars were waiting behind us. One of them pipped their horn. 'Damn.' He darted into the space and braked hard. He dropped his hands from the wheel. Clicked the CD player off and avoided looking at me.

I said, 'I'm going to start unloading.' I didn't wait for his response. I got out and opened up the boot. One of the orange-vested tip men came over to help. Erik stayed where he was. When I began clearing the back seats and the footwells, he just kept staring straight ahead, ignoring me. It was like he was imagining himself to be somewhere else, trying not to think of all the magazines being fed through the slots into the recycling crate, all that potential material going to waste. But for me, it was satisfying. I felt like we were getting somewhere. The boot, then the back seat, then the footwells were cleared. I was careful not to look at him when I got back in the car.

'That's everything,' I said when he didn't start the engine. I waited. 'Well, not *everything* but at least it's a carload. One of those a day and we'll be sorted in no time.' I was trying to fill up the silence. Then I noticed the tremble in his hand and stopped talking. Maybe everything was the right word after all.

11

It was raining when I went to his house again a day later. I knocked but he didn't answer and I started to wonder whether he had gone to London and forgotten to tell me. I was about to dial his mobile when he finally let me in. He must have seen I was annoyed because he started to explain as soon as I stepped inside.

'I'm sorry, Miriam, this is very difficult for me. When you're not here, I think that the place doesn't look so bad and that all this clearing is unnecessary. Then when you are here, and we can barely fit in the same room together and you can't sit down because there are no empty chairs, I see it more clearly. I sometimes think it would be easier if I was unseeing all the time. Then it wouldn't matter. I'd be happy.'

There were new magazines on the kitchen table. *National Geographic, Time, Newsweek.* He had them delivered by post. The reason he rarely used the front door was because there were piles of them sitting in the front porch, waiting for him to take upstairs and dissect with his scalpel.

95

I took off my coat and went to hang it in the hallway. When I stepped back into the kitchen he said, 'But then I think about how good it will be to have Chloe here. And I hear you knocking on the door and I imagine you walking all the way over here in the rain with your leaking shoes, and standing there getting wet and I think, I better let her in after all.'

'Thanks.'

He said, 'I know it is hard for you, too.'

'You can't just not answer the door.'

'I know. I was psyching myself up. I wasn't going to ignore you.'

I was ignoring him now, and I liked how it felt.

'Can you think of it as part of the job?'

I pulled out a chair. There was nothing on it and we both looked at it for a second. I sat down. 'So what are the perks of the job?'

'The money is good. And you get hot chocolate and Vietnamese food.'

I looked at him, thinking he'd missed the main one.

'And it is better than working in an office,' he added hopefully. 'Admit it, you love working here.' It sounded like a question but I didn't answer it for fear of giving myself away. He looked beautiful today. A soft grey jumper that matched his grey hair. Slight stubble on his jawline. High, shallow cheekbones that I would like to touch, just once. I got up and wandered over to the back porch, pretending to be interested in whether Micka was there on her cushion.

Erik said, watching me, 'And also, you like my cat.'

'She always hides when I'm around.'

'I know. She's under the table.'

'Who looks after her while you're away?'

'She looks after herself. I have this machine you can set to a timer to let out food every day.'

'What if it didn't work?'

'What if, what if?' He went to check the hot chocolate. I crouched down by the table to see if I could coax Micka out. She was sitting up, near the wall. She didn't move.

I sat down again. 'I'm thinking of getting an exercise bike.'

'Why not a real bike?'

'Because I want it for indoors. I get restless in the middle of the night.' I stopped. It suddenly sounded sexual.

He didn't seem to notice. 'You're an insomniac.'

'Sometimes.' I'd had restless legs last night. I couldn't stop them from moving – when I tried I got a crawling sensation that travelled up into my stomach. I'd wanted to walk, or swim, or cycle – anything other than lie still. If I hadn't been afraid of muggers, I would have gone outside and paced the streets just to tire myself out.

Erik said, 'That is when I do my sculptures, at night.'

'I thought it would be.'

'Why do you say that?'

'Because you work in the day. And it just seems like the type of thing you'd do at night. An artist in his garret working by moonlight...'

He turned from the stove. 'What is a garret?'

'It's like an attic at the top of a house.'

'Oh.' After a few moments he said, 'I have not heard that word before.'

97

He carefully poured the chocolate into two mugs and handed one to me. Micka padded out from beneath the table and brushed against his legs, winding between them as if binding them with rope. He knelt down to stroke her. 'Micka, why don't you say hello to Miriam.'

I didn't move. I had the feeling she'd run off if I did.

'She wants you to stroke her,' he said.

I'd never had a cat and thought I might have an allergy to fur. I ran my palm quickly over her back.

'Hold out your hand a little in front of her.'

I did as he said. She nudged her head and wet nose against it, and I snatched it away in response. She darted back, surprised.

He laughed. 'Poor Micka.' He ruffled the fur around her neck and ran his fingers down her back and tail. She rolled on the tiles in delight then twisted to standing again. I watched, locked onto the movement of his hand. It was lined and tanned and playful. It was hard to look away.

We spent the morning working through a stack of gossip mags. I wanted to get rid of them all – partly because of the space they were taking up, and partly because of the negative vibes they were emitting through their headlines about weight loss and weight gain, affairs and break-ups. But Erik was poring over them as if they were great works of art.

'Look at this typeface,' he said, turning a copy of *Heat* around so I could see. 'I need these for a sculpture I am thinking of making of a magpie.'

I wanted us to stay focused on the task. 'How many copies will you realistically need for that?'

'How can I know? I might need them all.'

I was about to protest when my phone started to vibrate. It was my sister. I went out onto the landing, glad for the break. 'Hiya.'

'Hi. Are you at your new job?'

'Yes.'

'How's it going?'

Through the half-open door, Erik was slicing out a headline from *Heat*. *Is she pregnant or is it a food baby?* 'Fine.'

She sighed. 'If you can't talk, just say so. Or else, don't answer the phone. I just wanted to see if you're free tomorrow night? We're going out for some drinks after work.'

This was new. She had never invited me on a work's night out before. 'Whereabouts?'

'Just around the Northern Quarter.'

The Northern Quarter was where Susie worked, in a converted mill transformed into offices for creative businesses. She was a PA for a branding agency with a lowercase name, all one word: seeingeye. At thirty-two, she was the second-oldest person in the company (the oldest being the guy who'd set it up). She said she thought they'd hired her because they had this idea of an organised, mother figure who would make sure they never ran out of bread for the toaster or milk in the communal fridge.

I leaned against the banister, trying to decide whether I wanted to go out with her or not. 'I might not have time to go home and change and then get out again.'

'Well try. What else were you going to do?'

'Go swimming.'

'Come drinking instead. We'll be in Bali Hai from half-five.'

I vaguely agreed and put the phone down. I had actually been meaning to go to this bar, as it was named after a song in one of my favourite musicals. My only favourite musical in fact, *South Pacific*.

Erik looked up from the dissected magazine. I sat down on the edge of the bed. 'My sister wants me to go out in town with her tomorrow night.'

'So...'

I'd figured out why. 'She must be trying to fix me up with someone.'

'Then you should go.'

'I don't want to be fixed up. I'll feel like a charity case.'

'So you're not going? You might miss out.'

'I haven't got anything to wear. Literally I haven't.'

He glanced at my black skirt which was getting greyer with every wash. 'You could buy something.'

'I don't have time.'

He put down the scalpel he'd been holding. 'Miriam, you need to just go with things sometimes. Stop putting obstacles in front of yourself.'

'I don't.'

'You do. It is like you are afraid of life.'

I looked away. Nobody else spoke to me like this. I wasn't sure how to take it.

'Tell me what is stopping you,' he said.

I shrugged. 'I tried to go shopping last weekend. I couldn't find anything I liked.' It hadn't just been clothes either. In record shops I'd forgotten the names of every band I liked. In Waterstones I couldn't decide what department I wanted, never mind what book.

He said, 'I will help you, if you like.'

'Will you?'

'Yes. It is late night opening tonight.' He smiled. 'I help you buy things. You help me throw things away.'

We ordered a taxi and waited for it under the beech trees in the light of the orange street lamp. There was more sky visible through the leaves now and I could see a bird's nest high up in the canopy. When the cab arrived Erik held the door open for me as I climbed inside. We drove down to Deansgate, then queued all the way along it, while people hurried for trains and buses, on a mission to escape the city until tomorrow. It was loud and fast out there compared to the stillness of Erik's house. People crossed before the lights changed, cars pushed in front of each other, it started to rain and umbrellas jostled for space at head height. The shop window signs shouted above it all. Last Chance To Buy. Sale Now On. Our Lowest Prices Yet. I couldn't tell whether they were gearing up or winding down, whether we were in the middle of a boom or a bust. It was a frenzy and I didn't want to step into it, especially now the rain had turned into a downpour.

We got out of the taxi at Kendals and pushed through the heavy doors into the brightly lit beauty hall. There were women armed with perfume ready to zap. Skilfully made-up girls behind the cosmetics counters. I usually only went as far as the high street fashion on the first floor but Erik said we should try the second floor if I wanted to find something of quality. Something expensive, I thought. Earlier he had given me an envelope with my pay in cash for Monday, Tuesday and today. After what I needed for rent, I had £200 to spend but I was hoping to buy an entire winter wardrobe with that, not just one item.

We stepped off the escalator and he looked at me, considering. 'So, when you come to my house, you wear jeans or this skirt. Do you have any dresses?'

'Not anymore.'

'Not one?'

'They were too try-hard.'

'I cannot imagine you trying hard.'

'You've not seen me drunk.'

He wandered over to a navy blue dress on a thick wooden hanger. It was tailored and petite and kind of French-looking. It wasn't something I would wear. 'I don't know.'

'Try it on.' He found a size eight, which was right actually, and hooked it over his arm.

'Are you my personal shopper?'

He smiled. 'I'm a fashion photographer. I know what will suit you.'

'What will suit me?'

He stood back and looked at me, with that same steady expression. 'I think that because you are a little bit shy, you want to blend into the background. But because you feel bad when you're ignored, you want to catch attention, but without doing anything to catch attention. So really, you just need to start dressing like a woman rather than like an awkward teenager, or like a boy.'

'Is that how I dress?'

'You dress like you are being very careful not to give anything away about yourself.'

'Yes.' I was pleased.

'It is like walking around with your mouth sealed up. Clothes aren't just for keeping warm, you know.'

He picked out a silk, orange chequered dress with buttons down the front, and a cerise woollen dress that looked like it would cling to my stomach. I didn't pick up anything. I felt completely intimidated by him at that moment, and by this place. I just followed along as we circled the floor, mumbling okay to his suggestions, not suggesting anything myself.

At the changing rooms, he handed the dresses to me. 'I will be sitting here.'

I wasn't going to ask his opinion, if that's what he was thinking. I took the clothes over to a shop assistant who looked like an out-of-work model. She led me to a cubicle and hung the dresses up inside. 'Isn't this lovely?' she said touching the hem of the cerise one. 'Just shout if you need different sizes.'

I closed the door and looked at myself in the three-way mirror. I was wearing my skirt and ballet pumps and my shapeless winter coat which hung badly when viewed from the back. My face was pale and my lips were dry. I needed a haircut. I thought of all the beautiful women he must photograph, and of how nondescript I must look in comparison.

Oh, what was the point? I had no chance with him. I tried to turn away from the mirror so I wouldn't have to see my sunken expression but it surrounded me on all sides. I felt like crying.

I sat down. I needed to get myself together but I just couldn't bring myself to try the dresses on.

After a while, I heard him outside the door. 'Miriam?'

'Yes?'

'Are you okay?'

'Yes.'

He hesitated. 'What is wrong?'

I opened the door. 'They don't fit.'

'I know you haven't tried them.'

I didn't answer.

'You're a size eight with perfect posture and this beautiful, English rose skin. If they don't look good on you, they won't look good on anyone. Just try them and see.' He closed the door. A second later opened it again. 'And stop being so vain. It's not the end of the world if they don't suit you.' He shut the door again. I heard him walk away.

Vain? I'd not been called that before. When I looked in the mirror now my face was flushed. English rose? Beautiful? I found myself suddenly smiling.

The orange silk one didn't fit at all. There were gaps between the buttons down the front where you could see my chest. It made me look like a girl trying on her mum's clothes. I took it off and tried the cerise one. It wasn't as tight as I'd thought. It was elegant in fact. I put my damp shoes back on, and feeling self-conscious, stepped outside.

Erik looked up from a magazine that would no doubt be coming home with us. His expression was neutral. 'Turn around.'

I did so, quickly.

'Buy it. It fits you very well.'

'Do you think so?'

'Yes. Go and try the other ones.' He looked back down at his magazine.

The cerise dress was £65. My usual limit was about £30. I hung it up carefully and put on the blue one. It was flirty rather than elegant with a high collar and an above-the-knee hem and demure, long sleeves.

I stepped out.

A shadow of something passed over his face. It was there and then gone. 'Yes.'

'Should I buy it?'

'Yes. You look very...' He didn't finish his sentence.

'What?'

'You look very nice.'

'Oh.' I went back inside the cubicle. The dress was £95.

I was getting it anyway.

After that, I bought winter boots and woollen tights, spending all my money and a bit more that went on my credit card. I had never been shopping with a man before but I couldn't imagine many were like this. Patient, interested, offering useful feedback. Erik wasn't your average man, though. The things that disturbed

105

me about his house were what made him a good shopping companion. He was into colours, shapes, patterns. Watching him flick, businesslike, through a sales rack of skirts, I had a heart-stopping thought that he might be gay. It would explain everything. A job in fashion, a failed marriage, a cat. Why hadn't this occurred to me before?

We stepped onto the elevator. 'So shall we go and get something to eat?' he asked. Then added, 'What is wrong?'

I was studying him a little too directly. 'Nothing.'

'Are you hungry?'

'Yes.' He couldn't be gay. Looking at him, I felt a tugging sensation, a dropping in my stomach that wasn't caused by the descending elevator. That surely wouldn't happen if he wasn't straight. But still, I needed to be sure. 'There's a restaurant on Canal Street that's good,' I said.

'Canal Street? Isn't it just bars?'

We stepped into the beauty hall. 'Mainly bars.' Canal Street was in the Gay Village. 'This one does food.'

'Okay, let's go there.'

I didn't really want to. 'Or we could go to Chinatown? Or the Northern Quarter?'

We were weaving through the counters towards the doors. He said, 'We can go to Canal Street if that's where you like.'

'It's not where I like,' I said. 'I'm not gay.'

He stopped and looked at me, that gently amused expression in his eyes. 'I know you're not.'

What was that supposed to mean? 'Chinatown,' I said.

'It's nearer.' I set off, crossing Deansgate and heading towards St Ann's Square, and he followed. Or I thought he followed. I looked back and he wasn't there. I saw him hovering by the entrance to Waterstones, looking over at me, then looking inside. I waited, two, three seconds then retraced my steps. 'Are you coming?'

He frowned. 'They have a sale on in the Art department.'

'You don't need any more books.'

'I just want to look. There might be something.'

'I'm really hungry,' I said.

'I know.' He was turned towards the open doors. 'Come with me just for a moment.'

He went inside and after a quick glance to check I was with him, forgot me entirely. The shop was busy with after-work browsers, scanning the shelves, picking up books and putting them back down again. But there was something different about Erik. He had none of their casual, half-hearted interest; he was intent. In the Art department, he stopped at a display of coffee-table books halved in price. His fingertips brushed the covers, his eyes were focused, when I spoke he didn't seem to hear.

'You don't have the space,' I said.

He looked at me like I was in a different reality to him then returned to sifting through the books, turning the pages carefully, putting some aside. He looked transfixed. Happy. I couldn't get his attention.

'Can we go?' I asked.

'In a minute.'

As the pile of books he wanted grew, I got more

and more depressed. The only reason we were spending time together was to reduce the number of magazines and books in his house. It was like that didn't matter, which meant I didn't matter. In Kendals he had seemed like a normal, reasonable man. Now he was immersed in his obsession again and I couldn't stand to see it. This nosedive in my mood, and the elation in his, was too much.

I picked up my shopping bags. 'I'm going,' I said.

I don't think he heard. When I left, he didn't even look up.

12

The books were on the kitchen table the next morning. I counted eleven in total. Erik saw me looking at the pile and turned away. He spooned cat food into a bowl for Micka. Watched her pad across the floor and take a few tentative bites.

'So you made it back okay?' he finally said.

'I got the bus.'

'We didn't go for food.' He pressed his fingers together. 'I thought you would wait. Sorry if I took too long.'

I met his eyes for a second. 'You seemed distracted.'

'Please, Miriam. I would rather not.'

So that was that. Closed book. Eleven closed books he would probably never look at again.

He said, 'I want to work hard today. I am going to order a skip to put on the driveway. I think we can find enough to fill one.' He wanted me to smile with him but I didn't feel like it. He was like someone with an eating disorder throwing up after a binge. It was private. Embarrassing. I didn't want anything to do with it.

That evening I took the bus to Piccadilly Gardens to meet Susie and her workmates. I always seemed to end up going out with other people's colleagues, normally Jessica's, rather than my own. It was two steps removed from having real friends; people you'd chosen because you liked them, rather than because they were the easiest available option at five-thirty on a Friday.

But it was better than staying in. And I had new clothes. I was wearing my blue dress and boots and was enjoying being warm and dry for once. I'd left Erik's house earlier than usual so I could get ready. We hadn't been making much progress. His version of working hard was different to mine. Maybe when the skip arrived, he'd focus more on throwing things away, rather than just endlessly sorting through them.

I crossed the gardens, my face wet as I passed through the fine spray from the fountains. Bali Hai was somewhere off Newton Street in what I thought of as old Manchester. Cotton warehouses and underground canals, backstreets as yet uncolonised by apartment blocks and delis. The businesses were the type that could only afford cheap rent: dance studios, fabric shops, youth hostels and takeaways. Bali Hai had a neon palm tree sign and a flashing arrow pointing down a flight of stairs. I descended to a garish pink door and was hit by the faint smell of disinfectant and a basement chill as I stepped inside. Synthetic palm trees, tanks of guppy fish, and a barman with a beard and a Hawaiian shirt. A TV screen showed young Elvis serenading a girl on a beach. The speakers above the bar played Katy Perry.

Susie was at the far end of the room, facing away from me. The boys at her table looked unsure whether to welcome me or not as I approached. I tapped her on the shoulder and she twisted around.

'You're here! I thought you weren't going to come. Everyone, this is my little sister, Miriam.' Then to me, 'Have you got new clothes? Take off your coat. Let me see.'

'In a minute.' I sat down with my coat on and she went round the table making introductions. There was a jolly-looking girl with tufty blonde hair, and three boys, all about the same age as me, dressed like they worked in the woods rather than in an office. Lumberjack shirts, jeans, stubble. They had the glazed eyes of people who have worked too fast all day and are now drinking too fast to try to slow themselves down. The one nearest to me, Ryan I think he was called, handed me the cocktail menu, saying I needed to catch up, they were all way ahead of me.

The drinks had names like The Zombie, The Painkiller, The Grog, as if describing the next day's hangover rather than that night's excitement. I ordered a Mai Tai at the bar and wondered whether I was supposed to clap when the barman tossed the cocktail shaker around, throwing it over his shoulder and catching it with his other hand. I turned my back on him because it seemed easier for us both. When he finally handed me the drink, it was the same sunset pink as the paint on

111

the door. Sweet and fruity, you felt the alcohol rather than tasted it.

Back at the table Ryan asked me about my job but I found it hard to explain and I think he got the impression I was a cleaner. He said he worked in brand identity and started to slide through images of logos on his iPhone. I wondered whether we were supposed to be getting together and whether another drink would make me fancy him, and whether it was worth sleeping with him even if it didn't, just so I could reset the clock at zero.

He went out to smoke and Susie sidled over. 'He's single, you know.'

I mustn't have looked sufficiently excited because she said, 'He's a nice guy, Miriam. Other girls fancy him.'

'Like who? You?'

'No but I would if I wasn't married.'

People in relationships who get their thrills from setting up single friends. It was the opposite of schadenfreude but somehow worse. I wasn't a reality TV programme.

I said, 'I'm not sure that he's my type.'

Susie lowered her voice to a stage whisper, the only kind that would work in a bar this loud. 'What about Jared then? I don't think he's got a girlfriend.'

'I don't necessarily have to find a boyfriend tonight in this particular bar. It's not a last-chance, end-of-year sale on men.'

'No but you are at the end of your twenties. You can't waste too much time.'

Was that an insult? I felt insulted. She must have

noticed because she changed the subject. 'I got a letter from Dad the other day.'

My head snapped around. I carefully reached for my drink. 'Where from?'

'Vancouver Island. Canada.'

'I thought he was in Denmark.'

'He moved.'

Oh. 'What did he say?'

'He said he was having classical guitar lessons. And that his girlfriend had a baby. A daughter.'

We didn't speak for a while. I took a long drag on my drink through the bendy straw. 'I bet he's gutted it's another girl. He's got two of those already.'

Susie said, 'He sent me a photograph of her. Do you want to see it?'

I'd be more interested in one of him. 'Okay.'

She took it out of her purse. A fat face with Cupid's bow lips and droopy eyelids. 'Cute,' I said and handed it back.

'She looks like him.'

'Does she?' I took it from her again and examined the baby more closely but I didn't feel any recognition. I couldn't picture my dad's face and I wasn't sure if that was because I was drunk or because I'd not seen him for eight years.

We stayed in Bali Hai until sometime after two. Ryan said he'd Facebook me, then as me and Susie were flagging down a cab, he ran over and asked for my number. Susie was delighted. It was the same expression she wore when her son Alfie scored a goal at his Sunday morning football matches. As we were going up Oxford Road in the taxi, my phone buzzed with a text message.

'Is that him already?' Susie clutched my leg like she always did when she was this wasted.

It was Erik. I clicked it open. *How was your night out?*

Susie said, 'Who's *Erik*?'

I reread it. 'The guy I work for.'

'Does he normally text you in the middle of the night?'

'He doesn't normally text me.'

'Best not to reply,' she said sagely.

'Why?'

'Overfamiliar.'

'But he's gorgeous.'

Her mouth dropped. Everything she did when drunk was exaggerated, as if she was making up for all the time she had to be level in the rest of her life. 'Why have you only just mentioned this, this man? I need to know everything.'

We were nearly at my house, thankfully. I gave Susie a tenner for the taxi and she pushed it back in my hand. 'You need to call me tomorrow about this.'

Inside I sat on my bed and reread the message for a third time. It was the time of night that made it significant. You couldn't send a platonic text at 2 am, could you?

I typed a reply. *It was ok. Just got in. What are you up to?*

Working in my garret. Hope you had fun. See you Monday. X.

No question for me to answer in reply. No easy way to keep the conversation going. Maybe he was just saying hello.

But that X.

Night night. I added a kiss. Deleted it. Added it again. Pressed send.

I wouldn't be able to sleep. I bit my hand and sat staring at the floor. I was bouncing around inside.

13

Alcohol feels like amphetamine to me on the morning after. Waking up after a big night is like being given a small electric shock. My eyes are wide open, I'm super alert, half of me feels like running, the other half like hiding under the covers. The only thing I've found that gets me back to the right speed is watching clouds being blown across a half-clear sky. But you need the right weather conditions for that and today it was a solid, unmoving grey.

I sat in bed with my laptop and ordered a discounted exercise bike I'd had my eye on. It was what I felt like doing, pedalling fast without going anywhere, but the website said it wouldn't arrive for at least a month. Then I ate breakfast at Jam Street Café, feeling an unfocused, panicky anxiety. I tried reading a newspaper that had been left on the table but I couldn't concentrate on the words so I finished my coffee and paid up, then set off walking. I covered miles that morning, snaking through Whalley Range, Chorlton, Withington, Didsbury and down Wilmslow Road until it became Oxford Road and I was amongst gym-bound students in hooded tops and jogging pants, and the first of Saturday night's drinkers starting early with a pint of bitter. I was thinking hard, about my dad and his new daughter, about Ryan and how he'd locked onto me, following Susie's plan as if it was another task to be completed before the end of the day, about Erik and his unexpected text message that seemed now to be a way of finding out whether I was alone or not. And whether or not this meant he cared. Was I growing on him like he was on me? He had slowly changed shape in my mind until he was this always-there, compelling thing I couldn't tire of thinking about. And I really wanted to be tired. Not just around the eyes but in my legs and head and chest.

I walked to Alexandra Park, telling myself he rarely went there, and saw that the lime trees bordering the long, straight avenue were dropping their leaves in a soft carpet of yellows and golds. The canopies touched high above the walkway that ran between them, forming an archway that stretched the whole length of the park. They were still full but the ground was covered, too, and the air in between swirled with falling leaves. It was beautiful. Perhaps I could call round to tell him to come and see. He was a photographer; he'd want to capture this. I left the park by the gate near his house and knocked on his back door. My nerve left me at the moment my hand rapped on the wood. I prayed he wouldn't have heard, then when he didn't answer, I wished that he had. I left quickly. He must have been upstairs, out of earshot, or just out. I thought about turning to look up at his bedroom window to see if he was watching as I walked back down the driveway. But he probably couldn't get to it for the stacks of books, and anyway, he wouldn't do that, would he, see me waiting and not let me inside?

An empty skip was on the driveway when I arrived at his house on Monday morning. I had to edge round it to get to the back garden, where I found him kneeling on the path by the kitchen window, examining something on the ground.

He twisted around when I said hello. 'Maybe don't look at this if you don't like dead things.'

'Who likes dead things?'

'Well, I do, in a way.' He stood up. It was a sparrow. Its small, soft body inert on the grass. 'Micka brought it. She thinks it is a nice present. I have tried to tell her.'

His camera was on the ground beside him. I said, 'Did you take a picture of it?'

He glanced at me. 'Don't look at me like that. It is how I make my sculptures, from studying photographs.' He went into the back porch and came out with a spade. 'Okay, I am going to bury it. Go inside if you like. Make yourself comfortable.'

I liked it when he joked about the state of the house. It made him seem more normal. Taking photographs of dead birds, less so.

I decided to have another look at the bird sculptures in his studio while I was waiting for him. The blackbird eyed me from the desk. Its sheet music feathers were congealed, one wing hung broken by its side. The seagull stood with its chest pushed out, its head high, ignoring the cavity in its side.

Erik came in and stood beside me.

I said, 'They look arrogant, even though they're dying.'

'They are used to being able to fly.'

'How do you decide what to make them out of?'

'I choose something that is also going to die. Phone directories, travel brochures, books. All this paper is being replaced by the internet and digital files. In twenty years, it won't exist anymore.'

'You're preserving it, like an archivist, or a taxidermist.'

'Yes.'

'Is that why you can't let go of your books, because you want to preserve them?'

He sighed. 'It is just a habit. It is in me.'

I nodded, not wanting to push him on it right now. 'So why birds?'

'I just like them.'

'Oh.'

'Shall we get started?'

'Okay.'

That morning I put into practice something I'd learned from a book on clutter clearing I'd ordered from Amazon. I'd noticed last week that Erik had lots of empty plastic boxes around the house that he must have bought with the intention of ordering his collections. I took them into Chloe's room and suggested we allow one box for each sculpture he was working on, or was planning to work on. Anything that wouldn't fit

119

in that box would have to be thrown away. I told him it was a way of limiting what he collected while still making sure he had what he needed for his art.

He had a lot of reasons why it wouldn't work, and it was only when I stopped arguing with him and started sulking, that he agreed to try it. I was surprised that this childish tactic worked but I didn't show it. By midday we had the whole room sorted into either boxes or bin bags, apart from one area that I'd been ignoring until now. Under the bed.

'Let's just leave whatever is under there,' Erik said. 'Chloe will not mind.'

'We're not leaving this room half-done.'

'But look around, it is clear. It is done.'

I lay on the floor and reached under the bed to pull out a shoebox. It was full of maps of the USA. California, Oregon, Washington State. A date on one said 1967.

He said, 'I do not want to throw those away.'

I put them aside to tackle later. 'There's something I want to show you at lunch,' I said, changing the subject.

'What is it?'

'Have you been to the park recently?'

'No.'

'It'll be a surprise then.' I reached under the bed again and dragged out another shoebox full of maps. 'Where did you get them all from?'

'A car boot sale.' He started flicking through them. 'I know what you want to show me. It is the turtles in the lake.'

'Turtles?'

'Yes.'

I couldn't tell whether he was serious or not. 'I've never seen them.'

'You don't believe me.'

'Not fully.'

'You think I am imagining turtles.' He reached under the bed to help me pull out a large plastic storage box. I took the lid off. There were five or six old cameras inside. Pre-digital and heavy in black protective cases. His eyes brightened. 'I have been looking for these.'

There was a Lomo. I recognised the make because Jessica had one of the new versions, though she'd never quite figured out how it worked. I studied it for a few moments then put it back in the box. 'Maybe you saw the turtles in another park? In another country?'

'There are turtles in Alexandra Park. They sit on the logs when the sun is out. It's not like I'm saying I saw a bear.'

I said, 'I need photographic evidence.'

'A photograph doesn't prove anything. It is easy to add a few bears, turtles, whatever.'

'Not with one of these.' I picked up the Lomo again.

'It is harder with one of those.' He took it out of my hands. 'It has a film in it,' he said, eyebrows raised. He held the viewfinder up to his eye and turned the camera towards me.

'No.' I looked at the carpet.

He put it down and smiled when I looked back up. Did he smile like that at everyone? His hand was close to mine on the carpet. It would only take a small movement to touch him. I couldn't do it.

'Shy Miriam,' he said.

I felt my face grow warm. Was he reading my thoughts? My body language?

'I will get you later,' he said.

The park was quiet that lunchtime. There were just a few fathers pushing toddlers on tricycles, a couple of schoolgirls holding ice creams in gloved hands. We followed the path between the lake and the road, passing a man teaching himself to walk on a tightrope tied low between two trees. He balanced for three steps, four before jumping off onto the long, leaf-covered grass.

'So where are we going?' Erik asked.

'Just along here.' I'd brought the camera. He'd brought our lunch, saying we should eat outside as it wasn't raining for once.

We came to the top of the lime avenue and stopped. It was as beautiful as yesterday, perhaps more so now the wind had dropped, keeping the moment suspended, the perfect balance between leaves on the ground and leaves in the trees. The avenue stretched away from us, symmetrical and straight. 'This is it,' I said.

He didn't speak for a moment and I looked up to see his expression.

He said, 'I get stuck in my house. I forget the park is here.' He took the camera from my hand. 'Shall I help you take a picture?'

He explained how to adjust the shutter speed, choose a focus point, hold the camera steady. He moved my finger onto the right button, and crouched slightly so that he was at the same height as me, seeing from the same perspective. He was standing close beside me. The world through the viewfinder seemed small and removed. I pressed the button and it clicked and whirred.

'You don't get that with digital cameras,' I said.

'It is exciting, isn't it?'

'I want to take another one.' I looked around, trying to spot a suitable subject. 'Let's go to that derelict house.'

'Okay but please can we eat our sandwiches first?'

He had bought one for me from the Barbakan delicatessen opposite the swimming baths yesterday. Cheese with gherkins on rye bread. We sat on a bench overlooking the lake. The ducks and geese were at the other side in a feeding frenzy around a gleeful little boy with a bag of bread crusts.

'Does this kind of food remind you of home?' I asked.

'This is home.'

'I know, I mean does it remind you of Slovakia?'

'Not really, but it is the kind of thing we would eat. My mother made sour gherkins sometimes.'

His mother and father lived in Bratislava. His brother, too. He had an uncle in London. He'd told me this last week.

A dog barked at another dog by the gates. The pigeons perched on the island took to the air, lapped the lake, and settled in the trees that bordered the park railings. Beyond them was Erik's house. I'd never seen it from this distance before.

'Look at your house,' I said. 'You wouldn't imagine what's in there when you see it from the outside.'

Erik followed my line of sight. 'That's not my house.'

He said it with such certainty. I smiled at him. 'It is.'
'Is it?'
'Yes, that's your driveway leading up to your door. Your windows.'
He said, 'I did not even recognise it.'
Sunlight moved across the lake and onto the trees, then onto the tiles of his roof. Two squares of glass lit up within them.
I stood up. Moved to the railings by the lake to get a better view then turned back to him.
'What's wrong?'
I said, 'What's up there?'
He sounded wary. 'Where?'
'There's a room in the roof.'
Erik was looking at the skylights, his eyes squinting across the water. Something wasn't making sense here. There couldn't be a room up there because there weren't any stairs. On the narrow L of the landing were doors to the bathroom, Chloe's room, his studio, his bedroom. Opposite his bedroom door were the shelves of bird books. I pictured them. They were about the same width and height as a door.
I remembered how he had left the second downstairs room off our plan, saying, 'It's full' as if that meant it didn't exist. Had he done the same with another whole floor?
He said, 'It's an attic conversion. It was our bedroom.'
Our? His wife.
'Oh.'
'We all slept up there. Chloe, too, some of the time. My wife thought it was safer to be out of the way of

124

burglars. She thought they'd take what they wanted from downstairs and leave us alone.'

I sat down beside him again. 'Did you get burgled a lot?'

'She thought she could hear someone breaking in every night. But in reality, it only happened two, maybe three times.'

I thought of Caitlin's sharp words on the phone. Perhaps what I'd taken for bitterness was more a brittle nervousness. I said, 'She sounds…imaginative.'

'That is one word for it.'

'What's another?'

'Manic depression. Two words.'

He was still looking at the house. I said, 'That must have been hard.'

'It was a long time ago.'

Two ladies in burkas passed us with their prams. The ice cream van stopped near the park gates and began playing its halting tune.

I said, 'So what's up there now?'

'I don't know.'

'Just more books?'

He didn't answer and I didn't ask again, knowing already it would be another level of paper-packed rooms. It was like being stuck in a repeating dream, the house rising higher into the sky in layers of books and magazines and every time you thought you'd reached the top, another stairway appeared.

Erik had put his sandwich to one side as if he'd lost his appetite for it. He was still looking at the roof of his house and those silver-lit windows. I wanted to bring him back into the present, into his good mood again.

'So the sun is shining,' I said. 'But I can't see any turtles.'

'They are on the island in the undergrowth, probably. They hibernate.'

'That's convenient for you.'

Erik said, 'My wife used to say that she wished people could hibernate. She thought it would solve the world's problems if we could all just hide away and sleep for three months a year.'

I glanced at him. 'I don't think I'd want to sleep for three months every year.'

'She thought it would make everything new again. She thought you'd wake up feeling enthusiastic and sociable with all your problems put back into perspective.'

'Most people wake up feeling like that after seven hours.'

'Yes, it's true. I suppose she found life harder than most people.' He stood up and took my empty sandwich wrapper off me, picked up his own half-finished lunch. 'Let's go and take another picture.'

The abandoned house was bordered from the road by a red brick wall. Broken glass was cemented onto the top, ivy and moss had grown over the shards. If it was meant to keep people out, it wasn't working. The wire mesh hoarding between the gateposts of the driveway had been ripped out and now lay in the overgrown grass in front of the house. You could just walk in, so we did. There were graffiti tags on the brickwork. Cigarette ends amongst the rubble on the driveway. I found myself checking the windows for movement, looking behind me when I heard footsteps, but it was just someone passing on the pavement.

'What if there's someone in there? Like squatters or a homeless person?'

Erik said, 'I don't think anyone is living here.'

'How do you know?'

'It is too still. It is lifeless.'

We walked up to the glassless bay window and peered inside. The plaster was falling off the walls. There were beer cans on the floor and it looked as though someone had lit a fire in the hearth but it hadn't taken hold. A half-charred chair leg stuck out of the grate.

Erik tugged at the front door, it swung open. I had been hoping it wouldn't.

'Shall we go inside?'

'No.'

He hesitated. 'Will you be okay here?'

I looked through the window again, imagining a figure taking form in the shadows, a face looking back out at me. 'Okay then, but I'm not going upstairs. And don't go off without me.'

The front door opened onto a hallway with broken black and white floor tiles and a staircase leading up in a curve. You couldn't see where it ended, just a wall halfway up graffitied with a spray-paint outline of a slender, sitting cat.

It was a similar layout to Erik's house, with the rooms going off to our left, the kitchen at the back, visible through an open door. We went into the room we'd just looked at from the outside. It smelled damp and stultified, as though the empty window frames weren't letting through any air. The floorboards were warped beneath our feet and there were water stains on the ceiling. Erik took a picture of the fireplace. I tried to imagine it as the heart of a bustling family home. Photographs on the mantelpiece. Armchairs and house plants and a piano. Had the owners known they were leaving for good, or had they always meant to return?

We went into the kitchen. The cupboards were still in place but most of the floor tiles had been taken and it looked as though someone had dug into the walls to prise out the pipes. I wanted to take a photograph of the cracked sink with its gathering of leaves. Erik helped me set up the camera and I was aware of his closeness, of the patient, careful movements of his fingers on the buttons.

We stood at the foot of the staircase, looking up at the cat silhouette on the wall.

'I'm not going up there,' I said.

'I'm not either.'

Thank God. I said, 'Why would you let a house like this fall to bits?'

'Maybe they went bankrupt.'

'Or something bad happened here.'

He turned to me. 'Why do you think that?'

'It's like the family who owned it couldn't stand to live here anymore, and nobody would buy it because it had this violent past.'

'Hmm. I think maybe we have stayed long enough.'

I took a close-up photograph of the gateposts on our way out. They were like the ones at Erik's house, but moss was growing in the letter carvings, filling them with green: *IONA*.

'Is that a girl's name?' Erik asked.

'It's an island off the coast of Scotland. What's your house called?'

'I can't work it out,' he said. 'Maybe it's an island, too. I might see it on a map one day.'

We walked back towards the park. I said, 'What would you do if one of the photos we took of the house shows a child's face at the window?'

'Like a ghost? I don't believe in them. I am like you with turtles.'

'It's not that I don't believe in turtles.'

'You think they are like unicorns. You think they don't exist.'

He was teasing me again. It was making me smile. When we got back to his house, I traced the eroded letters on the gatepost with my finger. Most were illegible. I could only make out an I and an L and the last letter, an E.

'Something Isle,' I said.

'It doesn't fit. There is too much space between the L and the E.'

'Isildur,' I said. 'From *The Lord of the Rings*.'

'I really hope my house isn't named after a make-believe place.'

'It's a person, I think.'

'A make-believe person? I will seriously have to rename it.'

'Shall I take a picture?'

He passed me the camera. 'It's the last one. I will send it off to be developed, then we can see what kind of photographer you are.'

14

The living room, he called it. Though it was clear that nobody had lived in it for some time. No people anyway. Who knew what creatures scuttled and scratched under that mass of books? It was a different scale entirely to Chloe's room. Bigger, fuller, darker. Standing in the doorway, at the start of the passageway that snaked between the stacks and shelves, I felt that this whole project was impossible. I was out of my depth; we both were.

That morning we had shut the door on Chloe's room – now the one clear space in the whole house – and I had tried to ignore the fact that very little had been thrown away, just moved into his studio and the hallway. There were thick green plastic bags full of magazines filling the area at the foot of the stairs. Erik said he would put them in the skip, later.

Now in the dim hallway light, his face was tense and still. I edged along the passageway between the books to the clearing with the armchair and sat down. It could all go. Couldn't he see that? If I could just get him to let me clear it without him, it would be done in a few days. He was going to London tomorrow for two nights. When he came back, this room could be empty.

He stepped into the clearing. I tucked my feet under the chair so our legs weren't touching, and he half-sat, half-stood against the curtained window.

'Is this where you sit?' I asked.

'Sometimes.'

His shoulders were sunken and his voice was low. This room weighed down on you. I wanted to reach out to him and pull him up, help him surface. I picked up the scalpel that was lying on the floor by the chair and moved the sharp edge lightly over my jeans. How could someone who had let their house get like this have the ability to put it back to normal? I told myself he wanted to do it, so he would do it. He was making room for Chloe. I was making room for myself.

'There is so much in here,' he said quietly. 'All these ideas I had for different projects. If I didn't have to work, I could be so productive on it.'

'Why don't you let me get started on the clearing while you're in London?'

'Because you would throw everything away.'

I twisted round to look at him. 'Isn't that what you want, really, an empty house?'

That guarded look in his eyes. 'I cannot imagine that.'

'I can.'

He shook his head, his eyes on the floor.

'Think how much clearer your thoughts would be if you didn't have all this stuff around you. It's like

131

having the radio on all day and night, it doesn't let you hear yourself think.'

'Maybe that's what I want.'

'What's so bad that you need to drown it out?'

He picked up a book on astronomy and opened it halfway through. 'Nothing. I collect stuff because it is useful.'

I turned away. 'It's the opposite of useful.'

'I know I have too much and that is why we are cutting it down. There is not a problem here.'

Except we weren't cutting it down. Later, chipping away at the rock face of books, I imagined this room empty, just swept floorboards and sunlight through the windows. I longed for space, for a break in the claustrophobia. It was a frustration similar to how I longed for physical closeness with him, or not closeness, because we had that in the narrow pathways and floorless hallway, but for contact. Sometimes I knew he felt my eyes on his jawline and sculpted, swimmer's arms. He accepted it, like he accepted everything else about me. He didn't seem to want to change this desire, or censure it, or do anything about it, which of course made it stronger still, until I felt like it was the thing taking up all the space in the house, not the books or magazines or piles of sliced-up paper.

He was away until Friday and time slowed down. I spent the days at home, reading the books I'd got about hoarding, hoping to find the solution that would break the wall we'd hit. Some had strategies to follow to help a hoarder clear a house. Others were case studies. I read these in short, anxious bursts. I couldn't help noticing how many ended with little or no change.

But, I told myself, Erik was different to these hopeless cases. He wanted to clear his house. Nobody was imposing it on him. It was his own decision and he had recognised that he needed help. This 'insight', as it was called, was a valuable thing.

The problem was, it slipped frequently and then it was like he had no idea why we were even trying to throw things away. I read that the hoarding impulse was like a pathway carved into his brain which his thoughts followed by default. He was sometimes aware of it but he could rarely reroute it or find another way. And according to the books, people who tried to redirect it would invariably end up in conflict with the hoarder, sometimes being cut out of their life completely.

But another difference was, I just wouldn't let that happen. I wasn't going to abandon him to this problem, no matter how hard it got. You didn't do that; leave someone you cared about in a mess. It wasn't friendship. It definitely wasn't love.

There was a mattress in the skip when I arrived on Friday morning. Blue, worn, and heavy with rain, it was bent over the side as if trying to climb out again.

I told Erik and he frowned. 'Where did that come from?'

'People think an empty skip is theirs to fill.'

He hadn't touched the bags lining the hallway. And the kitchen table was now covered in books he must have taken from the living room to sort through.

He looked at them and sighed, trying to find a space to put down his mug of chocolate. 'Sometimes things have to get worse before they get better.'

'They need to start getting better soon. It's seven weeks until Chloe moves in.'

'Well at least she has a bedroom.'

'I think she'd like a bathroom and a kitchen, too.'

I heard the thud of post hitting the letters already piled in the front porch. Erik went to gather them up. I had read it was a good idea to have hoarders taken off junk mail and subscription lists and decided to sort that today. It didn't seem to make him happy, the daily post delivery. Most days he carried it through to the kitchen as if it was heavier than it was, a burden he'd like to be free of but couldn't quite resist.

This time, though, he looked pleased as he brought in the post. 'Your photographs are back.' He handed me the envelope. 'Don't be disappointed if they're not what you expected. You get better with practice.'

I unstuck the envelope and pulled out the photographs. 'I'm not expecting much.'

They were in reverse order. The first was of the gatepost at the end of his driveway. The weather-worn letters still refused to form themselves into a word. Then the other gatepost. *IONA* spelled out in moss. Then the abandoned house itself. The kitchen sink with its crisp, dry leaves. The fireplace which somehow looked more desolate in his photograph than it had in real life. Then the lime tree avenue and I liked how the carpet of gold receded towards a point in the centre of the image, how it captured the cathedral-like canopies rising up and arching over.

'It's good,' Erik said.

'Thanks.'

'You could have it framed. Put it up in your flat.'

'I might.' I felt proud of it, even though he'd practically taken it for me. I hadn't created anything in a long time.

The next picture was of me, in the hallway, reaching up to unhook my coat from amongst the scarves. He'd taken it from the kitchen without me realising, and it had an other-worldly quality that my photographs lacked. I was blurred, indistinct and small within the sharp frame of the doorway. Maybe it was the disappearing light from where he stood to where I stood.

Then there were photographs that had been taken years ago. Chloe, about eight or nine years old, playing a recorder. In the background a green tiled fireplace with a vase of lilies in the grate. Then Chloe again, this time in a red hat and scarf, sitting on the low, sweeping branch of an oak tree, frost on the ground below.

'Did you take these?' I asked.

'Yes.'

'She's pretty.' She was one of those girls I'd envied at that age, whose thick black hair naturally fell in tangled waves onto her shoulders.

I couldn't see his expression but at the next photograph, his shoulders stiffened. It was Chloe and a lady who looked like her. Caitlin, I guessed. They were on a velvet, honey-coloured sofa, a thick, creamy rug in front of them, the green fireplace just visible in the corner of the shot. Chloe was pretty but Caitlin was beautiful. Her smile took over her face and she had big,

135

almond eyes. She wore wide-legged jeans and a man's blue shirt. Her feet were bare, her toenails painted red.

I saw all this in the second before Erik pulled the photographs out of my hands and pushed them back in the envelope. He went upstairs with them. I stood in the kitchen, waiting for him to come back down.

15

The photographs of Chloe and Caitlin were in the skip when I arrived the next morning. I lifted up a plank of paint-splattered wood, curious to see what had been dumped in there overnight, and there they were, still inside the envelope. Mother and daughter sitting on the velvet sofa in a room warm with sunlight. Then Caitlin on her own, lying on the same sofa, her hair over bare shoulders, naked beneath a soft white blanket. Then one of her half-sleeping, half-smiling, her face half-hidden by her hair.

There were more. Caitlin at the park, in the garden, drinking a glass of wine, laughing at the camera. I felt something breaking up inside me, and I told myself, this was in the past. She wasn't his wife anymore, or his muse. She wasn't in his life. I was.

But if she meant nothing to him, why were these photographs in the skip? They were the only thing he'd thrown away but they were the wrong thing. I brushed the rain off the envelope and slid it into my bag.

My own photographs were on the kitchen table,

alongside the ones that just showed Chloe on her own. I rehearsed a question in my head, *What happened to the pictures of your wife?* but it would be said too lightly, too carefully, I couldn't do it. Erik didn't mention them. He looked tired. He said he'd been up since five editing some photographs for the women's supplement of one of next week's papers.

I said, 'The skip is getting fuller.'

'Is it?'

I looked at him but he gave nothing away. Had he hidden the photographs underneath the scrap wood or had someone dumped the wood on top of them after he'd left them there? I couldn't picture him doing either – carelessly dropping them in, carefully hiding them away – and it made him seem like a stranger.

I was starting to believe that it wasn't the scarcity of a Communist childhood buried beneath the hoard, but something as commonplace as a broken marriage. I set about the clearing with a renewed vigour, sneaking books into bin bags when he wasn't looking, reducing towers into stubs. Whatever was hidden beneath it all, I would bring it to light.

We were in the kitchen sorting through a pile of encyclopaedias when the doorbell rang. He looked towards it but didn't move.

'Shall I answer it?' I said.

'No. It will be Jehovah's Witnesses or a salesman. They are the only people who knock on my door, apart from you.'

'It might be someone you know.'

'Then they'd phone me.'

It made it funny when his phone started ringing in his pocket. He looked at the screen and swore quietly, then put it to his ear. 'Hi Chloe.' His hand shot up to his forehead and he turned away. 'I didn't hear. I am coming now.' He clicked it off. 'She is here, with Caitlin.' He looked around at the chaotic kitchen, the table covered in books, the work surfaces, too, and through to the hallway lined with bags of magazines, the living room with its horror-house strangeness, its utter abnormality, and another room just like it next door.

His voice was stunned and slow. 'What should I do?'

I thought fast. 'Lock all the doors like you used to with me.'

'But the hallway, the bathroom. She has never seen it like this.'

'We'll keep them in here. It's not that bad in this room, just say you're having a clear-out.'

'But who are you? What are you doing here?'

'Your girlfriend?' My assertive tone had gone.

He stopped looking around and focused his worried expression on me. 'You're too young to be my girl-friend.'

'I'm twenty-nine.'

'You are my friend. A girlfriend is too complicated.'

'Okay.'

He took the keys from inside a jug on the windowsill. 'Please lock the doors. I will bring them round the back.'

By the time I'd locked his studio, bedroom, the living room and the back room, they were already in the kitchen. I paused for a second in the hallway, trying to get the flustered look off my face, then stepped inside, closing the hallway door quickly behind me. Everyone turned round.

'This is Miriam,' Erik said. 'Miriam, this is Chloe and Caitlin.'

I got the impression Chloe vaguely recognised me from the charity shop. She seemed to have lost that sheen of confidence she'd had that day, and was standing just inside the doorway, echoing the worried expression on Erik's face. I remembered how he'd said she never came here because of the 'bad vibes'. I doubted the state of this room was doing anything to change her mind about the place.

Caitlin was considering me carefully. Her face was a computer running too many programmes at once. 'Was it you I spoke to on the phone?'

'Yes, I think so.'

She looked at me. Looked around the cluttered room. 'Hi.'

'They were shopping at the Trafford Centre.' Erik's fingers were tensed and moving. He pulled out a chair and shifted its covering of books onto the floor.

Nobody sat down. Caitlin said, 'We thought we'd call round and surprise you, as we were so close. And because Chloe hasn't been here for so long. We thought it'd be a good idea to come and say hello before the big moving day.'

His ex-wife looked different to the photographs I had in my bag. In person, her features were set and unreadable, not fluid and expressive, as though she had been hardening over time. It was age, I supposed. And unhappiness. Her almond eyes were flat, her hair cut short, her smile gone.

There was an awkward silence so I asked if anyone wanted a cup of tea. They all said no thanks. I wanted to get out of there. Chloe and Caitlin were both looking at me curiously. I didn't think they meant to be unfriendly, they were just confused. Whatever they'd been expecting to find here, this wasn't it. And now Erik was trying to clear space on the table as if he was staging a family dinner in the middle of this book-strewn chaos. I took a pile of encyclopaedias out of his hands and put them in the back porch. I wished I knew how to make him calm again.

In the kitchen, Chloe said, 'Can I see my bedroom?'

Erik moved, subtly, so he was blocking the hallway door. 'I want it to be a surprise when you move in.'

'But I can't even remember what it looks like.'

He said, 'Right now, it looks a mess and I think you would be disappointed. Let me show it you when it's finished. Please.'

She was used to getting her own way with him, but in this strange situation, she was unsure and hesitant. He reached for the photographs on the table and went to stand beside her. 'I found these pictures of you.'

Her face broke into a reluctant smile. 'How old was I then?'

'You were nine, I think.'

'Look at this,' she said to Caitlin. 'Look how long my hair was.'

They were looking at the one of Chloe with a recorder,

141

a music stand in front of her, the green fireplace behind her.

'Where was it taken?' I asked.

Chloe looked at me like I was dim. 'Here.'

Of course it was. It was just another place entirely from what lay behind those doors.

'Have you eaten?' Erik asked quickly, looking at Caitlin.

'We thought we'd stop somewhere on the way home.'

'Then we can eat together,' he said. 'Maybe Croma? Or wherever you like.'

'Croma is nice,' Chloe said to Caitlin. 'Me and Dad always go there.'

'Yes, you've told me about it. Will you join us, Miriam?'

I sensed an agenda behind her invitation. Erik must have, too, because he answered for me. 'You have swimming, don't you?'

'So how do you two know each other?' Caitlin's question was directed at me.

'Through swimming.' I wondered how that would have worked. Striking up a conversation in the communal showers, chatting as we rested at the end of a length?

Chloe seemed happier now she knew they were leaving the house and going to familiar territory. She said, 'Swimming is *the* most boring sport. I don't understand how Dad can do it every single day.'

'I like to be bored. It's relaxing,' Erik said. 'So shall we go?'

'You like being bored?' Chloe said. 'I hate it. I can't

wait to get out of Sheffield. Did I tell you Jemma has swapped courses from Liverpool to Manchester? We'll be based in the same building next year.'

'That's great.' He picked up his car keys from the table.

'I need to use the bathroom,' Caitlin said.

'It is better to wait till we get to the restaurant, if you possibly can,' Erik said smoothly. 'I am having some work done. It's a little basic up there at the moment.'

Chloe looked concerned. 'It'll be finished before I move in, won't it?'

'Yes, of course. 8th of December.'

He ushered them towards the door. I grabbed my coat from the hallway and followed. Nobody mentioned the skip on the driveway. Underneath the beech trees I said to Erik, 'See you Monday?'

'Yes, Monday,' he said. 'Thank you.'

Caitlin looked from him to me. She was still trying to figure out who I was, what role I had in her ex-husband's life. 'Are you sure you don't want to eat with us?'

In this shadowy light she looked older still. How long ago were those photographs taken? Ten years at the most. What had happened to her in that time?

I made myself say no, thank you, I had to get going. I walked home under the dripping trees, thinking of the living room that existed in the photographs and the one that existed now, and of the Caitlin in the photographs, and the one I'd just met. On Demesne Road, just past the abandoned house, I stopped and took the pictures out of my bag.

I looked through them fast, then again more slowly.

It was the same room, yes. Not the same person. These pictures weren't of Caitlin, though the woman in them had her eyes and bone structure. Her cousin? Her sister? But why was she lying there like that, nearly naked, in his living room? I stood staring at that particular photograph, trying to work it out, but every conclusion I reached, I rejected. I wished I had left them in the skip, buried under the splintered wood.

16

When I was eight and Susie was eleven, we used to go on night walks with my dad. We would put on our trainers and anoraks and set off with him through the narrow lanes of our village, heading upwards to where the street lamps stopped and the fields began, then further still on to the first stretches of blank moorland. We didn't take torches. Dad knew the way. And we didn't talk. You had to be quiet to hear hedgerow creatures rustling, owls calling, cars approaching, their headlights illuminating tree trunks and stiles before they sped by us.

We sometimes stopped and stared up at the stars or at the swaying silhouette of a sycamore. Or we would step into a wood and let our eyes adjust to that deeper level of darkness closing in then opening up around us.

You wouldn't think two young girls would want to spend their evenings in this way. But I found it exciting to be roaming outdoors when everyone else was settled in their houses for the night. I was restless, wanting something outside my world, like you can be at that age, or at any age.

When we returned home, we would be glowing with cold. Mum would still be watching television, knees underneath her on the sofa. She never came with us and even back then I wondered whether she minded us all disappearing like that. Some dads escaped to the pub, mine went for night walks on the moors. It was the same thing, though, and Mum must have felt it more, with me and Susie going, too, as though she was the only one who wanted to be at home.

I decided I would ask Erik about the woman in the photographs. I would tell him the truth: that I'd wanted to see if anything interesting had been dumped in the skip by other people, and that I was surprised to see them hidden in there, so I'd taken them out. I wouldn't ask who she was, or why she'd been sleeping in his bed and lying half-naked in his living room when she wasn't his wife. I'd just ask why he'd thrown them away, and see what his reaction was.

Part of me knew it was a terrible idea. He would get angry or turn cold and quiet or just ignore the question all together. But a bigger part of me couldn't let it go unresolved. Was it an affair? With his wife's sister? Had it happened while he was married or after they'd separated? I had to know so that I could stop trying to work it all out in my head. I had to know what kind of man he was.

On Monday I had the photographs in my bag, ready to show them to him straightaway. But when he opened the door, I had second thoughts.

No smile. He mumbled 'Hi,' and turned back inside.

In the kitchen I saw why. The room was buried in books. It looked like he had spent all weekend dragging them out of the living room and dumping them in here. They covered every available surface, including the floor. I stepped carefully through them, steadying myself against the table, and saw that the hallway was full as well. The front door was blocked and you would struggle to get to the stairs. I didn't know what to say.

Erik gestured to it, speechless, as though this was something that had occurred when he wasn't there, as if he'd just come down this morning and found it like this.

'What happened?' I asked.

'I have been trying to get organised.'

'I think you need to stop.'

'I thought if I could just sort out what's important from what's not, I'd be able to move forwards. But I'm not getting anywhere. I am thinking of renting another storage unit.'

'Another?'

'I have two, but they are full.'

I felt my face slacken. I wanted to sit down but I couldn't without shifting a load of stuff first. I went out into the garden instead, wanting space and air. Whatever we were doing, it wasn't working. It was getting worse in there, not better. I leaned against the garage and tried to slow my breathing. When I went back inside, he was standing where I'd left him.

'I have been up since six working on this.' He spoke fast. 'I didn't go to bed until one. I feel so fucking confused, Miriam. It's making me feel insane.'

I gave him a sideways look. 'It's not that bad.'

'It is bad.'

His agitation calmed me somehow. It was like only one of us could be freaked out by this at once, and right now it was his turn. I pushed the tension in my chest down and spoke as if I was in control of the situation.

'You need to take a break from it. You're too caught up in it to think clearly and make decisions. Let's go to the park and just try to chill for half an hour.'

'I don't want to go to the park.'

'Well, what do you want to do?'

'Organise.' He moved towards the table and its thick covering of books. His expression shifted from confusion to something like fear.

I went over to him and took his arm. 'Leave it for now.'

He looked down at me. I pulled him away from the table, trying not to slip on the books on the floor. His muscles stayed tense but he stepped back. I felt like I was getting a firmer grip on him even though I'd let go of his arm. 'Shall we go for a walk?'

He didn't answer for a moment. When he did, he said, 'I want to go to the sea.'

I wondered about his knowledge of UK geography. 'We're landlocked.'

'Why do English people always forget they live on an island?' He got his car keys and wallet. 'Let's go now. Are you ready?'

'Where are we going?'

'Morecambe. It is beautiful there. Have you been?'

148

Memories of a shoddy Wild West theme park in the rain, a seafront without a sea.

'A long time ago.'

He was leaving so I followed, grabbing the Lomo off the table. He locked the back door behind us and I felt lighter straightaway. I wanted to get out of there, too. I hadn't realised how much until then.

'You didn't like it?'

'I don't remember it that well.' It was a half-lie. I remembered Morecambe as an ugly, run-down place. We went there as a family just before the family broke up.

In the car, I slipped the camera in my bag and pushed the envelope of photographs down to the bottom, beneath my purse and make-up and keys.

It was years since I'd been on a car journey this long. The furthest I travelled nowadays was by train to Mum's house, about fifteen miles from Manchester. Being transported out of the city and onto the fast, forward pull of the motorway was exhilarating. We climbed over the long, high curve of a six-lane bridge, and joined the flow of cars racing north past television masts and football stadiums, farmland and new housing estates, a space age service station with a hexagonal restaurant on a concrete tower. Then we turned towards the coast, passing through Lancaster and the suburban roads on the edge of Morecambe, all the time hoping for the first glimpse of the sea.

We parked in a place I thought I recognised from my last visit, although the whole town had the feel of a car park back then. That day we'd climbed out of Dad's car into wind and rain. Today the sky was a pale, cold blue.

Erik got us a day-long parking ticket and looked me up and down. 'Will you be warm enough?' He got a navy knitted jumper from the back seat and handed it to me. I put it on underneath my coat. I would be too hot but I liked the smell of it, of him, mixed with the vanilla of the air freshener in the car. We walked towards the seafront, crossing a stream of unhurried cars out to take in the promenade view. Then we saw it for ourselves.

How long since I'd seen a view so wide you could watch the light changing as the miles spread away from you? The tide was out and the blue sea and blue sky met on the long, straight line of the horizon. Even the mountains of the Lake District to the north were diminished by the scale of the vast, flat bay. They were a low, cloud-topped border in the distance, separated from us by miles of sandbanks and mudflats skimmed by sunlit, shallow water.

I smiled at Erik but he didn't notice. His hands gripped the promenade railing as if steadying himself against the expanse of space. He had been quiet all the way here. I imagined his tension as an iron bar across his chest, making it difficult to move and speak and breathe freely.

To the south, further down the promenade, were the remnants of the theme park I'd visited as a child. I'd queued with Susie for jerking wooden rollercoasters while Mum and Dad waited in a café amongst old ladies who hadn't taken their coats off. The rides were gone but the entrance was still there: a cowboy town water tower with the Frontierland logo bolted onto the front. Nearer to us was another tower, much higher, in the green and white colours of a Polo tube. I wondered what it was for and why they hadn't taken it down.

I remembered the camera in my bag. Erik tuned back in. 'You brought it. Good.'

I took a few pictures then wc set off along the promenade, passing a crescent-shaped white hotel which reflected the sands in its lines of windows. We followed a wide stone pier out into the bay. There were bird silhouettes everywhere; in the railings, welded on top of pillars, stencilled into the stone. Whole flocks of them, as if someone was worried the real ones would migrate across the mudflats and not return.

I stopped to take a picture of a lead cormorant sitting on top of a post. I thought of Erik's bird sculptures with their trailing wings and congealed feathers.

'Do you like it?' I asked him.

'I like the way it is looking at you. Like it is sussing you out.'

We sat on a bench at the end of the pier. There were oystercatchers and crows. Seagulls swooping in the air. Sitting beside each other, our arms touched through the thick, safe layers of our jumpers and coats. I felt the pull of his body. I wanted to reach for his hand but as always, doubts stopped me. What if he shifted away from me, or told me no, or suggested we go home? So I only moved when he said let's walk on.

We went back to the promenade and bought fish and chips in a side street then ate them on a beach where horses churned the sand. Then we went northwards, the bay on our left, the town on our right. On the other side of the strip were second-hand bookshops and charity shops and I quickened our pace, but he didn't seem to notice them. Soon we were on the edge of town, passing bed and breakfasts, old people's homes, a golf course. Out in the bay a tractor travelled slowly across the horizon. I took some more photographs, trying to capture the smooth lines where the water met mud, the silver reflection of the sun in the rippled sand.

Erik said, 'I came here once before.' He was speaking towards the bay, not towards me. Then he turned to see if I was listening.

'With Chloe and Caitlin?'

'No, just me. It felt like the right place to be, looking out at this big empty space. I always meant to come back.'

'Why didn't you?'

'I forgot, I suppose. I got busy with other things.'

'We could come here again.' I wanted a future with more days like this in it, not just today.

'Yes, we could.' He smiled. 'Can I take a picture?'

I watched as he unhurriedly chose a view and fixed it in the frame. When he turned to go, he stopped and took a photograph of me, standing on the pavement. I just looked at him, wondering what he was thinking and why he didn't want that perfect view as a backdrop instead of the ordinariness of the road.

We walked for another hour or more, dropping down from the road onto sand and pebbles, climbing back up again over storm boulders when the stretches of beach ended. After a while, the road curved away from the sea path, leaving it quiet. We crossed thin grass growing over mud, stepped between patches of reeds, around pools filled with broken white shells. The wind had picked up, sending shadows across the sheer water. When we came to a bench we sat down to rest.

He said, 'Did you know that when the tide comes in at Morecambe Bay, it travels faster than a galloping horse?'

'That sounds like a fact you got from one of your encyclopaedias.'

'I read them sometimes before I cut them up.'

'What else did it say?'

'It said that the channels where the water comes in are carved out by the tides. They stay the same for decades, always following the same route towards the land. I remembered it because I have read that people's thoughts work in the same way.'

'In what way?'

'They get into a channel like when water carves out a path through rock. It is the easiest way through so the water always goes that way. It is how we think. How a habit is formed.'

I turned to look at him, surprised at the turn in the conversation. He had never spoken about himself like this before. I wanted to encourage it, to get him to talk on. I said, 'You seem to understand how your mind works quite well.'

'It is how everyone's mind works,' he replied, looking steadily at me. 'But then there is a storm or just something changes out at sea, and overnight the channels

153

move. The sand gets swept away and new routes are formed, in a completely different place.'

'I like that idea,' I said. I imagined it happening below the surface of the murky water, invisible to us. The channels could be changing right now and we wouldn't know it.

'I like it, too.'

I fixed my eyes on the tractor as it grew in size, getting closer to the shore. 'So do you see your mind as like sand or like rock?'

He didn't answer and I wondered whether he had heard. I said, 'I mean, do you believe your thought patterns can change like sand, or are they fixed, like rock?'

'Like sand.'

Yes. It was true. He wouldn't be stuck in this problem forever. He believed he could change, and I believed it, too. I tried to hide my smile, dug my hands into my pockets. I sneaked a glance at him. He was looking back at where we had started from. All the while, the tide had been coming in, swallowing the mud and folding in around the distant pier. Boats that had been grounded were set afloat and the beach where we'd sat earlier was sea.

By the time we arrived back at the pier, the sky had changed, too. It was the colour of slate over the town and a clear, glassy yellow out to sea. The sun was setting into the clouds sitting on the horizon line and the light was becoming grainy.

Erik looked towards the road and the car park

beyond. 'Let's wait until after rush hour before we drive back. The M6 will be chaos right now.'

'Shall we find somewhere warm to sit? Like, in there.' I pointed to the long, curved hotel which bounced the last of the daylight off its white walls.

'If you like.'

We entered a cocktail bar centred around a huge Art Deco chandelier lit in lilac. The barman greeted us, meeting my eyes, trying to work us out. A man in his forties with a girl in her twenties. Did we look like a couple or like father and daughter? Erik ordered a soda water. I asked for a gin and tonic, wishing I wasn't drinking on my own. He chose seats at the window and arranged them so we were both looking out towards the darkening space of the sea.

I said, 'Do you wish you weren't driving?'

'It makes no difference. I don't drink anyway.'

'Oh.' That was depressing. 'Not at all?'

'Not at all.'

'Why?'

We stopped talking while the waiter placed our drinks on the table. Then Erik said, 'There's only two reasons people don't drink. They're pregnant or they have a problem with it.'

I looked at him without speaking.

He said, 'It's the last one.'

'Do you miss it?'

He rested his eyes on my glass for a second. 'I gain more than I miss.'

'Should I not have ordered a drink?'

'It doesn't matter. Alcohol is everywhere. You can't avoid it.'

I wanted to know if it was why Caitlin left. I thought of the photographs at the bottom of my bag, the woman who wasn't his wife. Was she the reason or just a catalyst? I could ask him but why make this time about someone else? Why couldn't I be the centre of his attention for a while? I went into the hotel lobby to find the toilets. I hadn't seen a mirror since we left his car that morning. My cheeks were flushed from the sudden switch from cold seafront to warm bar. I brushed my hair, put on lip balm, swept powder across my face. When I returned the daylight had gone, taking away the view.

'Do you want another drink?' he asked.

'Yes,' I said quickly, surprised. Maybe he didn't want to go home yet either.

When he returned from the bar, he said, 'Tell me what happened when you went out with your sister.'

He hadn't mentioned the text messages we'd sent. I wondered whether he was thinking of them now.

'Nothing much. We got drunk with some lads from her work.'

'Was she matchmaking?'

'Yeah.'

'So?'

'I wasn't interested.'

'Why not?'

'Not my type, I suppose.'

'What is your type?'

I felt suddenly nervous, suddenly brave. 'Older.'

He looked directly at me then, his brown eyes considering, his lips slightly open, and I made myself hold his gaze for a second, two seconds. I looked down.

A friend once told me it was very easy to seduce a man. She said you just had to let them know that you would sleep with them, and that it would happen soon. She didn't say how you let them know. Sitting there, I realised that even at twenty-nine, I didn't know how. We weren't drunk in a club, or suddenly clutching hands in a taxi, or pushed together in a busy bar. He was completely sober and I was almost sober. It would take an admission, a request even. I couldn't do that.

'What is wrong, Miriam?'

Was my frustration visible on my face now? 'Nothing,' I mumbled.

He watched me for a moment then stood up and headed to the door to the lobby. I sighed audibly once he'd gone. The barman glanced over. I took a long swig of my gin and tonic, then another. My glass was empty.

Ten minutes passed and he didn't return. My reflection in the window started to look like a stranger. I looked impassive, unconcerned. I looked like I had nothing to do with me. I thought of trains back to Manchester, whether or not he'd paid the bar bill, five more minutes, then another five, then I would leave. Then there was the shape of him in the glass, pulling out his chair, sitting down beside me again and waiting for my eyes to meet his.

He said, 'Would you like to stay the night?'

He waited, his face very still.

'Yes.'

He moved his hand closer to mine on the table but still didn't touch me. 'Do you want another drink?'

'No. Thank you.'

'Okay. They have a room available. I just need to move my car.'

'Shall I come?'

'If you like.'

I hesitated. 'I'll wait here.' When he'd gone, I tried to see the sea out of the window but it was hidden behind the mirror image of the bar, the cascading chandelier, my alien reflection. The room had closed in on us, shutting out the empty skyline and racing tide.

I felt him touch my shoulder, then his fingers were on the back of my neck beneath my hair. He took my hand as we left the bar.

We waited in silence for the lift. The sounds of the bar and lobby were extinguished when its doors shut and it began to climb. The intimacy between us felt fragile and unsure, and I didn't want to break it by speaking. Then we were on a long, empty corridor. He dropped my hand to slide an electronic key into a door. Inside the room, a muted, soft glow lit the bed.

Now we were here, I didn't know what to do next. Thick grey curtains covered one wall. I pushed them apart, felt the cool glass behind, and saw pink globe lights on the pier below.

Erik poured two glasses of water and brought one to me. Then he sat down on the sofa. He was waiting for me to go over. When I sat down next to him, he took the glass out of my hand and put it on the table. I turned to him and he kissed me and it was different to any way I'd been kissed before. He held my hands at my sides and made tight, teasing circles with his tongue on my tongue.

158

I stopped thinking then. It was just wanting and moving and he was so slow at first, making it worse. I spoke once – to ask if he liked something – and he said quietly, 'No talking.' Later, on the bed, when he was pushing me into this deep, all-over feeling, I said his name out loud, but I couldn't help that. He was inside me, I could feel him right through me, and I'd lost myself.

17

When I woke Erik was deep in sleep beside me. It felt early, before dawn. I sat up and studied his face and shoulders, his arms and hands in the thin light. His skin was darker than mine and worn. His body was broad and muscled.

I liked it that there was such a gap between us; his age, his accent, his life were all so different from mine. And I liked it that I could close this gap. When he'd kissed me last night I'd felt his full attention on me and it had made my mind go quiet. It was like being hypnotised, like being erased. Now I lay back down and moved my hand around the thickness of his waist. I wondered how anyone could live without that feeling once they had experienced it. I wanted to see if it would be like that again.

He was awake. He turned so he was facing me. He knew what I wanted. He'd known it before I did, all those weeks ago when he had looked at me with a flicker of surprise as I'd stepped out of the shelter of his umbrella and into the rain.

Afterwards he said to me, 'Sleep some more,' and lay with his arm across my back. That sleep was instant and deep. I lost a layer of myself in it. It was the contentment. The feeling I had what I wanted and I didn't have to wait anymore.

He woke me up by stroking my shoulders, putting his fingers on the hairline at the back of my neck.

'I thought you were an insomniac,' he said.

'I am.'

'You're not. You will have to wake up if you don't want to miss breakfast.'

He had a towel wrapped around his waist. I could smell the sharp citrus of the hotel shower gel. He sat on the bed beside me. I sat up and took his heavy hand in mine. He kissed the top of my head and held me against him for a moment. He let me go and I waited to see what he would do next.

'Do you want a cup of coffee?' he said.

'Yes.'

'Go and have a shower then we will go downstairs to eat. I am starving.'

I got up reluctantly, keeping the sheet around me out of shyness. I scooped up my clothes and took them into the bathroom, then showered and got dressed, wishing I had a clean outfit to put on. When I came out, he had opened the curtains. It was cloudy and the distant sea was grey. There were dog walkers on the pier. A woman on a mobility scooter. Erik handed me a strong, bitter espresso. I drank it sitting on the sofa, watching him tie the laces on his trainers.

'Does it look bad that we don't have any luggage?' I said.

'We have a camera.'

'I don't think that helps.'

'But you know, if I had a toothbrush and maybe a razor, I would be happy living like this,' he said.

I stopped myself from laughing, unsure whether he was joking. 'You wouldn't feel the need to add a few... books?'

'I feel like I would be a completely different person if I lived by the sea.' He turned towards the windows. 'How could you lose track of yourself when you have this to put your problems into perspective?'

'Maybe you wouldn't notice the view if you lived here all the time.'

'You would because it's always changing. You can watch it like you watch TV.'

I thought of what he'd said yesterday about his mind being like sand not rock. I imagined the patterns it followed being washed away by a wave. It was a good thought. I was smiling as we left the room. In the lift he said softly, 'It isn't that we have no luggage that looks bad, you know. You look a little younger than you are, and I look a lot older than I am.'

'You look gorgeous.' Now that I could, I wanted to say things like this to him all day.

He smiled in the way that lit up his eyes. The lift door opened and we were in the lobby. In the shower I had wondered whether we would know how to be with each other now we had done this, but it was easy, like last night was easy. At breakfast I held his hand across the table until the waitress brought a pot of tea and we had to make room for the cups and sugar bowl and milk. Her eyes darted between us. I didn't care if we looked strange together. I liked it in fact.

Before we set off home, we stood on the seafront again, watching orange-beaked birds running across the mud, the wind sending ripples across the silver water. The clouds were clearing to the north. I said, 'We could go somewhere else for the day and drive home tonight.'

He didn't answer for a while. 'No, I have to get back, I have too much to do.'

'Okay.'

He looked at me. 'We will come back another time. We can go further, to the Lake District or Scotland.'

'When?'

'In the spring.'

I thought of the skip on his driveway. The mess filling his kitchen. The tight spaces between the walls of books in the living room. I knew we had a lot of work ahead but standing there with the sands stretching out in front of us, it felt possible. It was just some paper, it was nothing compared to this. I took a last, long look at the open space of the bay, breathed it in and implanted it on my mind before I turned away.

He dropped me off outside my flat, pulling into a space between two vans and leaving the engine running. I asked if he wanted to come in for a cup of tea but he had to prepare for an assignment in London tomorrow. He would be back in Manchester on Friday and we would go out for dinner somewhere, he said. I kissed him. He took his hands off the steering wheel and put them on my waist. I wanted him to come inside.

When I let myself in, I decided it was probably better that he hadn't. Was this really where I lived? Gareth's bike was blocking our hallway and several pairs of his shoes were sticking out from beneath the sofa. There was a photograph of him and Jessica on the fridge, and his big plastic containers of protein shake powder were crowding up the kitchen surfaces.

He and Jessica were everywhere but there was no evidence of my existence here at all, apart from my jeans that were now tough and dry on the living room radiator. By throwing away so much of my stuff, I'd made myself disappear. But now I wanted to reassert myself. I wanted Erik to come round and say, 'So this is where you live,' and pick up interesting objects I had dotted around, look at photographs and ask, 'How old were you then?'

I thought of the hotel room, anonymous when we'd arrived and anonymous again when we'd left. Somebody else would sleep there tonight. Erik would be in his paper-packed house. I'd be in my three-quarter bed. We didn't have a place where we could be together. His home was taken up with the hoard. My flat was taken up by Jessica and Gareth. We'd have to spend our time in bars and restaurants, in the park, in hotel rooms.

I decided I wouldn't let it be like that. I took the sheets off my bed and put them in the washing machine, then hoovered the carpet right through the flat, and dusted all the surfaces in the living room and my bedroom. I put

Gareth's protein mix on top of the kitchen cupboards and moved his shoes and bike into Jessica's bedroom. Tomorrow I'd buy some flowers and a vase to put them in. I would go around the charity shops looking for things I liked, and buy some eggs and fresh bread for breakfast on Saturday in case we slept here. I imagined introducing Erik to Jessica and Gareth in the morning. Maybe they would feel awkward and out of place for once rather than me.

When Jessica got home from work that evening, she wanted to know where I was last night. I told her about it because we always told each other about our love lives but this time, it didn't feel right. It was private and I decided I wouldn't share that kind of information again. Then she moved on to talking about Gareth and I realised there was a lot she hadn't told me about their relationship, which made me regret talking to her about Erik even more.

'We're thinking about moving in together,' she said, letting the sentence hang in the air.

We were in the living room. I was sitting on a cushion in the bay window with a glass of wine. She was lying with her legs across the sofa.

She said, 'We practically live together already. Like you said, he's here all the time.'

I tried to keep my voice neutral. 'That's true. I guess I better start looking for another flatmate.'

'We've not really decided what we're doing yet. But I'll keep you posted.' She got up and took the wine out of the fridge. Poured more into our glasses. 'So when are you seeing him next?'

'Friday,' I said. 'We're going out for dinner.'

'I'm so glad you've met someone. Did you say he's got a massive house?'

'Yeah, but it's not...it needs a lot of work doing on it.'

'But at least he's got somewhere. Gareth's house is a right mess. With five blokes you'd think at least one would take out the rubbish before it spills all over the kitchen floor.'

'Erik's house isn't exactly tidy.'

'You could sort that out soon enough,' she said. 'It's easy if there's just two of you. It's when there's other people living with you that it gets difficult.'

Was she talking about me? It was one of those conversations where we weren't connecting again. There were things I wasn't saying but when I did say things, I regretted it. I was almost glad when Gareth arrived. I escaped to my room, claiming I needed an early night. They made jokes about that and I smiled, thinking how one of the best things about sex with Erik was how relaxed I'd felt afterwards, how my legs and body had sunk into the bed, giving me the deepest sleep I'd had in a long time.

In Barnardo's they were playing early Beatles songs over the stereo. 'Please Please Me' and 'I Saw Her Standing There'. I flicked through the stacks of framed pictures leaning against the wall. A genteel scene of a plump lady picnicking with a moustachioed man by a lake; an Egyptian mural on raffia that had the look of a misguided holiday souvenir; a line drawing of a cat that had somehow gone wrong. I was looking for something to give my room character but maybe pictures were unwise with Erik being an artist. He would know what was good and what was bad. Well, even I knew these were bad. I could buy some ornaments instead. I moved over to the metal shelves holding sherry glasses and butter dishes, plant pot holders and pottery figurines, searching for something I liked. The problem was, you needed years of experiences and travels to build up a collection of unique, significant objects that spoke of your life and your tastes, and I was trying to do it in one morning.

Annie was on the till. She waved and I went over.

'I watched that film of yours.' She was wearing an oversized shirt, the sleeves folded at the wrists, a bird-shaped silver pendant around her neck.

'*Diva*? What did you think?'

'Bit weird but strangely compelling. Kind of how I like men.'

'Hmm, me, too,' I said.

'We should go out some time. I'll introduce you to some.'

'I've kind of already got one, but yeah it would be good to go out.' I thought about telling her about Erik. She was there when we first met. I was about to say something when a young man with a quiff and square glasses brought a Lloyd Cole record to the counter.

'Good choice,' Annie said, putting it through the till and into a supermarket carrier bag. When he'd gone, she said, 'So, not seen anything you want to buy?'

'Not really. I need to make my flat look more... Miriam-like.'

167

'You want to buy your old stuff back?'

'No, I was thinking of other people's stuff. Pictures or art or something.'

'Oh right. So what was wrong with your own things? You had some really good books and clothes.'

Did I? When I'd been shoving it all in bin bags, I'd felt like I couldn't stand to look at it for even one more day. 'I think I was having some kind of personality crisis. A woman at work wrote this nasty appraisal of me.' I didn't know why I was telling Annie this. I hadn't told Jessica or Susie or Erik about it.

'Saying what?'

'That I was capable rather than bright. And possibly depressed.'

Annie's expression made me laugh. She said, 'No fucking wonder if you're working with someone like that. Was that what made you throw all your stuff away?'

I picked up a thin, gold bracelet that was hanging on a mug holder on the counter and ran it between my fingers. 'It was other things as well.'

Annie took a deep breath. 'Wow. So are you still working there?'

'No, I work with Erik now. You know, the man who was here when I brought all my stuff in.'

'Erik! He's in here like twice a week. He's a nice guy, isn't he?'

I smiled, probably right across my face. 'Yeah, he is.'

Annie paused, considering me. 'So you work together?'

'Yes.'

'What's that like?'

Frustrating, exciting, infuriating, addictive. 'Good.'

'He's completely obsessed with retro books and magazines. I bet he's got hundreds of them at his house.'

I said, 'He's a collector.'

'He's an addict.'

'Yeah but he's getting over his addiction. I'm helping him.'

She looked at me without saying anything. I was glad when a pale-faced man with greasy black hair stepped up to the counter, holding a digital alarm clock that had turned from cream to yellow with age. 'Does this work?' he asked Annie.

'It most certainly does,' she said.

'Can you plug it in to check?'

'This label means we've already had it checked. Believe me, it works.'

He nodded as if he understood. 'The thing is, I have a plane to catch to Sydney at 4 am. If I oversleep, that's it. I won't see my son again for another ten years.'

Annie looked levelly at him. I told her I'd come back another time. As I was leaving the shop, 'Love Me Do' stopped abruptly, replaced by a loud, insistent beeping from the alarm clock. Everyone turned to look at the counter and a baby in a pram started to cry. Annie seemed to be struggling to turn it off again. I closed the door behind me to shut out the noise.

When I got home I pulled out the box of photographs and letters from under my bed. I'd returned from my shopping trip with a bunch of pale pink hollyhocks, a clear glass vase, a little cactus in a clay pot, a thick white church candle, and three second-hand photograph frames that I hoped to fill with pictures from the box. It was the one possession I hadn't sorted through during my clear-out. Inside were stacks of birthday cards, photograph albums, letters from pen pals, old diaries. I took out the postcards I'd brought back from the inter-railing trip I'd taken the summer I'd graduated. I'd gone on my own but knowing I'd finish up at my grandparents' house near Alicante made me feel like it wasn't a big deal, just a long, meandering train journey. The postcards were from art galleries in Paris and Barcelona and Madrid. They were slotted in amongst photographs I'd taken myself. Red and yellow fish in a tiled pool. Rain running down steep cobbled streets in a storm. A view of Palma Cathedral from across the harbour.

I had caught a ferry to Majorca to visit my dad. It was the last time I saw him. He'd met me on the quayside in Palma and carried my rucksack to his car, then we drove along a twisting coastal road to a restaurant perched above a rocky beach. Later we went back to where he was living in a hilltop town with a Swedish lady called Grita. I'd thought I was staying for a few days but Grita was upset about me being there and I felt awkward so he drove me back to Palma. I stayed overnight in a hostel. My clearest memory of Majorca was lying awake in that airless mixed dormitory, waiting for it to get light so I could catch the first ferry back to the mainland. I hadn't taken any photographs of my dad. There hadn't been a chance.

I spent the next week sunbathing by the pool in my grandparents' retirement complex, sleeping late in the mornings and taking long, shadeless walks on the shores of the salt lake behind their house.

I put the photographs and postcards back in the box. None seemed worth framing. Then I got involved in reading the letters I'd received from my pen pal when I was in primary school, and the email correspondences I'd printed out from my secondary school friends when we'd all started at different universities. There wasn't much from after that, as if I'd grown out of documenting my life by then. From my twenties there were just a few birthday cards from my mum and grandma and a couple of tickets for gigs I could barely remember going to.

Erik called me as I was piling everything back into the box. He was in a hotel in Islington, waiting for the bath to fill with water. When he asked what I was up to I told him about my inter-railing trip and the failed visit to my dad. He said it sounded like bad timing. He thought I should write to him in Canada. I said I might. We talked about the job he'd done that day, and he suggested a pub we could go to on Friday, out of the city in a village near Altrincham. His voice lowered when he said he was looking forward to seeing me and I told him I wished I was with him right now, feeling nervous and shy as I thought of him waiting for the water to rise. When I put the phone down, the shrinking feeling I'd had when looking through my letters and photographs had gone. It was funny how he could make the past seem better as well as the present.

18

With the flowers and cactus and candle, my bedroom
looked inhabited again. It could have been anyone living
here, but at least it was someone. I was still embarrassed
by the size of it, by the bed that was for neither a child
nor an adult, but then I thought about Erik's house and
decided I had nothing to worry about. He could hardly
judge. And one of the things I liked about him was that
judging just didn't seem in his nature. Unlike many of
the men I'd dated he didn't seem to be subtly, or not so
subtly, trying to get me to be someone else. Someone
more successful, or ambitious, or impressive – the kind
of girlfriend their friends might envy. I put it down
to his age. He wasn't a striving twenty-something,
assessing and valuing a girlfriend in the same way he'd
assess a new job or a new car. He didn't need me to
complete a picture of a perfect life because he'd given
up on creating one of those a long time ago.

I had finished my make-up and was just putting my
boots on when he rang to say he was outside. I was
about to go and meet him when I suddenly thought he

might want us to stay at his. I grabbed my other bag, emptied my smaller one into it, and put in a change of underwear, my deodorant, my toothbrush. I ran downstairs to meet him, making myself slow down before I opened the front door and walked out to his car.

'You're wearing your blue dress,' he said as I got in. 'I like it.' He leaned over to kiss me on the cheek. I felt suddenly shy.

'You chose it,' I said.

He ran the back of his hand over the material, smoothing it out. 'I didn't know at the time what was going to happen.'

'Didn't you?'

'No. Did you?'

'No, I didn't think you were interested.'

He smiled, looking at me through the corner of his eye as he started the engine. We drove through Chorlton and onto the motorway that led past the airport. He had the same U2 CD on. He said change it if you want but I didn't want to.

'Where are we going?'

'To the countryside. Three days in London makes me want to run away to the seaside again but it is a little far for a Friday night.'

We came off the motorway and followed a dual carriageway bordered by fields and woods, then drove into the woods ourselves, along a narrow road without street lamps or white lines. I couldn't see much apart from treetops and hedgerows until we came to a hamlet around a village green. There were tiny cottages with big four-by-fours parked up

173

on the grass verges. An old-fashioned red telephone box with a flower garden around it. The pub was called The Swan and it had a ye olde look that didn't seem faked. We stepped out into the autumn night smell of woodsmoke and rotting leaves, then into that gorgeous pub smell of beer and home cooking. There was a dog sitting on the tiles by the bar. A fire in full flame. I sat close to it at a round copper table while Erik went to buy our drinks.

'How do you know about this place?' I said when he returned. He placed his soda water and my wine on the table.

'Do you like it?' he asked.

'I love it, but I don't even know where we are.'

'I didn't either when I first found it. I was driving around, totally lost. I thought I was never going to find my way back to Manchester.'

'When was this?'

'Oh, years ago. Then when I got home and I had relaxed I said, I saw this amazing pub somewhere but I've no idea where. It took me ages to find it again.'

I wondered who he had said that to. I could picture him zipping past this place in his car, but who had he gone home to? His wife or the other woman? Those photographs were still in my bag. I needed to either ask him about them or throw them away. Not now, though. He was stroking the inside of my wrist with his thumb while we looked at the menu. I moved closer to him. I didn't feel like eating.

'Maybe you can come to London with me next time I go,' he said, suddenly. 'You can explore while I work, then we can hang out in the evenings. It gets boring being there on my own.'

'Don't you have any friends around from when you lived there?'

'Yes but usually I'm nowhere near where they are. I will take you to a restaurant that serves Slovak food. Or we could just stay in, watch TV, get room service.'

He didn't have a TV at his house. Or if he did, it was hidden beneath the books. I was curious. 'What do you watch?'

'Football. Tennis. Rugby sometimes.'

'Really?'

He laughed. 'Why are you looking at me like that?'

'I just didn't see you as a sports fan. Who do you support?'

'Arsenal. It was where I lived when I first moved to the UK.'

His phone started buzzing in his jacket pocket. Caitlin, it said on the screen. I looked the other way, as if interested in the black and white photographs of shire horses on the walls, the brass tankers lined up along the mantelpiece.

Into his phone he said, 'She can bring furniture if she likes. I have everything, though, so it isn't really necessary.' Then, 'My battery is going. I will call you back.'

'Do you want to borrow mine?' I didn't want him to see that she bothered me. I handed him my phone and he dialled a number he knew off by heart.

'It's me,' he said. Then, 'It's Miriam's phone. I'm not at home.'

I wished I could hear what Caitlin was saying. They

175

were talking about Chloe again. Caitlin hadn't asked where we were or what we were doing. It occurred to me that perhaps they had spoken about me when they went out for dinner. What had he said that had left her totally uncurious about our relationship? Or was she just pretending not to be interested because she knew I was sitting there next to him?

He put the phone down. 'So, it is six weeks until Chloe comes. And we have only cleared one room.'

Back to this. And the worn, worried look in his eyes.

'We've got time.' I put my hand on his arm, wanting to reassure him.

A man came to take our order. When he'd gone Erik said, 'I don't want to think about the house. It is too depressing.'

But I could tell he was still thinking about it. He was talking less, and he had to keep stopping himself from tensing his hand. I took it in mine but he didn't seem to want that either. Unlikely scenarios started going through my head. What if he just sold the house and bought a new one? An empty one that we could live in together. What if I hired a professional clearing team to sweep right through it one weekend? How long would he be angry for, and would it be worth it for the end result? Our food arrived, steak and ale pies, I only ate half of mine before I was full. I went to the toilets, only realising once I was at the mirror that I'd left my bag with my lipstick in it at the table.

When I got back the plates had been cleared away. My phone was on the table. Next to it were the photographs. They had been in my bag.

Erik's voice was flat. 'Your phone rang in your bag so I took it out. I thought it might be Caitlin. Sorry.' He looked like he thought it should be me apologising.

I sat down, put my phone away again. His eyes were on the photographs.

I said, 'I found them in the skip. I was going to ask you about them.'

'The one thing I throw away, you want to keep.'

'I didn't understand why you would throw them away.'

'Why do you need to understand?'

The woman at the table across from us looked over then looked away.

My voice was small. 'I want to know you.'

He shook his head minutely, as if it was an answer.

I said, 'Who is she?'

'My wife, of course. Hannah.'

Who is *Hannah*? 'I thought Caitlin was your wife.'

He frowned. 'Caitlin is Hannah's sister. Chloe's aunt. Hannah died.'

She died. Oh. I didn't know what to say. I couldn't get my head around this new information.

He checked his pockets for his keys, reached over for his coat from the chair next to him. 'So I have paid the bill. Let's go.'

'Caitlin isn't Chloe's mum?'

'No.'

'So why does Chloe live with her and not you?' I turned to him. 'Didn't you want her to live with you?'

'What?'

'Didn't you want her?'

'Okay, we need to go. Will you please let me out?'

I stood up, put on my coat, hung my bag over my shoulder. The envelope of photographs was still on the table. I didn't know whether to pick it up or not. Then Erik took it and I thought he was going to put it in his coat pocket but instead he stepped towards the open fire and dropped it on. It sat there, on top of the wood, smothering the flames rather than stoking them. It looked like an image from the cover of one of the airport novels he had in his back room. Dramatic and ridiculous. The couple at the table opposite us were watching. Erik was standing over the fire, frowning. The flames still hadn't taken hold and the envelope was melting into the fire rather than setting alight.

I couldn't watch this. I walked out. Cold air bit through my coat. When I breathed in, my chest was tight. The car park was in darkness. I heard someone coming up behind me but I didn't turn round. I knew it was him when his car locks clicked open.

We didn't speak on the drive back. I wanted to ask if the photographs had caught light in the end. It somehow seemed like the most important question. He dropped me off at my flat and said he was tired when I asked if he wanted to come inside. Later, lying awake in bed, I realised I hadn't asked how his wife had died, or when, or offered any sympathy.

I told myself I hadn't asked because he seemed like he didn't want to talk about it, but in truth, it just hadn't occurred to me. Was that why he hadn't wanted to stay over? Not because I'd asked too many questions, but because they were the wrong ones?

I barely slept and in the morning, I had this ache in my chest I couldn't get rid of. I needed to put things right between us so I could breathe properly again. I called him to say I was coming round, then showered and dressed fast, and took a taxi over there. When I knocked on his door, he stepped outside and pulled it shut behind him. He had his coat on already, as if he had been waiting for me.

He said, 'I thought we could go to the park to talk.'

'Why not talk in the house?'

'The house has too much in it.'

We crossed the road and went through the iron gates, taking the path that led along the top edge of the park towards the avenue of limes. It was one of those late autumn days where the greyness is stunned and set by the cold. The grass was covered in frost and there was thin ice on the puddles, already shattered by footsteps. We walked in silence, my legs felt slow and heavy. The lime avenue had lost its covering of gold now. The canopies were bare and the leaves were turning to mulch on the cracked tarmac.

He wasn't saying anything and everything I rehearsed in my head sounded wrong. Then about halfway down the avenue, we took the turning that led back towards the lake. We weren't going for a long walk then, just a small circle. He stopped at a bench opposite the island, but it was covered in frost so he didn't sit down. He leaned against the railings by the water. I stood beside him.

'I have been thinking about us becoming involved,' he said. 'And about you helping me with the house.'

I was cold and tired. I wished we were indoors, waiting for the chocolate powder to dissolve into milk on the stove. When I drank it, it would melt this knot in my chest and take this dull taste from my mouth.

He said, 'And I don't think that either of these things is going to work.'

I said, 'Either of what things?'

'Us working together on the house, and us being together.'

I didn't speak.

'Miriam?'

'They will work.' My voice had shrunk.

'No, I'm sorry. I don't think they will.'

'But... they will.'

He said, 'I'm sorry.'

I looked at the water littered with bread crusts and plastic bags. My head felt as hazy and still as the frozen mist in the air. I said, 'If it's doing the two things together, you could find someone else to help you with the house.'

'It's not that. It just isn't what I want.'

All my words had gone. I felt a heaviness pushing me against the railings. Then he was getting something out of his pocket. Money.

He said, 'Here is what I owe you.'

I didn't move. If I didn't take it, he wouldn't be able to leave.

'Miriam, at the hotel, it was beautiful, and we will both remember it that way. But I was wrong to think

180

we could bring it back here. I cannot have a relationship with you. You are too young or I am too old and as you know, my life is too full already.'

'Your life isn't full at all,' I said, the numbness clearing for a moment. 'Your house is full. Your life is empty.'

'Maybe. But that is how I want it.'

'Because you're still grieving for Hannah?'

'Please, take this money. It's yours.'

I ignored him. He touched my shoulder gently and I turned quickly to face him, hoping he would put his arms around me. He put his hand in the pocket of my coat, it brushed against mine for a second. He took it out, leaving the folded notes.

I turned abruptly, walking fast away from the lake. I wanted him to follow. He didn't. But maybe he would in a minute. I sat on a bench halfway down the avenue of limes. A group of teenage girls in big coats and scarves were approaching from the far end of the park, shrieking and pushing each other, the loudest thing around. They kept stopping to take pictures of each other with their BlackBerrys, to pass headphones between them, even though their music, tinny RnB, was playing so loud everyone could hear. I thought, if he comes now, we'll have to shout over them, we'll mishear each other, we won't understand what each other is saying. I hated them. How could they be so noisy in such a quiet place? I wished they would all just disappear.

Then they had gone, taking the side path out of the park, and Erik still hadn't come to find me. The bench was wet, I realised. So was my face. I waited there a long time before I walked home.

19

I didn't normally answer the phone if it was an unknown number. Or if it was a known number when I was feeling like this. I liked to wait until the caller had left a message so I could think about what to say and summon up the energy to say it before I phoned back.

But when my phone buzzed now that tactic seemed reckless. If he was calling from another number. If he called once on impulse but never again. It was late on a Tuesday morning and I was lying in bed, hoping to slip back into sleep for another hour or so. The screen said Caller Unknown. I sat up, cleared my throat. Hoped it wouldn't be obvious that this was the first time I'd spoken today.

'Hello?' I sounded nervous and hopeful, like someone taking a call from a hospital.

'Miriam? It's Sheila at CBS. I've not disturbed you, have I?'

I could hardly wait for the call to end so I could lie down again. 'Hi. No, I'm just at home.'

'Not working?'

'Not at the moment.'

'I was hoping you might be free. Do you think you could come in and help us out a few days this week? Natalie's left us.'

Left us? Apart from Sheila's slightly miffed tone, it sounded like she'd died.

She said, 'Are you free tomorrow and Thursday?'

Treeless Ardwick on a dark November morning. If I'd been up and about, I might have said no. As it was, I was contending with the guilt about being in bed at ten to twelve, and with worry about how my bank balance was about to go into minus figures. It was over a week now since I'd been paid. Or paid off, as I was starting to think of it.

'Yes, I can be.'

'Smashing. You're a saviour. We'll see you tomorrow then.'

I got up and padded into the kitchen to fill the kettle. A saviour? I should probably think about getting dressed.

The office was the same apart from Natalie's absence. Neglected spider plants, tea-splattered notices about kitchen hygiene, a view through slatted blinds of the car park. A new quote was fading in and out on Natalie's computer. *Tomorrow could be the best day of your life*, it said in a swirling serif font.

When I asked Sheila where she'd gone, she said with a dry laugh, 'Weatherfield.'

I looked blankly at her.

'She's got an internship at *Coronation Street*.'

'Doing what?'

'Working with the storyliners,' Megan chipped in. She was lining up snacks on her desk: an apple, a sachet of porridge, a packet of crisps. 'She had to sign a form to say she wouldn't tell anyone what was going to happen.'

Sheila sounded less impressed. 'You'd think it was the Official Secrets Act, the way she was carrying on. And she's not getting paid for it. I don't know how she's surviving.'

'How did she get that?' I asked.

'Met someone through uni who had contacts,' Sheila said. 'Then she just announced she was leaving. Didn't give notice either which isn't on after how long she'd worked here. And she left things in a right muddle. Took me ages to get everything how it should be.'

How had Natalie managed to get somewhere in television so quickly when I'd tried and failed for years? 'So did they think she had potential or something?'

'Oh yes, we heard all about that. They told her she had "insight into character", whatever that means.'

I thought of her 'Notes on the Candidate'. The 'capable rather than bright' and 'possibly depressed', as if she was gathering observations for a bit part based on me.

'I think she thought working here was beneath her once she'd started that course,' Sheila continued. 'If I told my Jim I was going to work in TV, and not earning, he'd have a paddy. Some of us have got teenagers to feed. Still, she's a young woman with all her life ahead of her.'

'So what am I doing here?' Megan said.

Sheila turned back to her computer. 'You didn't want to go to college. That's why you're here.'

'True.' Megan slowly stirred her tea with the chewed end of a biro.

I expected to feel jealous of Natalie, but when I tested my mood, it was just flat. I didn't care and I wondered when it had happened, this death of ambition. Had I decided a job in TV wasn't for me? Was it possible I was depressed?

The two other ladies arrived, Deborah and Bernie, dressed for winter with fleecy scarves and big hooded anoraks. Deborah clicked on the portable heaters. Bernie put a box of Cadbury's Celebrations in the centre of their trio of desks.

'Of all the things to win when you're on Weight Watchers. Welcome back, Miriam. You'll help us get rid of these, won't you?'

Sheila, Bernie and Deborah chatted as they worked. Megan flicked between Facebook and a spreadsheet. The phone rang steadily all morning. 'Hello, how can I help?' worked best for finding out who I was supposed to be.

'Is that Synergise IT Solutions?' a voice asked.

'Yes that's right.'

Or, 'I'm looking for Tailormade Travels?'

'That's us.'

At half past ten exactly, I got up to make a second cup of tea. Megan was in the kitchen squirting syrup from a squeezy bottle into a bowl of microwaved porridge.

'Glad to be back?' she said.

'It's money.'

'Yup. Shit money. Or my job is anyway. Yours is probably better.'

'It's minimum wage.' I tried to fish out a teaspoon of sugar granules that hadn't been contaminated with coffee.

'So what were you doing when you stopped working here?' Megan asked, syrup still trickling. 'Didn't you get a job at the university or something?'

I had prepared an answer to this already. 'Yeah, just temping, doing the paperwork for job applications. It ended a few weeks ago.'

'What about that photographer you were working with? Natalie said he did a photo shoot with Keira Knightley once.'

I carefully poured milk into my tea. 'How did she know that?'

'She Googled him. She probably wanted him to give her a job. She was desperate to get out of here. When she got the *Corrie* placement, she literally left overnight. So did he decide he didn't need our help then?'

She was still talking about Erik. 'Um, I don't know. Just lost interest in it, I suppose.' My voice was trailing off. I turned my attention to her bowl of porridge. 'Do you think you've got enough syrup in that?' She'd covered the entire surface with the treacly gloop.

'You sound like Bernie. "How many points are there in a banana?" As if I'd know.' Megan stirred in the syrup, creating a whirlpool effect. 'It's a taste sensation, trust me.'

I felt every hour in that place. The phone rang often enough to make focusing on anything else difficult, but

not so often that the day went fast. I ate three choco-
lates with every cup of tea and changed the screensaver
from Natalie's peppy quote to a black and white
photograph of a spiral staircase. In my lunch hour I
heated up noodles in the microwave and ate them at
my desk. Then I went for a walk around the industrial
estate, feeling a heaviness in my legs as if I was wading
through mud or Megan's bowl of porridge.

I followed the empty, wide road that bordered the
car park to where it stopped at the gates of a storage
yard. Through the fence, cranes and forklift trucks lifted
shipping crates into stacks. They had Chinese symbols
and unfamiliar logos on the side. YANG MING.
HAPAG-LLOYD. SEACO. What was inside or were
they empty? Maybe it was a storage place for storage.
A yard full of crates waiting to be filled. I watched a
crane hoist one into the air. I waited to see where it
was going, but it just hung there, mid-air, until it was
time to walk back to the office. Someone had placed a
Celebration on my keyboard. I said thanks but nobody
responded so I wasn't sure who it was.

When I arrived home that evening, I couldn't open my
bedroom door. Something was jamming it on the other
side, allowing just a narrow gap. I rammed whatever
was blocking it ineffectually with the door. I'd taken
two buses home, waited in the rain at Piccadilly Gardens
in between, and now I just wanted to climb under my
duvet and bury my head into the pillows. I pushed the
door again. I couldn't think what had happened inside.

Jessica came out of her bedroom, wearing the

unimpressed-unsurprised look she often directed at me nowadays. 'You had a delivery. There was nowhere else to put it, unless you wanted it right in front of the TV.'

'A delivery?'

'Don't tell me they brought it to the wrong place? I signed for it. It was under your name.'

I remembered. 'My exercise bike.' I'd had a text message about a week ago saying they'd deliver it today. 'It's a good job you were home.'

'It's massive, Miriam. It takes up your whole room.' What did it matter to her? She wasn't the one who couldn't open her bedroom door. I put down my bag, turned sideways and squeezed inside. The room was dominated by an awkward, silver, ugly-looking thing with a solid black base and huge black handlebars. It was much bigger than a normal bike and I didn't understand why it needed to be. It didn't leave any space for getting dressed or standing at the window. Jessica squeezed in after me and sat on the edge of my bed.

'I didn't think it'd take up this much space,' I said.

'It's way too big for this flat.'

There were the sounds of someone coming into the living room, then Gareth called out hello. He must have his own key.

'We're in here,' Jessica said. 'But there's not much room.'

Gareth stood on the other side of the door. 'What's going on?' Then he squeezed inside, too, his legs and chest squashing against the door frame. The already full room was now cramped and claustrophobic. 'Jesus, Miriam, do you think you got one big enough?' Gareth sat on the bed with Jessica. There was nowhere else.

'Maybe I should send it back,' I said.

'What's your fella going to think about it?' Gareth asked, smirking. 'Does he like cycling?'

Jessica gave him a 'shut up' look then turned to me. 'You'll have to get them to collect it again.'

Gareth stood up. 'Can I have a go?'

I said, 'Maybe not if I'm returning it.'

'I'll take my shoes off. They won't know.' He slipped off his trainers and got on the saddle, pedalling with his arms dangling at his sides like a teenage boy on a BMX.

Were we supposed to just sit there watching him? 'Can I have a go?' I said.

He stopped, slid off. 'It's your bike.'

I got on the saddle and leaned forward to reach the handlebars which were low down and far away. It seemed unlikely that this position would help me fall asleep at night. I started pedalling, feeling the resistance in my calves and thighs. 'It's not very comfortable, is it?'

Gareth shook his head slowly. Jessica was staring at me.

I got a rhythm going, pedalled harder. 'I might keep it,' I said, glancing at them.

'You're going to need a bigger room,' Gareth said.

'Shall we swap then?' I smiled at Jessica, picking up speed.

'I didn't mean—' Gareth started.

'Let's go and make tea,' Jessica said, grabbing his hand and contorting herself to get out of the door.

When Erik left me in the park I hadn't wanted to go home and I hadn't wanted to stay there. I'd tried some options in my head, starting with the possible – my mum's house, my sister's, a bar in town, a cinema. When none of them appealed, I'd moved on to more extreme alternatives – a beach in Spain, a lake in Italy, a city in Canada. I'd gone around the world like that, trying to think of somewhere, other than with him, I wanted to be.

The feeling of homelessness had stuck. It was there whether I was walking the streets or in the flat, whether I was awake or asleep. At night my dreams were about becoming unexpectedly cut off from him. In one I left his house to buy milk and a storm rose up, closing all the roads, and making it impossible to get back. The shopkeeper told me it would be impassable for decades. I'd left my hat and gloves in his kitchen. I'd only brought enough money for the pint of milk.

In another I was on a packed train and he was in another carriage, but it was too crowded on-board for me to push my way through. When we stopped at a station, I got off and ran down the platform towards where he was sitting but the train pulled away before I got there.

I woke from these dreams with a jolt, an anxious, crawling feeling quickly establishing in my head. I grew calmer by telling myself that this separation was temporary, and that he would get in touch with me soon, and we would be friends again.

I imagined meeting him by chance in one of the bars across the road. It would be quiet, just us, no one to interrupt. He would reach for my hand across the table and hold it in his. He'd say he'd been taking out his frustration with the house on me, and he'd been wrong to say what he said, and he didn't mean any of it.

No, it didn't seem real enough. He would say he'd meant it at the time, but he'd changed his mind because he'd realised how much he liked me. We would leave our drinks unfinished, take a taxi to his house, climb the stairs to his bedroom. I'd fall asleep in his arms, my legs becoming heavy, my head empty.

In this way, I drugged myself back to sleep. When I woke a few hours later, the radiators clicking as they started to warm, I buried myself further under the covers. I wrapped daydreams around me in there then wore them all day like a long, thick scarf that covered my head and ears as well as my throat. I knew if I unwound them the air would get in. I felt it whenever I let my fantasies slip. It was a cold, sharp pain I wanted to avoid.

That night when I woke from anxious dreaming, my eyes fixed on the unfamiliar shape of the exercise bike at the end of the bed. Through the wall to Mario's flat I could hear a woman's mechanical, steadily building cries. He was watching porn and I wished he would switch back to football with its surge and fall of supporters' songs, or the relaxation CD with its sound of pebbles being dragged backwards by a retreating tide. The woman's cries went on and on without a climax. I put on a jumper and socks and got on the exercise bike.

The soft whir of the wheels blocked out the soundtrack of simulated sex, and the physical effort of pedalling slowed my thoughts. I cycled for forty minutes before getting back into bed. It was quiet next door by then. I fell asleep around five.

20

The bike was for night-times. On my days off I walked. The pavements were dry with grit for frost that hadn't fallen and the last few leaves rattled on the trees. When I stepped outside in the early afternoon, the sun was low and my shadow long. I usually followed the main road into town, lowering my eyes to avoid being blinded by sudden sunlight beaming between buildings. I would go to the bookshops and WHSmith, the art shop and stationers in the Northern Quarter. Or the other way into Chorlton, past the swimming baths and library to the charity shops.

In Barnardo's my heart sped as I pushed open the door, slowed when I saw he wasn't there.

Annie was usually behind the counter. I wondered what she thought when she saw me arrive, day after day. I guessed there was a steady stream of regulars like me. The jobless, the retired, the compulsive shoppers paying by credit card, all looking for a purchase that would give their outing a sense of achievement. I flicked through £2 CDs and rails of trailing scarves and belts, my eyes turning often to the opening door. It was never him and I never bought anything. On my third visit in a week, Annie asked if there was anything in particular I was searching for. She said she could put things aside for me, if she knew what I liked. I wanted to ask about Erik, when he came in, whether she'd spoken to him recently. I shook my head. 'I'm just looking, thanks.'

In the evenings when I returned home from work or wandering, I watched a box set I'd borrowed from Susie. It was a long, intricate police drama set in Copenhagen and I liked the way the female detective was never cold or hungry or tired. She walked alone through rain into dark buildings. She worked for two days without any sleep. I watched it in bed, eating popcorn from a bowl, sometimes fitting in three hour-long episodes in a row before I lay down to sleep.

It was a Monday and I was on my second episode of the night when Jessica knocked on my bedroom door and squeezed inside. I pressed pause on my laptop. The frame froze on a shot of a man with a punched-in nose slumped against a wall.

She'd been out most evenings since the bike arrived. I'd barely seen her at all over the weekend. She sat at the foot of my bed. 'What you up to?'

'Just watching a DVD.'

She'd already lost interest. 'We've just been to see one of those new apartments by the Parkway.'

'Oh right.' She'd not mentioned moving out since that day and I had presumed her plans had been forgotten or put on hold.

'It's the fifth one we've looked at in a week.'

194

So that's what she'd been doing every night. I turned my eyes back to the screen. 'No good?'

'It had way too much traffic noise, which is probably why it was cheap. Anywhere under £600 is a slum. I didn't realise this place was such a bargain.'

Perhaps Jessica wasn't as keen on moving as Gareth. With its massive sound system and weed-scented lounge, his house wasn't somewhere you'd want to be living after the age of twenty-five. But this flat was okay, with the eucalyptus shimmering outside and the flood of light from the bay window. Jessica's room was spacious and her balcony got the sun in the afternoons and evenings. I didn't see what the hurry was for her to leave.

'We had another idea, though.'

'What about?'

'Where to live.' She paused. 'Katie at work is looking for someone to move into her shared house in Chorlton. She says it's really nice. It's got this big garden, big rooms, huge kitchen, really cool people.'

'Sounds good.'

'Yeah, it is. So we wondered whether you might want to go and have a look?'

'Me?'

She nodded.

'Why?'

'Well, so me and Gareth can live here.'

I felt like the man on my laptop screen. Expression frozen. Stuck in a moment. Jessica started talking. 'We just thought that, well, you can't afford to live here on your own. You'll have to share a house either way.

195

So what difference will it make? We'd help you move. You've barely got anything to take anyway since you binned it all. And, you know, you might like living with more people. You might make some friends.'

'But this is where I live.'

She looked around my room. 'It's tiny. You've not even got a double bed. What if you want to invite someone over?'

'Like *who*?'

'I don't know. A man.'

'I don't know any men.'

'What happened to Erik?'

I hadn't spoken to her about him. The words were trapped somewhere. I said, 'I don't know,' and clicked play on my laptop and stared at the screen. The man slumped down onto a wet concrete floor. His groans weren't subtitled.

She was still looking at me. 'It was just a suggestion. I'm just trying to find a solution.'

A solution to a problem you're creating, I thought. The guttural Danish dialogue started again. Jessica sighed, then sighed again as she struggled to get out of the door.

The shared house was just past the four banks in the centre of Chorlton, down a little side street with a beauty parlour on one corner. Beside the front steps pale coriander grew in cut-off water bottles and a wheelie bin was covered with paisley swirls of paint. I rang the bell and waited. A man in a bobble hat and cardigan opened it without a greeting.

'Is Katie in?' I asked.

He left the door half-open and disappeared into the house. I waited outside. There were a lot of houses like this in Chorlton. I almost knew the room layout without going inside. Three storeys. Long narrow bathroom. Big unheated hallways. Kitchen extended into an unkempt back garden.

Katie appeared, opening the door fully. She had frizzy brown hair and the look of someone who'd slept in her clothes. Her fingernails were bitten and painted with flaking gold polish. 'Hiya.'

'Hi. I'm Jessica's friend.'

'Miriam! Come in, come in. I'm Katie. I totally forgot you were coming.'

'Should I come back later?'

'Nope. We're just doing a whole lot of nothing. I'm feeling a tad rough around the edges.'

'Late night?'

'Three late nights in a row. I can't keep doing this. Anyway,' she opened a door immediately off the hallway, 'so, this is the room.' Her voice was loud and bright in the empty space. I had another wave of déjà vu. There was a bed with a sunken mattress, a coarse blue carpet, off-white walls with Blu Tack marks from taken-down posters. The air was damp and the furnishings were IKEA's budget range – the landlord's favourite. A wobbly wardrobe, a slanted shelving unit, a chest with drawers that didn't quite close.

'I know it looks a bit grim at the moment but at least it's a decent size,' Katie said. 'Jessica said your room's really small where you are at the moment.'

'Yeah, it is a bit.'

'She was so giddy about moving in with Gareth. I'd never seen her look so happy on a Monday morning. I was like, what happened to *you* at the weekend?'

I'd not seen Jessica smiling for weeks. It must have been a different story when she was with other people. 'Yeah, it's all moving really quickly with them.'

'That's what I said. She said it does when you meet the right person. Bully for you, I said. Anyway, I'm sure they'll be very happy together. It's a bummer for you, though, having to move out. But, I mean, I love this place. It's great living here.'

I felt left behind by her enthusiasm. 'Great.'

She said, 'You could make it look really nice in here. You won't have to keep this furniture. The landlord will take it away if you've got your own.'

'I've not really got much. Just my exercise bike, really.'

Katie grinned. 'The exercise bike! Jessica said. There's loads of room for it in here.'

I wondered what else Jessica had said. Did she make a story out of me at work? Miriam's latest fuck-up told in a despairing tone.

I went over to the front window and pushed aside the office-style blinds to reveal a view of a hedge, too close to the glass. I would miss being at tree height, watching the leaves move from silver to green and back again.

Katie said, 'I'll take you on the tour.'

We went down a hallway into a big kitchen where a man with an Afro was eating a kebab, flicking through a free newspaper. Katie introduced him as James. He smiled as if apologising for something. The 9 am kebab maybe. Or just the kitchen in general. It had two fridges and two cookers like in a youth hostel. There were dirty dishes stacked very neatly by the sink and tea bag stains on the worktops.

I said, 'How many people live here?'

'Six officially,' Katie said. 'Then I have my boyfriend over a few nights. Plus, there's James's girlfriend.' James started shaking his head, as if to say, not anymore but Katie didn't notice. 'And people's friends come to stay at the weekend sometimes. One thing about this place is you'll never be bored. There's always something going on. In summer, we have these massive house parties on the solstice and the bank holiday weekend.'

I turned around quickly. The cavernous hallway, the gigantic kitchen, the paved back garden with algae-covered plastic chairs. 'I think I've been to one.'

That full-beam smile again. 'Most people around here have.'

'Most can't remember them the next day,' James said, his mouth finally empty.

It wasn't long after I'd moved to the area, when me and Jessica had decided Fallowfield was too studenty for us now we'd graduated. Chorlton had seemed hipper, cooler, more adult. I remembered dancing to house music in the living room, pouring vodka into a plastic cup in the kitchen. I'd met some boy while I was queuing for the bathroom. We'd gone in one of the bedrooms. I think it was the one up for rent. My room.

'It was a few years ago,' I said. It seemed like the distant past.

'Before my time then,' Katie said. 'I'll show you the living room.' We went into a cold, dusty room where two girls in dressing gowns were watching *Saturday Kitchen*, pint glasses of orange juice by their feet.

Katie introduced them as Ellie and Daisy. They both wore pyjamas and big slippers and the remains of last night's eyeliner. Ellie stood up with a luxurious stretch. 'I feel like a pig shat in my head.'

'Are you making a brew?' Daisy said. Then, looking at me, 'Don't move in here unless you like doing massive rounds of tea. You never get away with just making one for yourself.'

'Unless you're Chris,' Ellie said. 'He has never once made me a brew in the whole time I've lived here. Would you like a drink, Miriam?'

'I would but I've got another place to look at,' I lied. I turned to Katie. 'Can I let you know tomorrow about the room?'

''Course. No worries.'

Katie took me to the door. 'Do you want another quick look at it before you go? So you don't forget what it's like?'

We stood just inside the bedroom, taking in the bright, stain-hiding carpet, the marked walls, the bobbly mattress. The doorbell rang. It sounded like it was right behind the bed. Ellie answered it with, 'Dude! What happened to you?' A Scouse girl replied, 'What didn't happen?' as they went into the kitchen.

'I always get a photo if I'm looking at a few places, otherwise you forget which was which,' Katie said.

'Good idea.' I got out my phone and aimed it at the

bed and back wall. I remembered searching for my shoes in the dark, checking nothing had fallen out of my bag. Was his name Steven? Was this his room or had we borrowed a stranger's bed?

Katie said, 'It'll look loads better when you've got your own things in. Jessica told me you had this huge clear-out, your clothes and your books and everything. I thought it was really cool. A clean slate and all that. I totally get where you're coming from.'

21

I took a call at work from a lady called Lisa who ran a company called Space Reclaimers. She wanted a quote for a new website and gave me her current web address so I could have a look. 'I'm a clutter-clearer,' she said, as I waited for the page to load.

I had seen companies like this when I was searching around for solutions to Erik's problem. They were the experts who worked to strategies and seven-step plans. I hadn't suggested it to him because I didn't want to lose my excuse to see him. Looking back, it seemed like another way I'd gone wrong.

Lisa said, 'Any joy?'

'It's still loading.'

'Daft thing takes forever. It's a wonder I get anyone phoning at all.'

When her website finally appeared on my screen, I struggled to think of a tactful response. It had too much text and messy design. It threw information at you in no particular order. You had to search around to work out what service she was actually offering.

'What do you think?' she asked.

'I think we could design one that's a lot simpler.'

'I know, I know. I have so much to say about what I do, I keep adding bits to it. It's got a little bit out of control.'

'That look probably appeals to hoarders.'

She laughed. 'You're right. But it's not the hoarders who visit my website. It's their fed-up husbands or daughters or parents. It's the tidy people I need to appeal to.'

I wanted to know more but I was conscious of Sheila listening in on our conversation. I told Lisa I'd send her an email with a quote for our standard web design package, then put the phone down and saved her name and number in my mobile. I could pass it on to Erik, by text, or maybe I could call him tonight. It had been three weeks now after all. And professional help like this was what he needed. Not an amateur like me, blundering around in the dark.

I worked with a new sense of purpose that morning. I whizzed through the invoicing and the monthly figures, then after lunch I asked Sheila if there was anything more I could be doing.

'Aren't you good?' she said, distractedly. 'Can you have a look through Natalie's email account for a tax code for JL Fabrications.'

'What do they do? Make stuff up?'

'Hmm, curtains and cushion covers, that sort of thing.'

Natalie's email password was 'be-joyful'. I logged in and waited while it downloaded several weeks of weight loss spam and daily deals. I found the tax code and was about to log out when I saw a name that made my fingers freeze over the keyboard.

Erik Zeleny.

The date was a few months back. I clicked on it, cursing the two-second pause that followed everything you did on this old computer. He was so absent from my life now. I just wanted to read something he'd written, see his words on the screen. Then the email exchange finally opened up, and I saw it was about me.

Hi Erik
It was great to meet you this morning. I just wanted to check that you are satisfied with the service you received today. Miriam is a new member of staff. Please don't hesitate to contact me if you have any queries or feedback.
Natalie

Hi Natalie
Miriam is fine. I am satisfied with the service.
Erik

Then a few days later.

Hi Erik
I enclose the terms and conditions of the contract for you to sign and return to me.
On a different subject, I saw your name in the October edition of Elle. What amazing photographs! (And what a great job – flying off to Kenya. I'm jealous!!)
Natalie

Hi Natalie

Thanks for the compliment about my work. I am writing to let you know that I have decided to finish the work here myself. Miriam had to leave early for an appointment so please can you contact her to tell her I will not need her anymore. And please thank her for her assistance.

Send me an invoice and I will transfer payment.

Erik

Hi Erik

I'm sorry that City Business Services is of no further use to you at this time. Please don't hesitate to contact me if you require our services going forward.

RE your photography. I'd love to develop a career in this area myself! Can you recommend any books or websites that could start me in the right direction?

Natalie

Hi Natalie

I've attached a list of useful sources for when you are beginning a photography career. Also there is a photography network you might want to join in Manchester. Website link below. Good luck.

Erik

Hi Erik

Thanks for the list you sent me. It's really helpful. It would be great if I could meet with you to get some advice on my plans? We could go for a coffee in the city centre?

Natalie (07995 654 138)

The email conversation ended there.

I stared at her last message. That mobile number

tagged casually on the end. A scenario formed in my head.

He had called her. They'd met in a bar in town. She'd worn something bohemian and sexy that showed she wasn't an office manager on the inside, but a creative, artistic person trying to find her true path. How long had they sat in a corner chatting, his legs stretched out beside her, moving on from talking about photography to talking about their personal lives? I tried to remember whether Natalie had ever mentioned a boyfriend but even if she did, even if it was just a professional meeting, I hated it.

The afternoon dragged. A man in overalls cleaned the windows in the dark. The fuse blew on one of the electric heaters. Sheila invited me on the office Christmas do. Finally, by ten past five, everyone had left apart from me. Deborah and Bernie had turned off their computers but I knew where to find their passwords. I switched their machines back on, logged into their email accounts. I was looking for emails to Erik about payment but there were none. He must have been dealing with Natalie over the phone.

I couldn't handle the thought of it. I just couldn't let it sit in my head. I switched off the lights and computers and walked to the bus stop on Hyde Road. When I finally reached Piccadilly Gardens, the rain was falling at a slant that hit me in the face. People already rushing for trams and trains walked faster and I couldn't find a still, quiet place. I crossed between the wind-scattered fountains, stood under the shelter of the concrete wall separating the gardens from the bus terminal. I couldn't wait another thirty minutes until I got home. I called him. He didn't answer. I couldn't not know. I called again in case he'd not heard. On the bus home I called again.

I kept my phone close by me all evening. Jessica and Gareth were out so I didn't have to pretend to be okay. I called his home number at about nine o'clock. I imagined the long peals ringing in his hallway. I couldn't stand the sound of him not picking up.

I was sitting up in bed when my phone rang. I didn't know the number. 'Hello?'

'Miriam, it's Katie. I was just calling to see if you wanted the room.'

I tucked my legs up under my chin. 'Oh, sorry. I meant to call.' I'd been putting it off, telling myself each day that I needed to sleep on it to decide.

'We've got someone else asking for it, but you get first dibs, if you want it.'

'Oh thanks. But I think I'm just going to stay here.'

'Oh, okay. No worries.'

I put the phone down again.

When it got to eleven o'clock, I took two sleeping pills. They didn't work. I thought about Erik for hours, until the jealousy and sadness seemed so thick in my small room, I had to open the window. Damp air and the rumble of the night bus on the main road. I imagined the hotel room in Morecambe. His arm crooked around my waist as we slept. Sometime between three and four I heard someone on the pavement just outside the house. A boy shouted, 'Bye Kat.' A few moments passed then a girl shouted, 'Bye Jim,' from a couple of streets away.

About five minutes later, I heard them shouting again, further apart this time. 'Bye Kat' followed by 'Bye Jim' somewhere in the distance.

They repeated this every five minutes for about half an hour, each time their calls more distant. They were seeing how far their voices would travel across the city, stretching out their goodbyes for as long as they could be heard.

Jim stopped first. I lay awake listening to the silence after she'd shouted his name. When my radio alarm came on at seven, I felt like I hadn't slept at all.

All the next day I felt submerged by the sleeping pills still in my system. They made breathing difficult; I inhaled harder and deeper for less air. And the world seemed further away, like I was behind a mask. Low cloud hid the tops of the tallest buildings in the city centre and a thin mist of rain clouded the streets. I felt like I was snorkelling through the city. I didn't want to resurface.

By the evening, I was dog-tired. I didn't bother with dinner, just put the kettle on for a hot-water bottle to take to bed. It had just clicked off when Jessica arrived home. She came into the kitchen, her bag still on her shoulder, coat buttoned high. I knew what was coming from the expression on her face.

'Katie said you don't want the room.'

The thought of living in a house-share like an overgrown student had made me feel catatonic. I must have slept at some point last night because I suddenly remembered a dream where I was sitting cross-legged at the bottom of a swimming pool. It was something

I'd done in life-saving lessons when I was a teenager. Tracksuits over our swimming costumes, weights in our pockets like we were trying to drown ourselves.

She said, 'I mean, have you even looked at anywhere else?'

I refocused. 'I don't want to live in a shared house. Nobody lives with five other people at my age.'

'Loads of people do in London.'

I poured steaming water from the kettle into my hot-water bottle. 'We're not in London.'

'Have you found somewhere else?' A fast, clipped question.

'No.'

She turned away. Turned back again. 'Gareth wants to move in before Christmas.'

'I'm not moving out.'

'You said you would.'

'I didn't. And if I did, I've changed my mind.'

'Is this because you resent me being with Gareth? I thought you'd got over him.'

I laughed. It was easy to argue when you were zoned out on sleeping pills. I felt a calm control I'd never have if I wasn't this tired. 'You can't be over someone you were never into. I barely even liked him when we were dating. When I see him now, I think, what a dick.'

Jessica's face flushed. 'He doesn't like you much either.'

I moved past her. 'I don't care.'

'I can't believe you're being so selfish.'

I finally felt a prickle of anger. 'It's you who's selfish, not me. You act like my opinions matter less than yours.

It's like you think I only have half a vote because I'm single. You think I'll just go along with whatever you want because you're in a couple.'

'So, what, you're just going to stay here on your own?'

'Yes.'

'How will you pay the rent?'

'I have a job.'

'On minimum wage? Miriam, you're living in a dream world. You drift along, not noticing that you're getting older and you've still no career or boyfriend or house. You're not twenty-two anymore. You're nearly thirty. And you're not doing anything about it. I bet you'll be like this forever. God, I'm so glad I'm getting out.'

She stormed into her bedroom, slammed the door shut. I stood in the living room, still holding my fluffy hot-water bottle. Stand your ground, I told myself but it sounded uncertain and unconvincing, like when I'd typed 'be-joyful' into Natalie's computer just before being flattened.

22

Working at CBS cut time into chunks and sometimes seemed to devour it all together. Occasionally I became so involved in the mechanics of a spreadsheet, I didn't think of Erik and Natalie, and those frantic, unanswered phone calls, for a few hours. Then when five o'clock came and I stepped out into the freezing Ardwick evening, it slid back into my head, and the world seemed intolerable once more. Yet only ten minutes earlier I'd been chatting to Megan while washing out my mug ready for tomorrow. Part of me wanted to go back inside under the bright strip lights, start the next day's work now, and not bother with this going home, being alone bit in between.

I would stand in the potholed car park, my bag heavy on my shoulder, wondering how I would get from here to the flat without a teleportation machine because the thought of walking to the main road and taking two buses home was exhausting. I still couldn't find anywhere I wanted to be. Not here in this dark industrial estate. Not in my cramped bedroom. Yet when I tried to picture myself anywhere else, my mind went blank.

I couldn't move out of the flat because I couldn't think of anywhere I wanted to go. I wanted to explain this to Jessica but it seemed like we'd gone past the point of trying to understand how the other was feeling.

I barely saw her over the following week. She must have decided the toothpaste-caked bathroom at Gareth's house was better than the awkward atmosphere in our flat. I didn't blame her. If I'd had anywhere else to go, I would have. I hated having to plan my arrivals and exits from the kitchen and living room, half-wanting to avoid her and half-wanting to bump into her so we could clear the air. I heard her key turn in the front door when I was cooking dinner one night and waited in the kitchen, hoping she might come in and say hello. She went straight to her room, then straight out again an hour later.

Another time she mumbled Hi when she came into the living room to fish out a pair of Gareth's shoes from under the sofa. I said Hi, helpfully moving my feet out of the way so she could see better. I wasn't angry anymore. I wanted to make friends. But she retrieved the shoes and was gone again before I'd worked out what to say.

On Friday evening, I could hear her moving about in her bedroom. Gareth's car wasn't outside so I figured she must be on her own. I decided I would take her a cup of tea and see what happened from there. I went to fill the kettle. It wasn't there.

I scanned the kitchen surfaces, checked the cupboards.

It was gone. Other things, too. Plates, bowls, mugs and pans were missing. I checked the drawer where Jessica kept her food. Usually it was packed with tins of tomatoes, bags of dried apricots, packets of rice. Now there was just one stray pasta shell and a sachet of HP Sauce.

I heard her bedroom door open and quickly shut her kitchen drawer. She came through carrying an empty plastic storage box, which she dumped on the living room floor. Without looking at me, she started scooping up CDs and DVDs from the bookshelf and piling them inside.

I felt stupid standing there in the emptied kitchen, not knowing what was happening, and there was no way I was going to ask. I watched until she glanced back at me. Neither of us spoke and she went back to filling the box with magazines, a lamp, a photograph album. I wanted to casually hand her the photo of her and Gareth stuck to the fridge but I was too upset to carry it off with any nonchalance.

Later that evening as I was watching *The Killing* in bed, I heard Gareth's voice, and the sound of furniture being slid clumsily down the stairs. When I went to clean my teeth, the bookshelf in the living room was gone, and the TV, the stereo, the coffee table, and the curtains. The bay window was single-glazed and the air was cold without their barrier. Anyone looking up from the street could see me in my dressing gown in the bare room. I flicked off the light and felt my way over to the fridge in the dark. The photograph was still there. Out of all of this, it was what offended me the most. I went to put it in the bin, but when I opened the cupboard under the sink I saw she'd taken that as well.

In the morning, I heard them taking the sofa and armchair while I was getting dressed. Was anything in this flat mine, other than the exercise bike? When we'd rented it, there were just the white goods and the beds and Jessica had filled in the gaps with hand-me-down furniture she'd been storing in her parents' spare room.

I was sick of sitting around listening to her leave so I chose a moment when it was quiet and stepped outside the safety of my bedroom, hoping to escape unseen.

I met them on the stairs. We all stopped. Gareth a few steps below Jessica, me a few steps above her.

'We might be gone when you get back,' she said. It sounded like a challenge and I thought, was this all just a way of escalating the argument? And if so, how was I supposed to respond? Move cities? Leave the country?

She said, 'I'll push my key under the door when I lock up.'

'Okay.' I stepped down so they had to get out of the way. Nobody said goodbye.

In Chorlton I sat at the back of a café full of young couples eating elaborate breakfasts of waffles and poached eggs and home-made granola. I ordered a croissant and a coffee and waited for my mood to settle. I had wanted her to move out so it was a good thing, I told myself. But I couldn't help feeling like she'd won, or worse, walked out halfway through the argument. I called Susie and told her what had happened. She said

Jessica was 'passive-aggressive' then when Alfie had left the room, 'a skanky bitch'.

I finished my coffee and started my rounds of the charity shops. The list of things I needed was longer than ever now and I wondered when my life would stop emptying out and start filling up. I'd instigated the clear-out but it had picked up a momentum of its own, and now I wanted it to stop. In the last two months, I'd lost my clothes, shoes, books, DVDs, furniture, kitchen appliances, job, career ambitions, best friend, and Erik.

I started in British Heart Foundation, then moved on to Age UK and PDSA, leaving Barnardo's until last. Erik probably visited them all in his quests for books and magazines but I always felt I had more chance of seeing him in this one, as it was where we'd first met.

The shop was busy with Saturday browsers: young women looking for vintage fashion, retired men hunting for undiscovered antiques. I scanned their backs. He wasn't here. He was never here. It was possible I would never see him again in my life.

I headed towards the back of the shop where last year's literary hits and cookery books were shelved in almost alphabetical order. What did I want to read? I felt like I was playing a role even asking myself this question. I still had no idea what interested me. I'd erased myself when I'd cleared out my belongings and nothing had appeared yet to fill the space. Or rather, Erik had appeared, and filled my head so completely there hadn't been room for anything else.

I scanned the spines, still acting, wondering with every swing of the door whether it was him, stopping myself from turning round because the movement was too obvious. I wasn't taking in what I was looking at until I saw a book I recognised. *The Great Gatsby*, the Penguin Classics edition. I took it out. It felt so familiar, the slight crease in one corner of the soft cover, the wave in the pages from reading it in the damp air of the bath. It felt like it was my copy yet it couldn't be; Erik had bought that. I last saw it sitting on his kitchen table, next to his thick ash-grey jumper.

My throat tightened. I tried to remember what else had been in that box of books. *A Room with a View*. I scanned the Fs for Forster. Oh. It was there, too.

I opened it, flicked through the pages, no postcard fell out. Maybe it wasn't mine. But then I saw *Wuthering Heights* a few books along. I knew this was mine because I had written notes in the margins when I was studying it for A-Level English.

He had brought back my books. And he was a man who wanted all books, who couldn't bear to let them go even if they were torn and illegible.

'Are you okay, Miriam?' It was Annie. How long had she been there? I wondered what expression I wore to make her sound so concerned.

I straightened. 'Just browsing.'

She looked quizzically at me.

'It's just. I think these are my books.'

She relaxed. 'Well that's not surprising. Half the shop is yours. We've never had so much stuff in from one person, unless they'd died.'

'I mean, I know they're mine, but I thought they'd been sold.'

'That happens with books. People bring them back when they've finished with them. It's like they don't know there's a library up the road where you can do that for free.'

'But I don't think he's finished with them yet.' My voice sounded choked.

Annie paused. 'You're talking about Erik.'

My eyes filled with tears. It was embarrassing.

'Oh, don't do that.' Annie looked around, as if searching for something that'd make me stop crying. 'Okay, I finish here at two. Go and wait for me in Dulcimer.'

I pulled down the sleeve of my cardigan to wipe my eyes. I wasn't going to fall apart amongst the chick lit novels and Mills & Boons. 'Okay.'

I didn't scan the shop as I headed towards the door. If he was in there, I didn't want to know.

Dulcimer was reassuringly dark. When I ordered a drink, the tremor had gone from my voice. I'd finished my half-pint by the time Annie arrived. She asked if I fancied sharing a bottle of wine and I nodded. I didn't know her really. And I'd started crying in her shop. Wine would help.

Dulcimer was a folk-style bar with retro-rock artwork on the walls and scratched wooden tables. Girls in woollen 1970s coats made roll-ups to take into a yard at the back. A couple of young men sat at tables on their own, tapping into laptops. Annie returned with a bottle of red wine and two glasses. She filled them almost to the brim.

She said, 'I like this bar because you can forget it's daytime. There's no kids pestering their mums for a taste of their lattes.'

I said, 'I've never been in here before.'

'But you live in Chorlton, don't you?'

'Whalley Range.'

Annie was wearing what looked like a charity shop outfit. All a little bit worn and not quite the right size. A sleeveless cream dress over a soft pink blouse. Grey tights and electric blue ballet pumps. By her feet was a plastic bag spilling out jumpers and scarves.

'Do you get stuff for free?' I asked.

'No but I'm always buying stuff there. I can't help it.'

Was she another one? 'You must have a lot of clothes.'

'Not really. Every few months, I scoop together a load of stuff and bring it back to the shop. Otherwise I'd be buried in it. That's what I meant about your books. That place is like a conveyor belt. Things come back round.'

I looked at my glass of wine. 'Sorry about that before.'

'Don't be daft.'

'I don't know what's up with me.'

She looked like she didn't believe me. 'Is it to do with Erik by any chance?'

'How do you know him?'

'He comes in the shop. Almost as often as you actually, though not recently. He brought your books back about a month ago. They've been in the back room waiting for someone to put them out.'

It was about a month ago that he'd ended our... whatever it was.

Annie said, 'You're going to have to fill me in here.'

I finished my glass of wine. She refilled it. I said, 'Do you remember when I brought all my stuff into the shop and he was there?'

She nodded. I told her about meeting him at his house just a few days later. His nervousness when he showed us the paper-packed room. I was certain he was looking at me that day, not Natalie. I described the masses of magazines and books, the creations he fashioned from them, his refusal to let go of any of it, even my postcard. And I told her how despite this, I'd become fixed on him, how from nothing, he'd grown in my mind until he was all I thought about. The feelings had formed deep down, so far below I wasn't even aware of them at first. Then when they'd surfaced they were already strong and rooted. Even when I wasn't thinking of him, his shape and presence were in the background, a constant that followed me through my days and nights.

Then Morecambe in the curved white hotel with the muted room by the faraway sea. Then nothing. The park. His emails to Natalie. His phone ringing out. This last, long week, ending with today. 'The only thing he can throw away,' I said, 'is me.'

'You mean your books.' She sounded like she was getting the facts straight. 'And didn't you say he binned those photographs of his wife as well?'

'Oh yeah, he did.'

'So he gets rid of things that have some kind of emotional power for him.'

I liked this idea too much. 'But the phone calls. I rang him like ten times.'

'If he'd picked up, you wouldn't have had to.' Annie leaned forward slightly. 'What I'm saying is, anyone would act crazy in that situation. You fall in love with him, he sleeps with you, then he cuts you off a few days later, and won't even talk to you when you call. Obviously you're going to go a little bit mental. It's normal.'

'Would you do that?'

She considered it seriously, as if she was picturing herself ringing someone over and over. 'Not now I wouldn't. I just can't get interested in a man unless he likes me back.' She took a swig of wine. 'Sorry, I mean, unless he likes me equally. Erik must have liked you.'

'He did.'

I could see her holding back her words. I didn't need to hear her telling me to give it up. I changed the subject. 'Shall I get us another bottle of wine?'

'If you insist.'

We moved into the covered yard outside so she could smoke. It was cold, even with the heaters on, but I felt like if we kept talking and drinking, I could keep my unhappiness at bay. It was just a few books, I told myself, and for a second, I could see them as only that – just some books he'd decided he didn't need. But a second later, they were everything; the curiosity about me that had made him ask me to stay that first day, the hours we'd spent together in the enclosed corners of his house, the closeness that had grown slowly between us. I imagined him seeing the books after he'd returned from the park and feeling repulsed.

'Did he say anything when he brought my books back?' I asked.

Annie's cigarette smoke hung in the air. 'Not really. I think he just mumbled something about having a clear-out.'

'Did he look like he was in a bad mood?'

'I can't remember. Sorry, Miriam.'

I could picture him. His worn hands taking the weight of the box. An anxious frown shadowing his face. I felt the gap like an ache.

We stayed out there as the afternoon slid into dusk, pressing the button for the heater every five minutes, wrapped up in our coats, hats and gloves. Annie pulled a red chenille scarf from her plastic bag, and snapped off the price tag before giving it to me.

She was an upholsterer, she said, when she wasn't at Barnardo's. One reason she worked there was to get materials and old furniture she could bring back to life. She said she did commissions and asked if I had anything I wanted upholstering. I said I didn't own any chairs, unless you counted my exercise bike.

'Bicycle seat covers would go down a storm around here. But why have you got an exercise bike? Why not just get a bike?'

I was sure there was a reason but I couldn't remember what it was. It was dark now and we'd drunk two bottles of wine between us. I thought of the empty flat, my lifeless phone, felt the burn of rejection flare up again. I really didn't want to go home.

'I don't suppose you know anyone who needs a room, do you?' I asked.

'Not off the top of my head.'

'My flatmate moved out this morning. We fell out.'

'And she moved out because of it?'

'Kind of. It was on the cards before that.'

I wondered how I must look to Annie. Two people in one day who had cut me off. 'My life isn't normally like this.'

'Like what?'

'Like, a mess.'

She shrugged and lit another cigarette. 'You're just separating the good stuff from the bad, getting rid of the people you don't need anymore.'

'They're getting rid of me.'

'It's the same thing in the end.'

I poured the last of the wine into our glasses. 'I've never lived on my own before.'

'I prefer it. Forced cohabitation is the worst thing about being in your twenties. I'd rather have a bedsit than a flatmate.'

'Where do you live?'

'In a bedsit. Well, "studio flat". It's got a separate kitchen and bathroom and one room for everything else.'

'Is that where you do your upholstering?'

'No, it's way too small. I share a studio in Ancoats with a milliner.' She added, 'Hats' when I nodded blankly.

She mentioned a birthday party later at a bar in town, and it seemed like it was hours away, then it was that time, and we were there. It was another place I'd never been. Red vinyl seats, a jukebox, a beer-wet floor. There were fairy lights behind the bar and a sleek, black dog weaved between the drinkers. A lot of people told me their name. A couple of men bought me a drink. One with a broken tooth and warm eyes told me Annie was one of the nicest people you'd ever meet. Another, tall and crumpled in a dark blue suit, said, 'Where have you appeared from?' Someone handed me a shot of Pernod. I looked at my phone at half-two, then again at four. Annie had gone by now and I felt strangely clear-headed as if I had drunk myself sober.

I got a taxi home, remembering as I unlocked the door that I didn't have to be quiet because there was nobody here to disturb. The flat looked like it had been burgled. No furniture, no TV, no rug on the floor, no pictures on the walls. I went in Jessica's room. She'd left the bed and mattress and clumps of dust where her wardrobe had been.

I stood on her balcony looking out onto the street. I wanted to call Erik and hear his warm, curious voice. I wanted to go round and have him make me hot chocolate in his kitchen. It was five in the morning but that made no difference. Whatever time it was, he wouldn't answer the door.

The return of those books had left me no space to dream in. Thinking of him, of the end of him, made me flinch. The pain cut through the haze I'd surrounded myself in; the fantasies, the maybes, the sleeping pills, the fourteen hours of drinking with Annie. I had a shower as if it would somehow wash away all the alcohol still inside me. I was sick in the toilet before I went to bed.

23

In the days after Jessica left, I kept thinking I could hear her in the next room. The drone of her hairdryer, her heels clip-clopping across the floorboards. They were the background noises I'd grown used to over four years and now my brain was finding them in the sound of cars outside and the muffled noises from the flats next door. It was like she'd died, and I felt embarrassed at myself for reacting like this. I'd wanted her to go. I'd craved solitude. But the stillness was heavier than I'd imagined. It was that sense of doubt that crept into empty weekends, except now it was every morning and every evening as well. I left work each day at five and didn't speak to anyone until I arrived back there the next morning. In the evenings, I went on my exercise bike, counting up how many miles I was covering. One long Friday night, I cycled as far as the coast and back without leaving my room. Or I moved about the echoing flat, rearranging my few belongings to try and make it look more homely. I stuck a sheet over the bay window as a makeshift curtain. I put a few cushions against the radiator for a sofa. I was sleeping in Jessica's room now. My clothes were in piles against the wall. My alarm clock was on the floor by the bed. I left the exercise bike where it was.

It was the bedroom of someone who's only staying for a few nights so doesn't bother to unpack. I felt like a guest in there, as though it was still her room and I was just borrowing it for a while. But it was bigger and quieter than mine. I couldn't hear Mario's television in there, though when I returned to my own room to use the bike at night, I sometimes heard his abrupt, frightened shouts. Nobody seemed concerned so I kept pedalling. The next day he'd be sitting at the bus stop in the sunshine, unshaven, hood up, saying hello to everyone who walked past.

By the following weekend, I'd stopped instinctively looking up when I heard the other inhabitants of the flats on the communal stairway. So when the doorbell rang not long after I'd got up, I sat still, unsure whether or not I had imagined it. It was repeated again, louder and longer. I said hello into the fuzzy intercom.

Susie and Tom, bringing a sofa they no longer wanted. They'd said they might be round today. I buzzed them in downstairs, then opened the flat door.

'The sofa's in the van.' Susie was coming up the stairs, Tom behind her. 'We thought we better check you'd cleared a space for it.'

I led them through to the empty living room. 'Space is not a problem here.'

'This is bloody brilliant, Mim.' Tom turned to Susie. 'Why don't we have a proper clear-out? Get rid of all our shit and start again with just the things we need.'

'I'm sure the kids would love that. No TV and no sofa. They'd go into meltdown.'

'We could bin all their toys. Tell them we got burgled.'

'I'll let you break it to them.'

I liked Tom. I remembered feeling at ease around him even the first time we met, on a family pub lunch for Susie's birthday when I must have been about fifteen. He had a big smile, boyish looks, and in Susie's words, 'no sides to him'. Everything was laid out on the surface and it was easy to see why she had decided on him straightaway.

He said, 'Are you definitely sure you want this sofa? You look well set up here with your cushions.'

'The thing is, I'll have to get a flatmate soon, and they might want to sit down.'

'Fair enough. Come on then, Suze, let's get it in while Mim makes us a brew.'

Luckily a kettle was the first thing I'd bought. I only had two mugs, though, so I pretended I didn't want a drink myself. They struggled in with the sofa which had been Mum's before she'd handed it down to them. A silky grey 1980s velour with a pattern of pastel geometric shapes. I'd watched hours of CBBC on it, drinking Vimto and eating KitKats. It felt strange having this visual flashback to childhood in the middle of my adult life.

The three of us sat down on it in a row, looking at the wall where the television had been.

'We're on a plane,' Tom said. 'I've got the window seat.'

'You're going to need some more furniture,' Susie said. 'Go and have a look in Mum's garage. It's rammed with stuff she doesn't want.'

'I've not spoken to her for weeks.'

'She's got Alfie and Isabel today while we go Christmas shopping.'

'Buying more toys. There's a patch of carpet in the lounge we haven't covered yet,' Tom said.

Susie ignored him. 'What do you want for Christmas, Mim?'

I thought about all the things I was missing. 'A sharp knife?'

Tom gave me an amused look. 'Intense.'

'Jessica's taken all the kitchen stuff.'

'Unbelievable,' Susie said.

'I suppose it *was* hers. Or you could get me a frying pan? I'm starting from scratch here.'

'Get yourself to Asda,' Tom said. 'They've got all that kind of stuff. Or a charity shop.'

I didn't like to say I went round the charity shops about three times a week. When they were getting up to go, Tom suddenly said, 'Did you bring Mim's letter?'

'Well remembered.' Susie rooted in her handbag and pulled out an envelope with my name on it in handwriting I knew.

It was from my dad.

I held it in my hands. 'What does it say?'

'I don't know. Try opening it.'

He never wrote to me. 'Did you get one?'

'Yes but that's nothing new.'

Susie wrote to him every year or so with pictures of

Alfie and Isabel. He usually wrote back. Without their sporadic correspondence, he would have disappeared from my life completely. In the past when Susie had suggested I write to him, I'd always said no. He was the parent. It was his job to get in touch, not mine.

Inside the envelope was a single sheet of A5 paper filled with his neat, narrow handwriting. I skim-read it for bad news and big announcements but it wasn't that sort of letter. It was something you'd send to someone you hadn't seen for a few months, rather than eight years; full of inconsequential news about DIY projects and changes in the weather. It could be addressed to anyone, apart from one line near the end where he said he'd watched some orca whales in the bay near his house and thought of me.

'What's up?' Susie said.

'Why would he see orca whales and think of me?'

'You used to like them. You had a poster of them swimming into the sunset on your bedroom wall.'

'Did I?'

'What else does it say?' Tom asked.

I summarised some of his news. 'They're having a hot tub installed in their garden. The wind blew a pine tree across the driveway. The baby is sleeping through the night.' I stopped.

Susie said, 'Will you write back?'

I said I wasn't sure. What could I tell my dad about my life? *I'm making macaroni cheese for tea. I bought an eye mask to wear in bed because I haven't got any curtains.*

Susie studied me. 'Well, if you're okay, we best get off.'

'I'm fine.'

I read the letter again when they'd gone, more slowly this time. It had no explanations and no questions. It didn't skirt around issues. It acted like they didn't exist.

Susie must have told Mum about my empty flat. That evening she called me and asked if I wanted to go round the next day to look through her garage. She seemed to think that Jessica was a trickster who had stolen not only my boyfriend but also my furniture and kitchen implements. I started to tell her that none of it was mine in the first place but she didn't want to hear it. 'You were with him first and that flat is your home. Who does she think she is?'

The next day was a Sunday. I took the train from Piccadilly and watched the city turn into countryside as we sped towards the moors which bordered this side of Manchester. Mum lived in a cottage in a deep valley where the woods along the river hid the remains of cotton mills. It was the house I'd grown up in and I wondered now how its small, poky rooms had fit four people. Mum had gradually expanded into the empty bedrooms left by me and Susie, and her own bedroom seemed only big enough for one, as if Dad had been a holiday guest the house had stretched to hold before gratefully shrinking back to its natural shape. There was no sense of an empty nest, rather it seemed like the house had been made for her alone.

When she opened the door, she hugged me, rubbing my arms as if I'd had a fall or lost something important. Mum had a habit of mothering me, which would be understandable except she didn't do it with Susie, whom she seemed to regard as beyond the need for that kind of attention.

The kitchen smelled of roast chicken and lemon. In the living room the gas fire was on, its regulated flames burning steadily between the decorative coal. There were tulips in a vase on the dining table and a scattering of magazines and local papers. On the sideboard was a collection of seaweed-green plates, bowls and teacups I remembered from years ago, and a plastic bag containing a selection of mismatched knives and forks. Mum brought through two mugs of tea and a couple of KitKats, and we caught up on each other's news. Mum's was about pub quiz wins, a new tai chi class in the community centre, comings and goings at the bowling club. Mine was about Jessica leaving, my job at CBS.

'Did the job at the artist's fall through?' she asked. Considering she hadn't wanted me to work there in the first place, she sounded overly disappointed.

'It ended about a month ago.'

She nodded, probably trying to work out whether or not I'd been sacked, and deciding she couldn't very well ask. 'But this new job is at a proper company, isn't it?'

'Oh yeah. It's an office job. Just admin really.'

'Perhaps something else will come up in the New Year. It said on the news that businesses are starting to hire again. Might be a good time to get your CV out there.'

I nodded. I didn't want a new job. The effort of learning new systems and meeting new people seemed too much right now. CBS was dull but easy and the office had a cosiness to it with its plants and biscuits and predictable routines.

'Jackie's daughter is going off travelling for a year. She's got a volunteer job in Thailand.'

'Oh right.'

'I made a note of the website in my diary. She says they're still looking for people.'

Was she trying to persuade me to move to Thailand? 'I'm happy where I am.'

'It was just an idea.'

'I like my life.' I wished I was better at lifting my voice, injecting enthusiasm into it. I said, 'Shall we go and have a look in the garage?'

The push-up door was jammed as if it hadn't been opened for a while. I pulled on it hard and it slid up towards the roof, then stopped halfway. We stooped beneath it to get inside and I flicked the light switch but nothing happened. The air was dry and dusty and we couldn't see much in the grainy light. A corner of a painting, the back of a wicker chair, a roll of carpet, soft bin bags of bedding.

'Take whatever you want,' Mum said. 'The more I get rid of, the better.' A phone rang in the house and she went to answer it. There was a torch on the floor beneath the light switch. I shone it into the corners, hoping the beam wouldn't fall on any spiders. It lit a coffee table with a tiled top which had been at my grandparents' house. An Acorn computer Dad had brought home, creating much excitement in me and Susie. A heavy, gold-framed mirror turned against the wall.

231

I searched through it all, spending a good hour shifting boxes around, peering inside, pushing the things I wanted out onto the driveway: the blue velvet curtains that used to be in Susie's room, a mahogany bookcase that had once been in the living room, a rug which had lain across the landing. It had all migrated in here over the years as Mum had slowly redecorated and replaced old items with new. In the furthest corner, I found a box of Dad's things: a heavy camera on a green and blue woven strap, a pair of Aviator sunglasses. His belongings and clothes had stayed in our house long after he'd left. It was why me and Susie had thought he was coming back. That and the way he had never actually said he was leaving. He'd gone on a work trip to France and hadn't returned. After a few weeks, we spoke to him on the phone. Mum for a long time. Me and Susie just to say hello.

I remembered Mum going out into the garden after that phone call to rake up the leaves from the lawn, even though it was raining lightly. When she came in, there was mud streaked on her face. She washed it off and life went on as normal for a while. He often went away so it didn't feel strange at first.

I don't know how long it was before she said, one evening, sitting at the dinner table, 'It looks like it'll be just the three of us from now on.'

'Is Dad not coming back?' I asked.

'It doesn't look like it.'

Me and Susie were speechless. It was one of those situations where I couldn't think what questions to ask. We carried on as if nothing much had happened. Over the next five years or so, his belongings were slowly cleared out, or moved into the garage, until there was little trace of him in the house. By then, Mum had started seeing someone else, a man she'd met at work, who wasn't on the scene anymore. Not that bothered, was how I'd describe her reaction to Dad leaving. It was as if she'd accepted it before it had happened, and when it did, her sadness had already been felt.

The roast chicken was ready by the time I'd got everything I wanted into Mum's car. We ate with our plates balanced on our knees in the living room, looking out at the garden through the patio doors. The lawn and flower beds were fading into the dusk and I remembered sitting there on the sofas, the four of us, perhaps not long before Dad left. There was a cat that had started peering through the glass doors as we were eating our dinner in the evenings. Mum used to close the curtains when she saw it. She said she didn't like it staring in at us. It stopped visiting after a while. I don't know who it belonged to.

Mum said, 'Will you be going out with friends when you get back?'

'I'll probably have an early night. Work tomorrow.'

'I don't like thinking of you going home to an empty flat.'

'Why? You live in an empty house.'

'I've had my years of a busy household. It doesn't seem right at your age.'

'Lots of people my age live on their own these days.'

'I know, but I'm worried about you.' She rested her cutlery on her plate. 'Can't you tell me what's wrong?'

I didn't know how to answer. I filled my fork with potato and put it in my mouth.

Later, loading a box of mugs and plates into the car boot, she saw Dad's camera. She picked it up and studied it for a moment before putting it back down again without comment. I'd already checked to see if there was any film inside. It was empty and when I'd pressed the buttons, nothing happened. But I thought that maybe I could get it repaired. I kept it in my lap as we drove out of the valley and back towards Manchester.

The weather turned colder the following week. I woke one morning to find an early frost melting in the weak sun. The trees and telephone lines and roofs were streaming with water that caught in the light; it looked like rain falling out of a cloudless sky. On the Saturday the frost stayed into the afternoon. I walked into Chorlton to see Annie, wearing double socks inside my boots, passing pavement trees with tinsel wrapped around the trunks. It was December and the shop windows were decorated with spray-on snow and flickering lights.

I'd arranged to meet Annie in a café that specialised in health-boosting juices and smoothies. The chalk-written menu above the counter listed the benefits of each concoction of puréed fruits and vegetables: energy lift, hangover cure, positive thinking. I decided on one that offered mental clarity. A wan-looking girl in a long denim apron scooped beetroot and spinach into a blender then pressed the on button, staring into space as the counter shook and the grinding noise drowned out all conversation in the café. She poured the smoothie into a tall glass – it was a thick, murky mixture the colour of stagnant pond water.

'What is that?' Annie, just arrived, her face glowing with cold.

'Spinach and beetroot with ginger,' rapped out the girl in the apron, unsmiling.

'It's going to give me mental clarity,' I said.

Annie picked up the coffee menu. 'So is my double espresso.'

We sat down by the window with our drinks. There were bikes with handlebar baskets chained up outside, and adverts for Pilates and reiki on the door. Annie pointed to a flyer for her upholstery business which was called 'Recover/Recline'. It was a Roxy Music reference, she said, though most people didn't notice that.

'So, how was your week?' I asked.

'Profitable. I've got a commission for a chaise longue. And someone else wants their dining room chairs doing.'

'Brilliant. How did you get those?'

'From these flyers. I've been leaving them all over the place.'

'My sister's given me a sofa.'

Her eyes widened. 'Do you want it reupholstering? I got this gorgeous sunflower yellow material from a mill sale. I'd do it for mates' rates.'

'Great, yeah, when I've got some money.' My phone was ringing in my bag. I dug it out. A number I didn't know. 'Sorry, I better see who it is.'

'Hello?' The blender started rattling on the counter again, making it hard to hear. I turned away and put my hand over my ear.

'Miriam?'

'Hi.'

'It's Caitlin, Chloe's aunt. I'm trying to get hold of Erik. Is he with you?'

The blender stopped, sudden silence. 'No, I've not... he's not here.'

'I thought he might be.'

'No. Sorry.'

'Right.' A pause as if she was considering whether or not to say more. 'He's not answering his phone.'

That sounded familiar. I said, 'I've not seen him for about six weeks.' Six weeks exactly in fact.

'Oh, I thought. Well, never mind. Thanks anyway.'

She was about to put the phone down when I remembered what day it was. 'Isn't Chloe moving in with him tomorrow?'

'That's why I need to speak to him. I need to know what time to drop her off. And check he's actually going to be there. Chloe's not got through to him for days.'

That was odd. He always answered the phone if it was Chloe.

Caitlin said, 'I'm starting to think he's changed his mind.'

I pictured Chloe all excited about starting this new phase with her dad in a new city, and now not knowing what was going on. I said, 'He really wants to have her there. We spent weeks getting her room ready.'

'So where is he? I'm going to keep trying his phone.

If he doesn't answer, I'll drive over there and break down his door.'

I couldn't tell whether or not she was joking. I said, 'I hope you sort it out.'

'Me, too. Sorry to drag you into it. Bye.'

I clicked the phone off. Put it on the table. 'That was Chloe's aunt.'

'What did she want?'

'To see if Erik was with me. She can't get hold of him. Have you seen him in the shop recently?'

'I would have said.'

'I wonder where he is.'

'Not your problem.'

I said, 'Shall I go round and just check he's okay?'

'Well, you could.' It sounded like a no. She pushed the mental clarity smoothie in front of me. 'I think you need to drink some more of this.'

'But something might have happened to him.'

'Seriously, Miriam. Don't get sucked back in. You'll only end up more hurt.'

I nodded. The smoothie tasted wholesome but plain. A cold, unseasoned soup. Condensation ran down the window. Annie waved through the misted glass at someone she knew passing outside. When we'd finished our drinks, she said she was heading to her studio to get started on the chaise longue. 'Where are you off to?' she asked.

'Back to the flat, probably.'

She paused, waiting for me to say something more. When I didn't, she said, 'Call me if you need to.' She knew I wasn't going home.

24

As I walked from the café towards Whalley Range, I started to think that the smoothie's promised powers were real. The sun was bright and the air was sharp and everything seemed so clear and simple: if I wanted to see him, all I had to do was go and see him. I didn't need an excuse, even though I had one now. I just needed to knock on his door. I walked fast and reached Alexandra Road in no time. Then I was on his street, outside his house.

A branch lay across the driveway. It looked like it had been ripped from the beech tree when the truck came to collect the skip. I wondered how long it had been lying there and why he hadn't moved it out of the way. I stepped over it and followed the driveway down the side of the house, rehearsing my words in my head.

I would say that Caitlin had called, and she was worried about him, and I just wanted to check he was okay.

It sounded reasonable. Caring. Like what a friend would do.

But I was breathing too fast. I needed to calm myself down. Look relaxed and normal. At the back door, I waited, trying to get my breath to slow. Although, what if he was watching me from the kitchen? I turned to look through the window. Saw my blurred reflection and behind it, a room submerged.

Paper had washed through the kitchen like a wave. Every surface was flooded by a sea of books and magazines with the table and chair floating on top. I stared. Taking it in. Then knocked hard on the door.

Silence inside. I tried again, waited, still no answer. The kitchen had been the only normal room in the whole house. Now it looked uninhabitable. And yet Chloe thought she was moving in tomorrow. What had happened in there? What had happened to him?

I backed up to the middle of the lawn, hoping to see a movement or a light in the still, dark windows. The house seemed solid and airless, like it wasn't a shell containing rooms and hallways but a dense, heavy mass of paper and books.

My concern was real now, not just an excuse to come here. I found a broken brick by the wall at the bottom of the garden and took it to the door, then put my gloves on to protect my hands and smashed one of the square glass panes. I reached through to unfasten the lock on the inside. My hand was shaking when I brought it out. I pressed down the handle, pushed the door against the magazines crowding the floor, and went in.

The air was stale and heavy with the smell of newsprint as if the house had been sealed up for weeks. I forced open the door to the kitchen so that I could squeeze through. There wasn't even a pathway between the books. The floor, the work surfaces, the table where we used to sit, they were all swamped. I started to doubt he was even living here.

My phone went in my pocket. I silenced it before the second ring. Caitlin again. Then the phone in the hallway rang; ten long, drawn-out peals into silence. Then a fainter sound from further away. His mobile was ringing somewhere upstairs. Did that mean he was in here? I clambered over the books, dropping to my knees at times so I wouldn't fall. I reached the hallway, then the stairs. Books crowded each step, a frozen waterfall of paper between floors. I gripped the banister to steady myself as I climbed between them. The landing was paper-packed as well. I said his name, my voice sounded unsteady. No reply.

In Chloe's bedroom, all our work had been undone. It looked much the same as it had when I'd first visited except there were books mixed in with the magazines now. I went along the landing towards his bedroom then stopped.

The bookcase full of bird books that had stood opposite his bedroom door had been emptied onto his bed. Beaks and eyes and feathers covered the duvet. The bookcase itself had been shifted to one side. Behind it was a half-open door.

It led onto a staircase that looked newer than the rest of the house. I stood at the foot of the steps, stopped by a sudden fear of what I might find up there. Of what he might have done. It wasn't just that nobody had heard from him for days. It was the change in the atmosphere of the house. It was collapsing in on itself. The hoard had reached every corner and Erik had stopped trying to push it back. It was the home of someone who had given up.

I climbed slowly up the stairs to a small square landing with two unpainted doors. I had a strong urge to turn around and leave. I turned the handle on the first door, expecting to have to push hard against a carpet of magazines or a blockade of books. But it swung open easily with no resistance or scraping. Sunlight fell on bare floorboards inside.

No magazines, no books, no packed-in mass of words and pictures. Just a wide attic room with a roof sloped into an A.

And Erik, sitting on the floor against the far wall, looking utterly unsurprised by my being there, by the world in general.

'Miriam.' He was unshaven, the angles of his face sharper as if he'd lost weight. His eyes were flat and still as they rested on me.

I didn't know what to say so I just stood there, the stretch of clear, bright space between us. I felt that same dislocation I'd had when I'd first discovered the hoard downstairs.

'What are you doing here?' He sounded like someone who hadn't spoken in a while.

'I was worried about you.'

'Why?'

I wanted to go over to him, make a connection that way, but stepping closer felt impossible. 'Caitlin called me. She said you're not answering your phone.'

His iPhone was sitting on the floor beside him. He put his hand on it as if checking it was still there.

I said, 'She's worried. Chloe's worried. She thinks she's moving in with you tomorrow.'

'She *is* moving in with me tomorrow.'

I paused. 'Have you told her what it's like here?'

'No.'

'She can't come when it's like this.'

'She is coming.'

I thought of the time he'd said the house didn't seem so bad when there was only him around. Had he been here alone so long he couldn't see how awful it was downstairs? 'There's nowhere for her to sleep or eat or wash.'

'She will see, when she arrives. It is too late to do anything.'

How could he think of surprising her with this? The shock of this house when she still pictured it as the tidy home of her childhood. Having to return to Sheffield with Caitlin when she'd thought she would be starting a new chapter of her life here. I said, 'You can't do that. You have to prepare her for it. She's already upset you haven't spoken to her.'

'I spoke to her a few days ago. At the start of the week.'

My words came faster and sharper than I intended. 'She wants to speak to you again. You can't just ignore her.'

He looked at the floor to the side of me. 'I'm not ignoring her. I just don't know what to say.'

'It's the same thing.'

'Please, Miriam. I don't know what to do.' He pulled his knees up and put his head in his hands. I went and sat beside him, waiting for him to look up but he didn't. I wanted to see his face, take in this new sunken self in this new empty room but he seemed so unhappy that studying him felt like more of an intrusion than breaking into his house. Then something changed in his posture and I realised he was crying. I touched his arm, took his hand, and felt something that had been cracked inside me fusing together. Touching him made me feel more normal despite the abnormality of the situation. A selfish part of me didn't care that he was in pain and crying. I just wanted to sit there holding his hand.

I tried to think of something comforting to say. I wanted to tell him it was okay, but I doubted I could make the words sound convincing. I said, 'It will be okay,' instead, trying to picture a future time when all this would be resolved: the house, his relationship with Chloe, the hopelessness that had settled over him. But I didn't even believe it myself.

He wiped his face dry with the sleeve of his jumper. He said quietly, 'Thank you for coming.'

'It's all right.'

He said, 'I was supposed to be moving the things in Chloe's bedroom up here so that at least her bedroom is ready. I thought if she just has that space, she might be able to live with the rest of it.'

But there was nowhere to cook or wash. One empty room wouldn't be enough to make her stay. I felt like he hadn't got a grip on reality. I was still catching up myself. After all these weeks of absence, I was sitting beside him again. I had imagined it so many times but never like this, in this unexpected space at the top of his house.

He must have known all along that it was empty.

I said, 'I thought it would be full of books up here. We could have brought loads of stuff up if I'd known.'

'I don't use these rooms. I only opened them up because I am desperate.'

'Weren't you desperate before?'

'Not this desperate. Chloe wasn't about to arrive before.'

He had hidden this empty room while we struggled to deal with the claustrophobia and chaos downstairs. I wondered what else he was keeping from me. I had an ungrounded sensation like when I'd crossed the sliding floor of magazines downstairs. I felt like I would never really know what he was thinking, what he was hiding, what he was feeling beneath all the layers he'd built up over the years.

I said, 'What's in the other room?'

'Nothing. It's a bathroom.'

'Is it clear?'

'Yes.'

'I don't understand why you didn't come up here earlier.'

He didn't answer and I let it go. I was thinking about these two rooms – a mini-loft apartment that would delight an eighteen-year-old girl. I thought about how much time was left, about how bad it was downstairs, how fast I'd be able to make it look like a normal house if I shifted all the books blocking the hallway and kitchen into the rooms that weren't essential for day-to-day living. If he wouldn't let me do it now, he never would.

His phone rang on the floor by his leg. Chloe's face flashed up. He said, 'I can't tell her that she can't live with me.'

'You don't have to.'

'You think I should just let her arrive?'

'Tell her what it's like downstairs, and tell her she can live up here in the attic while you sort out the rest of the house.'

'No, I can't do that.'

What was wrong with him? 'You can. She has a bedroom in here, a bathroom next door. And I'll clear the kitchen and hallways before tomorrow.'

The phone was still ringing. I wanted to push him forwards into this sudden solution. 'Answer it,' I said. 'Tell her she'll be living up here.'

'I can't. She won't.'

He looked at the screen in the palm of his hand. I knew from calling him myself that it would go to voicemail in a few seconds. I felt my eyes fill with tears. He wasn't going to talk to her. I said, 'You don't care about her.'

I turned my back on him. Then I heard him say 'Hi Chloe,' and turned around. He had the phone to his ear. He stood up and walked towards the door and the stairway. 'I'm sorry. I was about to call you. I'm sorry.' His voice faded out as he went downstairs. I strained to hear what he was saying but I couldn't make it out.

I stood at the skylights looking out at treetops and dusky sky. I heard a police helicopter flying over the park then saw it briefly in the squares of glass before it moved away. I felt something like vertigo. Possibilities were forming in all directions. Chloe would live up here. I would call the lady from Space Reclaimers to help him sort out the rest of the house. Erik and I would be together again. It could all happen. I could see it clearly.

Then Erik was coming back up the stairs. When he saw me beneath the skylights something flickered across his face, a memory perhaps. I stepped away.

'What happened?'

'I told her about the house,' he said.

'What did she say?'

'She doesn't understand. She says she doesn't mind if I am untidy because she is untidy, too.'

If he'd said 'hoarder' she'd have understood fast enough. She must have seen the TV programmes. Erik didn't watch much television. Maybe he didn't know they existed.

He said, 'So they are coming tomorrow at ten.'

'Did you tell her she's having the attic rooms?'

'No. I will tell her tomorrow.'

'She'll prefer being up here, with her own bathroom as well. We'll need to bring up her bed. Get rid of all this dust.' I went to check out the bathroom. It was as normal and empty as the bedroom. When I came back in, I said, 'And then I'll clear the kitchen and hallway and landing. You can show her the other rooms when it's the right time. Just say you're using them for storage. It's true, in a way. I've found someone who can help you clear them – a professional clutter-clearer. It'll work this time.'

Erik was standing by the door. 'I don't know about this. Why don't we put her in her old bedroom?'

'Because we can't. It's a mess and she needs a bathroom. And having a loft apartment might make up for the rest of the house being like it is.'

'This room has a lot of memories.'

I could see him sinking again. I said, 'Don't go under. There isn't time.'

He seemed to gather himself. 'You are right. There's no time.' He looked around the room as if he was taking it in anew. 'How can I have let this go on so long? I have had years to myself and I'm only doing this now when she is coming back tomorrow. What was I doing all this time?'

My voice was quiet. 'Collecting books?'

'The mess that I've made. Literally, the mess down there.'

He opened one of the skylights, letting in the wintry air. He was tall enough to see out properly. His shoulders filled the square frame. When he turned back he said, 'Until today, I had not been in here since Hannah died. I forgot how this room makes me feel.'

'How does it make you feel?'

'Like I'm being suffocated.'

'But it's empty.'

'Yes, it's empty.' He sank down onto the floor then, sitting against the wall, looking into the space between the roof and the floor. I sat beside him, holding his heavy hand in mine, the air getting colder and the room getting darker. He wasn't saying anything and I didn't know what to do. After a while I went downstairs to find a cloth and some bleach so I could start cleaning the room.

25

Erik took apart the bookcase that had been hiding the door and brought it up in pieces, then began methodically fixing it back together with a hammer and a screwdriver. He was quiet and he felt far away from me even though the attic space wasn't even that big. He was thinking about Hannah, of course. I wondered whether he felt close to her up here, whether my presence in the room was an annoyance.

I wiped thick layers of dust from the skirting boards and the cloth turned black. I rinsed it in the sink in the bathroom and began again. The hope I'd felt earlier was cloudier now. Erik didn't look relieved or happy or excited about Chloe's imminent arrival and the solution we had found in these two rooms. He just looked distant and sad.

I would help him tonight and then, well, I tried not to think of what would happen after today. I couldn't be separated from him again. I swept the floor and mopped the spaces around us. In between the skirting board and the floorboards, I found an earring – a plain, gold bar. I gave it to him and he looked at it in his hand.

'Was it Hannah's?' I wanted a way in. I felt like I was the ghost in here, not her.

'Yes.' He put the earring in the pocket of his jeans. Then turned the bookcase frame onto its back and put the first shelf into place. I knelt down to hold it steady while he tightened the screws.

He spoke without taking his eyes off the bookcase. 'When she died,' his voice got stuck on the word, 'I emptied out this room and took everything of hers to a charity shop miles from here. It had to be faraway so I wouldn't see anyone wearing her clothes. I gave them everything. Jewellery, shoes, books. But when I got back and the house was missing all her things, I changed my mind. I went to pick it all up again the next day, but it was gone. They had already sent it off to a warehouse to be sorted and distributed to other shops. They said there was no way of getting it back unless I went searching round every shop in the North. I had to go home without it all.'

He stood the bookcase the right way up, the screw-driver hanging at his side. He looked at it for a while then said, 'This is not quite straight.' He knelt down, focused on redoing the screws on the side.

'Was that when Chloe moved away, after Hannah died?'

'That was later. It was just supposed to be a holiday at Caitlin's but then Chloe didn't want to come home and I didn't make her.'

'Why didn't she want to come back?'

'Because it was miserable here. I was miserable. Chloe

was miserable. She kept threatening to run away. Once I found her schoolbag packed with clothes and biscuits. So I thought it was better for her to be at Caitlin's for a while. We fell apart, in different directions. And I didn't do anything to bring us back together.'

He carried the case over to the far wall, stepped back to look at it, then looked at me for the first time since he'd started talking. 'I will go and dismantle her bed.'

When he'd gone, I looked around the sparse room, trying to picture it full of Hannah's clothes and belongings. And then with just his. I imagined him returning to the charity shop to claim back her possessions, all those memories, her smell, her choices, her favourite things, and having to leave without them. Was it then he'd started to fill up all the spaces she'd left behind in the house? Everything that looked like her absence, or felt like it, or *might* feel like it, if you gave it half a chance? It was fear of something, of emptiness, and he had been living with it for years.

I went down to the kitchen and began carrying armfuls of books into the living room and back room. It looked like they had migrated from there, as if he had been attempting once again to sort through them on the table, weed out what he wanted and what he didn't. In the living room, I edged along the pathway to the chair where I'd found the scalpel and poetry feathers. Micka was sitting there, dozing. She squinted her eyes at me as I approached. The paper feathers were scattered on the floor around her as if she'd caught a bird in her claws and it had narrowly escaped. The scalpel was dusty and the book of Romantic poetry was where we'd left it, as if it hadn't been touched since that day. Micka stood up and followed me into the kitchen, mewling against my legs. There was cat food in her bowl but it looked like it had been there a few days. I tipped it in the bin and refilled it with a fresh sachet then refilled her other bowl with water. She lapped up the water speedily and delicately nibbled the food.

I wanted to make a cup of tea but there was no milk in the fridge, just a carton of butter and a loaf of sliced bread. I had the impression Erik had been holed up in here, not eating proper meals, drinking nothing but water. I watched Micka for a while then started clearing the floor of books.

It took most of the evening to put the kitchen back into place. I moved the books out, bleached all the surfaces, and put away cups and plates in cupboards that had been full of paperbacks.

Later, when I had cleared the hallway and stairs, and Erik had rebuilt Chloe's bed in the attic room, he ordered us Singapore noodles from the takeaway. We sat down at the now-empty kitchen table, taking seats opposite each other, the food poured onto plates, holding real knives and forks rather than the plastic ones we usually ate with.

He kept looking around at the bare surfaces and floor. The plants watered on the windowsill. Micka's bowls lined up by the door. It was like he didn't trust his surroundings, as if he expected them to revert to the chaos of before at any moment. Finally he said, 'This is nice.'

'The kitchen?'

'Yes and the hallway, the stairs. It's like a real house.'
He looked unsure. 'I don't think I will be able to keep
it like this.'

I got my phone out of my pocket and opened up my
contacts list. 'I know someone who can help you with
that.'

Lisa, Space Reclaimers. I wrote down the number on
the edge of the takeaway menu. 'She's a professional
organiser. She helps people who can't throw things
away.' I sat back down. 'She's nice. You should phone
her.'

'Maybe I will.' He paused as if choosing his words.
'You are a good friend to me. I'm sorry I didn't answer
when you called.'

I swallowed. 'Why didn't you?'

'I couldn't give you what you wanted. I thought it
was for the best.'

I thought about that for a moment. I put my fork on
the edge of my plate. 'Are you seeing Natalie?'

'Who?'

I said quickly, 'It doesn't matter.'

'I'm not seeing anyone. I have been trying to sort out
my house. Then I got the flu and was in bed for two
weeks.'

'I missed you.'

'I missed you, too.' He said it like someone standing
at a window saying 'It's raining' or on an empty train
platform, saying 'It's gone'. He had stopped eating. He
met my eyes for a moment then asked if I had finished.
I nodded. He stood up, took our plates over to the
sink, watched the water falling from the tap into the

253

bowl. He took the food cartons into the porch to put them in the bin. I could see him looking at the broken window in the door. I'd swept up the glass and fastened some cardboard over the gap. When he came back in he said, 'You broke into my house.' He almost sounded impressed. 'You don't let go easily, do you?'

'What do you mean?'

'You're like me.'

I didn't answer. It wasn't a question anyway. He sat down opposite me and looked at me, a faint, sad smile on his lips. Trying to fill the silence seemed worse than letting it go on.

He said, 'It's late.'

'It's nearly midnight.'

'Shall I call you a taxi?'

I looked at his hands, resting on the table. 'Can I stay?'

There was a gap before he answered. 'I'm not sure that it's a good idea.'

I looked away.

'With Chloe arriving tomorrow, you know.'

The chair legs scraped against the tiles as I stood up. 'My bag's upstairs. I'll get it.' My legs felt heavy as I went down the hallway and climbed the first set of stairs. My energy leaked out with every step. On the landing I thought I might just sit and rest for a moment. I kept going. My limbs were like lead.

In the attic room, my bag and coat were by the bookcase. I gathered them together then sat on the bed in the dark. There was no sheet on the mattress and no covers on the pillows. I took off my boots and lay down, pressing my face into them.

A while later I was aware of Erik coming in and looking at me. He went out again then, after a few minutes, returned with something in his hands. Could he see that my eyes were open and I was watching him? He lay a blanket over me. He pulled the blinds down on the skylights. The room was pitch black. As he left he shut the door softly behind him. I heard him moving about in his bedroom before it went quiet and I fell into a deep, exhausted sleep.

I woke with a confused, sinking feeling. In the seconds it took me to remember where I was, and why I was still dressed, my body too warm beneath my jeans and cardigan, my thoughts gathered into an anxious assault. I tried to replay the conversation we'd had last night. He'd said I was a good friend. He'd said he missed me.

He'd asked me to go and I'd stayed.

I heard the door open at the bottom of the attic stairs. I sat up, my head still fuzzy with sleep, and pushed the blanket away, swung my feet round to the floor.

He opened the door, wide awake and panicking. 'Miriam, they are here.'

'What time is it?'

'Half-nine. I overslept and they're early. Can you make sure it is okay in here? I have to go and let them in.'

He pushed up the window blinds, letting in the weak morning sunlight. He turned up the radiator. Looked at me still sitting on the bed.

There was a rap on the front door far below followed by a drawn-out ring of the bell.

I said, 'Go and answer it. I'll come down.'

He ran his hand over his hair. 'Okay.' I watched him composing his features into a calmer expression as he crossed the room.

I put on my boots. Folded the blanket and placed it at the end of the bed, straightened the pillows. I could hear them in the hallway. Chloe's voice the loudest, telling Erik she'd barely brought anything with her – just a few bags of clothes, her Kindle, her iPod and her Mac. I shouldn't be here, I thought. Why am I still here? I got my bag and went downstairs to the kitchen where they were all standing, coats still on, bright, tense looks on their faces. Chloe had a laptop bag on her shoulder. She let it rest on the floor then picked it up again, as if unsure whether it belonged there or not. Caitlin smiled at me as I walked in. 'Hi Miriam.'

'Hello.'

I had the impression that Chloe was finally wondering who I was and why I was always around. I don't think she'd reached a conclusion. The idea that her dad and I might be together must have seemed impossible to her. I was closer to her age than his.

She turned to him. 'Can I see my room?'

'Yes, let's go up.'

'Finally. I can't remember the last time I even went upstairs. We never hang out here.'

'Because you never wanted to. And we are always going somewhere or doing something when you visit.'

'I'm not a visitor anymore. This is where I live.' She was asserting her territory. Claiming the house as her home, Erik as her father. I wondered how Caitlin felt, faced with Chloe's enthusiasm to leave her behind. As Erik and Chloe went into the hallway, Caitlin held back and began a conversation with me as she started upstairs.

'The house doesn't look that bad to me,' she said quietly. 'From the way he was talking to Chloe yesterday, I was expecting it to be a right state.'

I said, 'You've not seen the rest of it.' As if it was a joke we were sharing. Caitlin smiled, puzzled. Erik would have to explain later about the full rooms, his book-buried bedroom, the unusable bath.

When he passed the door to Chloe's room and continued down the landing, Chloe stopped. 'Am I not in here?' she asked his back.

He didn't answer. Maybe he hadn't heard. He opened the door to the attic stairs. I saw Chloe turn to look at Caitlin, her cheerfulness abruptly gone. She climbed the steps slowly, her laptop bag banging against her legs. I followed. I had that same sick, fearful feeling I'd had when I first climbed these stairs yesterday, and I didn't know why it had returned, and so strongly.

In the attic room, Erik's eyes were on Chloe's face as she stepped inside onto the sunlit floorboards. He spoke fast, a little too loud. 'So this is your bedroom, and you have the bathroom next door. I thought it would be like having your own apartment, your own space for you to do what you want with. We can redecorate it if you like, or keep it the same, it's—'

'I thought I was having the little room, at the back. My old bedroom.'

'Yes, but this one is bigger.'

Caitlin was looking between the two of them. She smiled, nervous, forced, like she was posing for a photograph she didn't want to be in. 'It's okay, Chloe.'

Erik went over to Chloe and touched her shoulder. She shook him off, stepped away, so her back was against the far wall. 'I want my old room. I'm not sleeping in here.'

'But there's nothing in here now.'

'But it's where Mum...' Her voice caught. Her bag fell from her hand onto the floor.

I saw Caitlin glance at the beam across the ceiling then quickly look away. The room changed character in an instant, as if the sun streaming through the skylights had disappeared behind a cloud. But it was still bright, turning the golden floorboards a sickly shade of yellow. I tried very hard to not look at the ceiling.

'Dad, I don't want to.' A teenager's whine now, like she was refusing to wear a coat on a night out. Her face crumpled. She pushed past us all and onto the landing, heading downstairs fast. Erik followed, then Caitlin. I stayed where I was.

Above me, the beam joined the rafters a few feet above head height. The open space between it and the floorboards was denser than the rooms compacted with books.

I picked up my bag and went steadily downstairs. On the first floor, Erik and Caitlin were outside Chloe's bedroom. Caitlin was looking inside from the doorway. Erik was slumped against the landing wall, his face drained.

Chloe came out. 'Why is it like that?'

She didn't get it. Erik looked at me like he thought I might be able to do something. I followed Chloe downstairs. Not to help. I was leaving.

Everything Erik had done to avoid that scarred attic room. Ignoring it, hiding it, pretending it wasn't there. He'd done it for years, letting the empty space grow unwatched and push the whole house out of shape, creating a life so warped he could barely live in it. It was what happened when you held inside you something you'd already lost. It was what would happen to me if I didn't walk away from him.

I reached the foot of the stairs. Erik was behind me. Chloe had opened the door to the front room. She turned to Erik with an expression like disgust.

I wouldn't look at him. I went into the porch and out the front door. As I left I heard Chloe saying, 'Why didn't you tell me? Why didn't you say?' but I was too far away to hear his reply.

26

On Saturday mornings I went to the Aquatics Centre for my diving lesson. It was a New Year's Resolution that had stuck. The memory of that girl launching from the highest platform into empty space had kept returning to my mind. I pictured her descending fast into the deep pool then shooting up to the surface and thought, I want to do that.

When I'd told Susie my plan she'd misheard and squealed with delight. 'You're learning to drive! Finally!'

'Dive,' I said. 'Into water.'

'Oh. Well. Great!'

For a month now, I'd been taking the first bus into town with the shop assistants and waiting-on staff. It was quiet, cold and still dark. At this time of day, the city hadn't had time to arrange itself into an acceptable pose. The streets were uncleaned, the dramas of the night before were still playing out. Things people thought wouldn't be witnessed were happening in full view. A girl pushed party balloons out of an apartment window, not seeing they were getting stuck beneath the balcony above. From another balcony, a blank-eyed boy in a dressing gown dropped a bulky holdall bag onto the trimmed grass below.

Through the thick windows of the Aquatics Centre the first swimmers in the brightly lit pool looked like they were on a television screen rather than sharing the same grey, winter city. Hot air pumped out at me as I went into the foyer, and I felt the prickle of sweat forming. Even now, on my fourth lesson, I had butterflies as I changed into my swimming costume. There were about ten of us in the class, ranging from a first-year uni student to a lady in her sixties. The coach was an unsmiling sports science graduate who gathered us round him for on-land demonstrations then issued one-word encouragements as we each took our turn at diving. Good. Better. Almost. As one by one we jumped and surfaced.

For the first few weeks we dived from the poolside, learning how to hold ourselves, how to angle our bodies to make the cut through the water smooth and controlled. Last Saturday we progressed to the spring-board a metre above the pool. I had been timid, walking carefully along the board, trying to contain its bounce. Today I jumped lightly and the springs magnified the movement, as though I was supposed to be going this way.

Diving was fast then slow; once submerged the pool stretched away beneath me, with nothing to kick against, only water to break the momentum. When I'd watched divers jumping from the highest platforms, I'd assumed they would like the descent best, the exhilaration of flying through air with gathering speed. But perhaps it was the underwater part that was addictive; the sudden slowing as you broke through the surface, the muted sounds, the sense of being cut off from the world in that boundless, airless space.

At CBS they'd advertised Natalie's job, full-time, permanent. Sheila had encouraged me to apply so I'd spruced up my CV and written a covering letter outlining what they already knew – that I'd been doing the job for months already, that I knew how their bizarre systems worked.

The job advert had appeared in the *Manchester Evening News* and sixty-five people had applied. I was filing the shortlisted CVs, including my own, in the walk-in cupboard when my eye caught on my original job application and Natalie's form with her 'Notes on the Candidate'. I reread it then put it to one side while I finished what I was doing. Then I took it into the office and fed it into the shredder: Natalie's comments, my old CV. When it had all been swallowed by the machine, a red light flashed to show the bin beneath was full. I took off the lid and ran my hand through the shredded, straw-like paper. It was a satisfying sensation, like reaching into a lucky dip at a fair.

I started when Sheila said my name. 'Miriam, phone.'

I hadn't noticed. I went back to my desk and answered the call standing up. 'Hello?'

Sheila turned her computer monitor to the side so I could see her frowning. I'd not been thinking and hadn't given one of the standard greetings. Still, she didn't need to glower. The pretence involved in this phone-answering system suddenly seemed like the height of stupidity.

'Is that Judy?' said the caller. 'I'm looking for Perfect Day Wedding Planners?'

'No, it's Miriam at City Business Services.'

Bernie and Deborah were looking at me, too, now.

The lady on the phone said, 'Wrong number. Sorry.'

'No, it's the right number. We run a telephone-answering service for Perfect Day. If you give me your number, I'll email it to Judy and she'll call you back.'

'Okay. Fine.' She reeled off her name and number and I wrote it down.

When I'd ended the call Sheila said, 'That's not how we answer the telephone, Miriam.'

'It worked, didn't it?'

'It created the wrong impression. Businesses hire us to make their clients think they're a large, established company.'

'But they're not. Why not just be honest?'

My mobile started ringing then, unknown number, and I had a moment of confusion about who I was supposed to be when I answered it. I took it into the corridor where a fig plant had dropped leaves onto the corrugated carpet. 'Hello.'

'Miriam?' A lady with a broad Lancashire accent. I placed her just before she said her name. 'It's Lisa, from Space Reclaimers. Are you at work?'

'Yes.' What did she want and how did she get my mobile number? 'Shall I call you on the office line?'

'No, no. This is a personal matter. I wondered whether we could meet for a chat one day this week?'

'Er, maybe, why?'

'It's just something I want to talk through with you. Are you free on Saturday morning by any chance?'

I was confused. Full of half-formed questions.

She said, 'How about half-nine in Debenhams café, city centre? Breakfast is on me.'

I couldn't think of an excuse fast enough. I said I'd see her there.

Erik had called me a few days after that final morning at his house. I didn't answer and I didn't call him back when he left a message asking me to. Then I deleted his number. I liked the feeling it gave me to cut him out of my life. To make a fresh start and leave the experiences of the last four months behind me. I imagined him looking at his phone, wondering, waiting, and it gave me a sense of power and control. I hadn't realised how little of that I'd had before.

Then just before Christmas, I'd arrived home from swimming one Saturday afternoon to see he'd posted an envelope through my door when I was out. It was a handmade card. Fixed on the front was the photograph I'd taken of the lime avenue, printed in black and white so the fallen leaves looked like snow. Tucked inside the card was the postcard from Dad, the one he'd refused to give me back all those weeks ago. And a message from Erik, in his steady, flowing handwriting.

Dear Miriam
How are you? I am writing because I wanted to return

your postcard. I'm sorry I held onto it for so long. And I also wanted to wish you Happy Christmas, and tell you that I am sorting out my house and my life.

Chloe didn't move in with me but we are building a good relationship now that things are more open between us. She lives with her friends in Fallowfield and I see her every week, sometimes more.

I called Lisa at Space Reclaimers (thank you for giving me her number). She is going to help me with the house in the New Year, when she has some free time in her schedule.

You've given up on me and I understand why, of course. But I think you gave up too soon. Maybe when you get this letter you could call me, or knock on my door like you used to.

Love Erik

I picked up my phone, forgetting for a moment his number wasn't saved. This was exactly why I'd deleted it.

I reread the card quickly. No, I didn't think I'd given up too soon. He'd given up on me, when he said it wouldn't work. All I had done was let him go.

I didn't go round to his house and I felt like I did the day after giving all my belongings to Barnardo's. Free and weightless, like my future self wasn't tied to the self I had been.

I put his card on the bookcase with the other Christmas cards I'd received from work. But it kept catching my eye every time I went in the room. I considered burning it in the sink, or feeding it into the shredder, or keeping it in my Memory Box, which was where I put the returned postcard from Dad. But in the end, I just hid it away between some books Annie had lent me, out of sight.

Several times during the week after Lisa called me at work, I almost phoned her to cancel our meeting. I knew she must have got my number from Erik and I was worried she'd want to talk about him. I remembered how I had wanted to speak to someone who understood what it was like in that book-buried house, who knew the frustrations of battling against a brain that kept misfiring, and I didn't want to get involved. I didn't want to talk about Erik, and there was a part of me that didn't want to help her succeed where I'd failed.

In the end, it got to Friday evening and I still hadn't cancelled, and by then it seemed too late. I would be in town anyway so it wasn't a big deal. And if she started asking about Erik I'd just say, sorry, I can't help, and leave. I imagined myself standing up in the café, putting on my coat, and walking away. It would feel good. I was almost looking forward to it.

Debenhams had only just opened when I arrived on Saturday after my diving lesson but it was already filling with shoppers: people on a mission to buy rather than casual browsers who would still be in bed. The background music was interrupted every few minutes by a silky voice enticing you to take advantage of exclusive offers and one-day-only savings in homeware and furnishings. I was early so I filled the time by poking through the dregs of the New Year sales. Odd or slightly damaged clothes at seventy per cent off. A leather jacket with a broken zip. Jeans that looked fine from the front but had a pink cat etched on the back pocket.

I saw a few things I liked but nothing I could afford. After rent, bills and bus fares I had £40 a week for everything else: food, clothes, socialising. I liked living alone but solitude cost more than you earned on minimum wage. I met Annie sometimes for nights out that consumed that week's budget in one go. I'd advertised for a flatmate in the newsagent's window but the three girls who'd responded left quickly when they saw the tight space and narrow bed. It was a child's room really. The only people who'd want it would be desperate or temporary.

At half-nine I headed up to the café on the fifth floor and scanned the customers already at the tables. There was an olive-skinned girl flicking through a magazine, an electronic cigarette glowing in her hand. An elegant lady in a caramel mac, pouring a carton of cream into a teacup.

'Miriam?' An older lady with a square face and an enthusiastic smile. Lisa was dressed in ironed jeans and pointed ankle boots and on her shoulder hung a blingy leather handbag with big buckles and a shiny strap. She had a gypsy look to her with all that gold, on her belt, her bag, her boot fastenings.

'Hi.'

'See, I knew it was you. Erik gave me a good description. Thanks for coming. Are you hungry? I'm starving.'

So he knew she was meeting me. I followed her through the self-service counters collecting sugar, milk, a mug of filter coffee. Lisa was a wide, slow mover, and I wondered whether she found Erik's narrow hallways and packed rooms difficult to navigate. She picked up a slice of carrot cake and a fruit salad. I was hungry after diving practice but I passed by the hot breakfast counter and put a blueberry muffin on a small plate, in case I wanted to leave in a hurry.

She paid and we sat in a booth at the back of the café. When she handed me a napkin, I saw she was wearing a wedding ring. It was only then I realised how worried I'd been about her taking my place in his house. The relief made me feel light and open towards her.

Lisa began rooting around in her bag. 'My sweeteners. I know they're in here somewhere.'

I watched as she began emptying the bag's contents onto the table. Makeup, tissues, a diary, a phone, a dog biscuit, a clothes peg, a Lego man in a builder's hat. She finally found the sweeteners and clicked one into her coffee. 'I know, I know,' she said. 'For a home organiser I'm a right one for making a mess.'

She scraped carrot cake icing onto her fork to eat first and began telling me about Space Reclaimers. She'd set it up after working as a home carer for elderly people. She'd had several clients who were hoarders and Social Services didn't have a specialist who could help. So she thought she'd do it. She trained in cognitive behavioural therapy, set up her website, and started getting calls almost straightaway. That was five years ago. It was a full-time job now with a waiting list of clutterers wanting her assistance. Erik had jumped the queue because he could see her at unusual hours. She said, 'Thanks for passing on my details. He said you were working for him for a while.'

'Yes, well, kind of.'

'You did a good job.'

I held my coffee cup mid-air. Was she having a laugh?

She took another bite of her cake and nodded. 'I was impressed.'

'But we only threw away one carload of stuff. We were supposed to be clearing the whole house.'

'He'll never clear the whole house.' She spoke as if it was a simple fact and I felt myself blushing, even though I knew she was right. 'It's not how some people live. A tidy space makes them feel as uncomfortable as we do in a cluttered house. But Erik is making good progress and I've only been working with him two weeks.'

'Does he throw things away?'

'After much thought and deliberation, he does.'

'Well done.' I sounded bitter. I couldn't help it.

Lisa put down her fork. 'I don't try to change people. I support them when they're ready to change themselves. In my view, it's the only way.'

I thought I'd read a similar line on her website. 'He said he wanted to change when I was working with him, but he didn't.'

'He wasn't ready.'

'But he is now?' I couldn't keep the cynicism out of my voice.

'He understands his hoarding better now. By the time he'd called me, he'd more or less worked out the cause of it himself.'

I'd seen that up in the attic when he'd sunk to the

floor. I didn't know it at the time but it was the break-through I'd been waiting for. And yet it hadn't changed anything. He was still a hoarder.

I stared past her, looking for something to distract me from this conversation and her sympathetic gaze. I'd told myself I wasn't going to talk to her about Erik. I wanted to go but standing up and walking away wasn't as easy as I had imagined. 'The thing is, if Erik understands it, why is he still doing it? Why can't he just stop and move on from it? It doesn't make any sense!' I stopped. I needed to leave. I pushed back my chair but Lisa put her hand out across the table to stop me.

'Understanding why you behave in a certain way doesn't make that behaviour magically disappear. We're not like a blackboard you can wipe clean and fill and wipe clean again.' She leaned forwards slightly. 'Miriam. You did well with Erik, especially considering you had no experience. You set up those systems for him. You took him off the subscription lists. You got him thinking about why he hoards. It may not have got the results you wanted but it was a decent start.'

'Right. Thanks.'

'He said you weren't that into your job at City Business Services.'

'No, I'm not really.'

'I'm looking at finding myself an assistant. There's the admin side of things, and there's working with the clients. I need someone I can train up. I was going to advertise for two people part-time, but then I thought, Miriam could do both.'

I looked at her. It almost sounded like she was offering me a job.

'You would be learning a very in-demand skill. There's a lot of people out there who need home organisers, and believe me, it's a growing marketplace.' She nodded, not very discreetly, towards a lady weighed down with four big carrier bags while pushing a pram with more bags hanging off the handles. 'Most people are better at buying than throwing away. My caseload is getting too big for me.' She fixed her eyes on mine. 'I need another pair of hands. Are you interested?'

'I don't want to work with Erik again.'

'You won't have to. I'll handle that case. This can be the last time we talk about him.' She waited. 'You won't be struggling on your own like you were there. You'll probably find it dull at first. You'll mainly be helping me set up organisational systems in people's homes.'

'I can do that.'

'I know you can. I've seen it.'

We moved on to talking about pay and hours and how much notice I needed to give at CBS. It was the thought of leaving that place that finally made it sink in.

Walking through the Accessories department after she'd left, I worked out that I would be earning nearly double what I did at the moment. I saw some shoes I liked: black, chic and low-heeled, they seemed very 'me'. I tried them on and took them to the cash desk, wondering whether it was wrong to celebrate getting a job as a clutter-clearer by going shopping for fun.

27

I spent my weekdays with Lisa helping people empty their homes, and the weekends and evenings filling my own. As well as new clothes, I'd bought a collection of glass vases, a second-hand armchair that Annie had reupholstered, plus I had the bookcase from Mum's house that held my expanding collection of novels and films, including a few of my old ones I'd bought back from Barnardo's. I'd also invested in a new box set with my first paycheck: that zombie drama I'd liked the look of. And I'd sorted out the internet connection so I could watch TV online. It was how I spent most evenings, that and pedalling away on my exercise bike.

I'd turned thirty at the end of February. Displayed on top of the bookcase now were birthday cards including one from Dad. I'd written back to his letter about the whales. He'd replied with another two sides full of small, everyday news, then later sent this card. I also had one from Annie, one from Mum, and one from Susie's family that my niece had made herself. I got nothing from Jessica.

Her post was piling up in the hallway. At first I'd brought it into the flat but seeing it sitting there on top of the fridge began to bug me so I put it back downstairs in the entrance hall. I didn't regret the end of our friendship. When I arrived home from work and stepped into my quiet, unchanged living room, I felt my spirits lift then settle. My space, my belongings. I'd stopped looking for someone for the spare room. My new job covered the rent and I didn't want to share again. I walked around the flat in the evenings, watering the plants, seeing that everything was in place, my birthday cards, my books, my DVDs. I liked being alone.

I also liked going out into the world again every morning. My working week was split between admin in Lisa's home office and accompanying her on visits to clients. She lived in Sale with her husband Peter, an energetic, retired man who made us cheese toasties for lunch and gently nagged Lisa not to drink so much Diet Coke. Her office was in the conservatory and I typed away in there while sparrows landed on a bird feeder in the garden, and Peter cooked curries and sponge cakes in the kitchen.

On Tuesdays, Wednesdays and Thursdays I went with Lisa on her appointments. Most of her clients were in their seventies and eighties, like Margaret, a Jamaican lady who lived in a tobacco-stained flat in Hulme. Her hoarding seemed a result of confusion rather than compulsive behaviour. I created a simple filing system for her bills and documents, separated and discarded several months' worth of recycling, watched

Lisa as she helped Margaret sort through rooms she could no longer use.

They tracked the same thought-processes again and again, with Lisa steering Margaret back to the task when she went off course. It was repetitive, slow work, and we spent a maximum of two hours on each visit. It wears them out, Lisa said. Even the younger ones can't focus for any longer than that. Every week she set her clients homework. A drawer to empty. A worksheet to complete. She said note down on a scale of one to ten how bad you think you'll feel before you throw something away, then note down how you feel just after you've done it, then again ten minutes later, then again in twenty minutes, and so on up to an hour later. The more time passed, the lower the numbers became. You'd have thought that seeing this would solve their problem but it wasn't that simple. The next week, the process started again. There is no cure for this, Lisa kept telling me, but there are ways to manage the situation.

How is Erik doing? I wanted to ask. Is he managing it? But I never let the words out of my mouth. We had agreed not to talk about him so we never did.

I liked being alone but weekend evenings still had to be carefully planned. If I wasn't going out I needed nice food, a film or box set, someone to see the next day so the hours passed more easily.

Right now, I was rewatching *Buffy the Vampire Slayer*, series six. Some nights after I'd made dinner, eaten it, washed up, and got ready for bed, it was only eight o'clock, so I carried the duvet onto the sofa and watched three or four episodes in a row until I fell asleep. It was just what I felt like doing. It was like hanging out with an old friend.

Tonight I had my DVD, duvet and popcorn all set up and ready to go but when Annie called to ask if I fancied a drink in Chorlton with some guys from her studio, I was pleased. She said she'd pick me up at eight. I had a shower and began planning an outfit. The doorbell rang when I was still drying my hair. She was always early, I found it flattering rather than annoying. I picked up the intercom phone. 'Hiya, I'll let you in.'

A crackle and a distant voice. 'Hi, it's me.'

I pressed the button on reflex and heard the door click open downstairs. That wasn't Annie.

Erik, climbing the stairs in the hallway, then he was at the door. I froze on the other side for a moment, my mind blank, then opened it. He was smiling, hesitant, handsome in his dark blue jumper and jeans. I'd had no time to think. He said, 'Can I come in?'

We went through to the living room. I hadn't shut the curtains yet and it had turned dark outside. I caught a glimpse of myself in the window: pale, serious, as if dealing with a crisis.

I said, 'Annie's coming round. I thought it would be her.'

'Annie from Barnardo's?'

I nodded.

'I didn't know you were friends.'

He was standing in the middle of the room. I said, 'Sit down' then followed my own instructions as if showing him how, then got up a second later to close the curtains.

'How are you?' he said.

I was about to answer when Mario next door startled us with one of his sudden shouts. A long, wordless cry followed by silence. Erik stared at the wall where the noise had come from.

I said, 'That's Mario.'

'He sounds like he has just seen something really bad.'

'He does it a lot.'

'You have to let it out somehow, I guess.' Erik sat down on the edge of the armchair, his body turned towards where I was sitting on the sofa. The fingers of his right hand were moving against each other lightly. He seemed about to say something but didn't. For the first time, it was him who was nervous, examining his words before he said them. 'I usually meet Chloe on Friday nights.'

'That's a weird night to hang out with your dad.'

'Not for students. Their big nights are Tuesdays and Wednesdays. Weekends are when they work or catch up on sleep.'

'You and her are getting along okay then?'

He hesitated before he answered. 'More or less.'

'She seemed pretty shocked, at your house.'

'Yes. And embarrassed. She was ashamed of me.' He looked at his hands. 'But it is getting better between us, especially now I am getting help from Lisa. And perhaps it is right that she didn't move in with me. She likes living with her friends. There are six of them, all girls, in one huge house in Fallowfield.' He looked up. 'So, you work with Lisa now.'

'Yes.'

'Does she tell you anything about me?'

'No.' I added, 'It'd be unprofessional.'

He shrugged. 'I wouldn't mind her talking to you. You know everything anyway. I thought she might have told you that I am making progress. She says I am a star pupil.'

'No, she never told me that. But she never says anything about you. We just don't talk about you.' I'd over-made my point. He looked like he wasn't sure how to take it. I said, 'So it's going all right?'

'Yes, I think so. You probably know about the techniques we use. And I know what to do, to get perspective. It is just that it's difficult, and sometimes I don't want to work that hard. But the house is definitely more normal now.' He looked at me when he said this. 'I have more space in my life now. Much more than I did before.'

It felt like he was waiting for a reply. I wasn't going to answer a question that hadn't been asked. I said, 'My life isn't as empty as it was before.'

'Do you have a boyfriend?'

'No, I mean, my job, my flat, new friends, and I'm learning how to dive.'

'Off a boat?'

'Off a diving board.'

'Oh.' He thought for a moment, then said, 'So you don't have space for me? Or you don't want to make space for me?'

A pause. 'Is that what you want?'

'Yes. It is why I came here.'

I had a sense of openness and fullness, of something filling and expanding and filling again.

He said, 'I have been thinking a lot about what to hold onto and what to throw away, not just with my books, with everything. I made a mistake with you. You're something I should have kept hold of.'

His voice was quiet but his eyes were on me. I felt the buzz that ran beneath the surface of my life when we were connected. But now it was different: calmer, steadier, easier perhaps. I smiled, not at him, just to myself. There were things I'd given away that I'd later bought back, parts of myself I'd tried to erase that would always be in me. I thought of Lisa saying how understanding something doesn't make it go away. I loved him and I understood it. Its roots, what they grew out of, why they reached down so far. But this knowledge didn't make them any weaker. They were just as strong as ever.

He was still watching me. 'I found out the name of my house.'

'What is it?'

'Thirlmere.'

I'd been there. It was a beautiful valley in the Lake District. A long, narrow lake bordered by larch forests and snow-topped mountains. Wooded islands reflected in the water. I remembered it as a dreamland, a place so idyllic, you wouldn't think it could exist.

'How did you find it out?' I asked.

'I found the deeds while I was clearing. I want to go there and take some pictures. Will you come with me?'

'When?'

'Tomorrow?'

'Yes.'

He moved towards me then stopped when the bell went on the intercom. We looked at each other, both unsure what to do next.

I said, 'That's Annie.' Terrible timing. I stood up, thinking I should warn him to expect a cold reaction from her. I hesitated at the intercom speaker.

Erik said, 'What's wrong? Do you want me to leave?'

'No, it's just. She'll think this is a big mistake.'

'You and me?'

I nodded. He was going to say something sensible and cautious, like, we'll have to wait and see, or, how can we know unless we try it.

He said, 'Then we will have to prove her wrong.'

www.sandstonepress.com

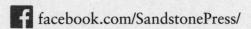 facebook.com/SandstonePress/

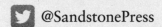 @SandstonePress